JUV YEA
Yeager, Jackie
Pop the bronze balloon

THE CRIMSON FIVE

JACKIE YEAGER

AMBERJACK
PUBLISHING

CHICAGO

For my parents, my very first preceptors—
the ones who've taken me on many *trips of a lifetime*.

I'll treasure those memories forever.

AMBERJACK
PUBLISHING

Amberjack Publishing
An imprint of Chicago Review Press Incorporated
814 North Franklin Street
Chicago, Illinois 60610

Publisher's Cataloging-in-Publication data available upon request

10 9 8 7 6 5 4 3 2 1

ISBN 978-1-948705-561
eBook ISBN 978-1-948705-578

CONTENTS

CONTENTS

NAIL BUTTER

THE HALLWAYS OF Crimson Academy are just like I'd imagined they'd be. Concrete floors and concrete walls—everywhere! Even the number reader inside the doorway is the color of cement. The green dot blinks, waiting for me to swipe my student number card.

But I don't have to swipe *No. 718* anymore or be called by my number. It's just one more amazing thing about reaching the top level of the Piedmont Challenge, the most incredible task-solving, invention-building competition in the whole world.

My teammates and I step in line behind Principal Bermuda, our principal at Crimson Elementary. This procession through the school is supposed to be a celebration parade for Ander, Mare, Jax, Jillian, and me, a chance for our classmates to congratulate us for placing second at the Piedmont Global Championships a few weeks ago. But it's like we're being marched through a prison. And I knew it. This school is just like Crimson Elementary, but even worse because the kids here have been separated into learning pods. They've been programmed to study one category for all of seventh and eighth grades. That's practically forever.

As my team turns the corner, Jillian tugs on my sleeve. "Kia, what are you staring at? Come on. We're almost to the Art Forms pod."

I don't know why the awful grey boxes still make me so mad. We've been saved from using them, from being called by numbers instead of names, and from being programmed to study one category—all because of our success at the Piedmont Challenge. Soon, we'll be leaving on the worldwide Swirl and Spark Creativity Tour for a whole year.

Ander snaps his fingers in front of my face. "KK, I see you staring daggers at those number readers."

I snap out of my trance and skip to catch up with the rest of my team. "Not anymore, Ander. I'm done thinking about them. Do you realize that when we get back home next September from the tour, we'll be enrolling in PIPS, the amazing Piedmont Inventor's Prep School? I'll finally get to build my sixty-seven inventions!"

He pulls a golf ball out of his pocket and rolls it in his hand. "Don't forget about our two awesome team inventions."

The Ancestor App and the Satellite Spectacles.

"I would never forget about those."

Principal Bermuda, with his grease-slicked hair and bulging belly, leads us out of the main corridor and into a colorful classroom pod. Sunshine streams through the windows casting a glow over more than a hundred kids who've been programmed to study Art Forms. They're working—some on art projects, others on music lessons, and several on theater sets.

As we walk through the area, they stop what they're doing, stand up, and clap. I feel their eyes all over me. They seem happy for us, or maybe they're envious, I can't tell. But they make me feel like we've accomplished something important, and I know we have. No one from Crimson has even made it through the first level of the Piedmont Challenge, and we've made it through three. Principal Bermuda, like always, is puffed up with pride.

Mare whispers, "Principal Backstabber can call this stroll through Crimson Academy the Crimson Five Celebration Parade, but I call it his sad attempt to make peace with us."

"I think he's changed, Mare. He did acknowledge that Martina from the Michigan team is his granddaughter, and he did apologize for being a little intense about us winning the Piedmont Challenge and everything."

She rolls her eyes. "A *little* intense?"

We make our way around an open area full of musical instruments, craft materials, art supplies, and a stage. Jillian's eyes are bigger than oranges. I think if she had an invisible backpack, she'd stuff all the glitter and fabric into it and smuggle them out of the room.

"Isn't this pod the best? If I was programmed here, I would never leave."

I laugh because that's such an understatement. "We know, Jillian."

Kids in one corner are making pottery on potter's wheels, while others gathered in the back are playing the harp. A few more are wearing harnesses, suspended midair, painting a mural on the ceiling.

Jillian points to the kids dressing a mannequin. "I wish we could try that."

Principal Bermuda hikes up his pants. "There's no time, Miss Vervain. The next stop is the Communications pod. Please follow along." Jillian practically deflates.

We wave goodbye to the students, and I think about what Jillian said. She might not want to leave this pod, and I think drawing, painting, and playing instruments would be so much fun, too, but when I look over my shoulder, I realize that *only some* of the kids programmed here look as ecstatic as she does. Only some of them are smiling the way she is. The others look like they're trapped.

We continue our mini parade through the Communications pod, the Human History pod, the Earth and Space pod, the Math pod, and the New Technology pod, where kids working on their studies stand up and cheer. My face flushes, and I wonder how many of them wish they were coming with us—or are happy right where they are.

Principal Bermuda opens the front school door. "Well, that certainly was a nice send-off by your classmates. They're all extremely proud of you. What did you think of the learning pods?"

I bite my pinky nail, wondering how I should answer. But I quickly take it out of my mouth because it tastes so bad. Grandma Kitty's nail butter is working. Maybe soon my nail-biting habit will be broken for good.

"I liked them," Jax replies. "The New Technology pod was my favorite by far." I'm amazed that Jax answered before anyone else. That's a first for him.

"Well, I adored the Art Forms pod!" Jillian exclaims. "The others aren't even close."

Mare's expression is stone cold. "I thought they were all good in their own way. I don't have a favorite."

Ander hides the golf ball behind his back. "I have two favorites: New Technology and Human History. Hey, do you guys want to hear me name all the presidents? I can list them in order."

"Ugh, no," Mare snaps. "There've been like fifty-five presidents. We'll be here all day."

"Miss Barillian is right, but thank you for your enthusiasm, Mr. Yates."

Ander shrugs, and my teammates wait for me to answer. Should I tell Principal Bermuda how I really feel, or make something up? I decide to be honest. "Well, I think they're all horrible."

"All of them, Miss Krumpet?"

I bite my thumbnail, then pull it away. "Yes, how can people be expected to study one category for the rest of their lives?"

"I believe that's an exaggeration."

"Kids get programmed to study one category for all of seventh and eighth grades and then they attend a specialized high school after that. That's practically their whole lives!"

"Please keep your voice down, Miss Krumpet. That's no way to honor the school system that propelled you to success in the Piedmont Challenge. You will be more respectful in the future, understood?"

My face burns like a million flames, and I stare at my shoes. "Understood." I start to bite my thumbnail, but . . . the nail butter.

"Now, children, you may be nervous about the journey you're about to take. But I have confidence in all of you and suggest you head home to finish packing. Your preceptors will be arriving at the Sapphire Terminal at 4:00 p.m."

Finish packing? My suitcase has been packed for days!

He hurries down the steps of Crimson Academy and across the schoolyard to Crimson Elementary. Mare nods at me. "Way to stand up to Principal Backstabber."

I smile, but I don't think I did a very good job of standing up to him. I was just saying what I thought.

We grab our helmets, hop on our aero-scooters, and one by one glide up to the treetops, riding single file. This is the last ride I'll be taking for a while. The Piedmont people said we won't need our aero-scooters, but I'm not too sure about that. My best invention ideas come to me when I'm riding through the air. But not today. Today, my brain is tangled up like a plate of spaghetti.

The October breeze sends chills through my whole body, as light raindrops sprinkle my face. It's not the rain I'm thinking about, though. Soon, I'll be leaving the town of Crimson Heights, my home, and my family for a whole year. And even though it's going to be the trip of a lifetime—just like Seraphina said, a year is a lot of days.

The butterflies in my stomach are still fluttering when I land in my driveway. My family is scattered in the yard—even Grandma Kitty. They fuss over me, like they have ever since we found out about the tour, and I like that they're being so nice to me. Malin hasn't screamed at me once to get out of her bedroom. But everyone is making such a big deal about this whole trip that I wish we could just leave already.

While Dad packs up the aero-car, Mom, Malin, and Ryne disappear inside the house. Grandma Kitty, dressed in her favorite tracksuit and pearls, leads me to the back porch. And that's when I feel the butterflies in my stomach light up like fireflies.

"Thank goodness, the rain has finally stopped." She pushes a button on the house, our couch slides out of the wall, and she fluffs the cushions. "Come have a seat with me right here, Buttercup. How's my girl doing? Are you all right? You don't look all right."

I bang my head against the cushion. "I don't think I can do this, Grandma."

She squeezes my arm. "Yes, you can."

"But I'll be gone for a whole year! I won't see you at all. I'll be so far away!"

"Sugar Dumpling, this is the year 2071. Nothing feels as far away as it is anymore. We can talk through air screens every day if you like. Besides, the Piedmont Organization has a revolutionary invention all set up for the five of you. Apparently, you'll feel just like you're home when we talk. It'll be fine. Mark my words."

"But I don't know how to speak any other languages. How am I supposed to inspire kids all over the world with our inventions when I can't even talk to them?"

"Well, you'll just smile and do the best you can."

My eyes get watery. "And what if I get sick, or miss you or Mom, and want to come home? They won't let me leave the tour early, I know they won't, and what if I need to?"

"Sweet Tart, you're spiraling. Now take a deep breath."

But I can't take a deep breath.

"Deep breath."

I let out the deepest breath I can, and then slowly breathe in again. But it doesn't make much difference.

"I'm going to be away for my birthday, you know."

"I know, and I wish you weren't. But you're going to have an experience—and a birthday—that you'll never forget. Mark my words. I wouldn't tell you that if I didn't believe it right down to my glitter toenail polish or believe that going on this tour is what you really want. It may feel scary at this very moment, and you may be physically far away in miles, but you won't be far away in any other way. I promise. Plus, we'll all be together in Norway for Christmas. How exciting will that be?"

I picture all of us exploring the fjords of Norway together. "Really exciting."

"Besides, if you don't go, who's going to inspire all those kids with inventions that *you* created with your *own* brain and your *own* hands? You are meant to go on this tour, Buttercup. I knew it all along."

The sparkles in her hair shimmer; it's like they give me the confidence I need. She's right. I get to spend this next whole year with my teammates—my friends—showing off our inventions. I know how lucky I am.

WE STAND AT the Sapphire Terminal and watch the Piedmont aero-bus fly into view. My teammates and I gasp. A grin the size of California spreads across Ander's face. "It looks like Air Force One! Look at the American flag painted on the side."

Jillian grabs my arm. "And the Piedmont crest!"

"This aero-bus is massive!" Jax inches closer to the roped-off area.

When it finally lands in front of us, my insides explode like fireworks. This aero-bus *is* gigantic! The door slides open, a staircase slides out, and a blur in a purple dress races down the metal steps.

We charge at her. "Seraphina!"

Our team preceptor hops to the ground in her purple platform heels. Her ponytail, pulled back higher than usual, is wrapped in a bright purple band. "Oh, my Crimson Kids! I'm so happy to see you!" She scoops us into a hug. "Are you ready for our *trip of a lifetime?*"

Before we can answer, Gregor, our other preceptor, appears at the top of the stairs dressed in grey pants and a white shirt. "Hello, children. We're off to Brazil. Climb aboard!"

Seraphina claps like a cheerleader. "You heard him! Set your travel cases inside the loader compartment and hug your families. Your flying home awaits!"

Ohmygoshohmygoshohmygosh!

A compartment on the side of the aero-bus splits open, exposing an empty storage bin. I lift my suitcase, but Dad takes it out of my hands and sets it carefully inside. Malin and Ryne wrap their arms around me, practically knocking me to the ground. I'm shocked that Malin doesn't say anything about boys, though—not about cute boys or stories about boys. All she says is, "Call me later, okay, Kia?"

I nod quickly. "For sure."

Ryne refuses to let go of me until Dad pries open his grip. He barely budges, though, and stays close—like he's trying to stay near me for as long as he can. We do our special handshake, and he finally turns away.

Dad kneels to my height and swallows hard. "Have I told you lately how proud I am of you, Little Bear?"

My eyes get watery, but I blink them dry. "Have I told you that I'm going to miss you?"

He wraps me up like a burrito. "Have a good ride. We'll call you tonight."

Mom's crying so hard, her eyes have turned puffy. I wish she wasn't so sad. I wish I could walk back to the aero-car and stay with her for a little longer. But I know I can't. My team is waiting for me, so instead I squeeze her tight. "It's okay, Mom. I love you so much. I'll talk to you in a few hours."

She whispers in my ear, "Be safe, my sweet girl. I love you, too."

Grandma Kitty walks me to the aero-bus door, a door so tall I can hardly see the top of it. "You're going to have an experience you'll never forget, Sweet Tart. Mark my words!" She grabs my wrist, and her bracelets jingle next to my wristband—the silver one the whole team wears, our gifts from Seraphina.

Be Curious. Be Creative. Be Collaborative. Be Colorful. Be Courageous.

I bite my thumbnail, swallow the awful nail butter, and start up the steps. My family waves and I wave back, trying to forget about all the miles between New York and Brazil. I tell myself it's going to be okay. My best friends and I get to travel all over the world telling little kids about Seraphina's words and our inventions. So I'm not going to be nervous about leaving my family. I'm not.

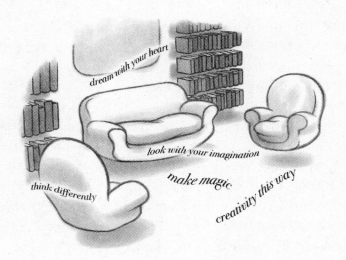

dream with your heart

look with your imagination

make magic

think differently

creativity this way

FLYING SOUTH

WE CLIMB EIGHT steps into the aero-bus. The door
swiftly closes behind us, and we're squashed inside a small
space. The mirrored walls stretch up to the ceiling and
puffs of cool air send shivers up my legs. We shuffle
around shoulder to shoulder and look at one another,
confused.

"Welcome aboard the Team USA aero-bus, my Crimson Kids! We're headed on the most amazing adventure
ever. But before we let you inside, Gregor and I want to
explain how the aero-bus is set up. Then we'll let you
explore."

Gregor stands tall, looking like a teacher. "Your airborne
home is divided into eight chambers. Chamber one is at
the front, through this door next to me. That's the driver's
chamber, and it's off limits to you for safety reasons."

Ander jumps, trying to look through the chamber one window. "Who's driving the aero-bus?"

Gregor grins. "I am."

"You know how to fly an aero-bus?" Jillian asks.

"The aero-bus is self-driven. Automatic. However, a human backup pilot must be present, and I do have my aero-bus license."

Wow. Gregor's even smarter than I thought.

"The other chambers can be found through this door next to Seraphina. You'll enter chamber two first, which is the living chamber. Next to that is chamber three, the dining chamber."

"So, we ride in the living chamber?" I ask. "Just like on the other aero-buses?"

Seraphina nods. "If you like, but you may also ride in the dining chamber or even in your bedchambers."

"Where are those?" asks Mare.

"All the bedchambers are located behind the living and dining chambers. Gregor's bedchamber is number four and mine is number five. Your bedchambers are located behind ours. The boys' bedchamber is number six and the girls' is number seven."

"What about bathrooms?" Ander asks. "I mean, when you gotta go, you gotta go."

Seraphina shakes her head. "Yes, Ander, that's true. We have bathrooms inside our bedchambers."

"You said there are eight chambers," Jax points out. "What's the last one?"

"Chamber eight is located behind your bedchambers in the tail of the aero-bus. It's a common area for the five of you. It will give you privacy for times when you need to be away from us older folks."

Hmm. Seraphina and Gregor aren't really that *old.*

"The flight to Brazil is about twelve hours, so this will be a fairly long trip," Gregor explains.

"Why so long?" asks Ander.

"We're riding in an aero-bus, not a commercial airplane, so it takes longer to travel."

Mare nods. "That means we'll get to Brazil in the middle of the night, right?"

Seraphina's purple nail polish shimmers as she replies. "Yes, when we wake up in the morning, we'll be in the sunny city of São Paulo!"

This is going to be amazing!

"After you explore the aero-bus, please unpack. The loader compartment, which contains your travel cases, can be found in the living chamber. Then, meet me in the dining chamber. We'll have dinner, and I'll explain our itinerary for tomorrow."

Ander bounces on his toes, like he's ready for a big game. "Can we look around now?"

"Well," she replies, "every adventure begins with a first step. So, step inside and let the adventure begin!"

She flips a switch, a pocket door slides open, and out pops twenty, no, thirty or forty colorful glass-like messages. They float, appearing and disappearing all over the living chamber. If you blink, you miss them, they're so quick.

Creativity this way. *Make magic.*

Dream with your heart. *Think differently.*

Look with your imagination.

We step into the chamber, and I don't know where to look. It's like they're everywhere and nowhere. We walk around them and under them, step over them or through them—they're transparent, no, translucent, like a rainbow or an opal. They float like magic—just like the air-purification sparkles at Camp Piedmont!

Jillian spins around. "What is all this?"

"Yeah, how is this even happening?" I reach out to touch one, but my hand moves right through the ghost-like letters.

Ander jumps to swat one over his head, but it disappears before he can reach it. "Aw, man. I almost had it!"

Gregor leans against the wall. "No, you didn't, but nice try."

The living chamber is filled with white puffy furniture. But the couches and chairs have no legs. They're suspended in air. Plants grow from the ceiling, and an invisible bookshelf makes it look like the books are floating, too. Mare jumps onto one of the legless chairs. "Hmm, comfy."

Seraphina opens her arms wide. "Well, what do you think of the living chamber? I think we should call it the 'floating chamber' instead."

"It's pretty cool," Jax replies. "No, definitely cool."

Ander hoists himself onto the big couch. "Yup, this'll do."

I spin around and around trying to read every message—and commit each one to memory. But most of them disappear before I can. Gregor strolls over to the bookshelf and waves his hand in front of a panel where a world map lights up. "This map shows where we'll be traveling over the next year. It'll tell you the miles between the countries, the dates we'll be stationed in each one, and how long it will take for us to travel to them—plus other interesting navigational facts." Ander jumps off the couch and races to the bookshelf. He waves his hand like a circus clown, but nothing happens. Gregor shakes his head and shows him how to work it.

Mare curls up like a ball. "This is the perfect way to travel. You guys know where to find me if you need me."

Ugh, Mare! "Don't you want to see the rest?" I pull her off the chair because if I leave her there, she'll sleep all day.

She lands on her feet, but still, she glares at me. "Seriously, Kia? Like I wasn't going to explore with you guys."

"Team, this is where I shall leave you," Gregor announces. "One of us must ensure that we arrive in Brazil on time."

"See you later," Seraphina replies. "I'll take it from here." She flips a second switch, another pocket door opens, and we follow her into the dining chamber. A wall of windows paints a view of the sky on the other side of the aero-bus. The table in the center holds a spinning food flower.

Ander tries to spin it, but it doesn't budge. "I was wondering if we'd see one of these food flowers again."

We climb onto stools at a counter. Buttons with food selections pop out from an air screen. "Well," says Jax. "It looks like this is where we come for snacks."

We pass through a third pocket door into a narrow hallway. The doors to chambers four and five face each other. Seraphina stops in front of them. "This is my bedchamber and that's Gregor's. Keep walking, and you'll find the last three chambers. If you need me, I'll be in here." She disappears into her bedchamber, and we race down the hallway to chambers six and seven. The two chambers, across the hall from each other, are marked in colorful letters, and for a split second, I feel like we're back at our bedchambers at Camp Piedmont and our tree suites in Québec.

Chamber 6
Ander Yates and Jax Lapidary
Swirl and Spark Creativity Tour

Chamber 7
Mare Barillian, Kia Krumpet, and Jillian Vervain
Swirl and Spark Creativity Tour

Ander and Jax barge into their bedchamber, and Jillian, Mare, and I open the door to ours. We stand in the doorway for a moment—temporarily frozen. We're bombarded with flowers, so many flowers all over the chamber. Daisies, tulips, lilies, carnations, and daffodils . . . they're everywhere! They're in vases. They're growing up the walls. They fill the center of our bed—a triangle-shaped bed. It's like three mattresses have grown into an equilateral triangle!

Mare climbs the two-step staircase to the bed first and claims the one covered with blue blankets and pillows. "This bed is *perfect*."

I follow her up and pick the bed covered in swirls of yellow and orange, and Jillian takes the last one splashed with streaks of pink. I arrange my pillows and lean against the headboard. "This is almost like the star bed at Camp Piedmont."

Jillian reaches into the center of the triangle, pulls up a daisy, and sticks it in her hair. "Except it's a flower bed!"

I jump off and mist-like droplets fall onto my arm.

"What the—" says Mare. "Is the roof leaking?"

I look up at the sky window, but it's not leaking. There's nothing but bright sunshine and clouds floating high above the aero-bus. It takes me a second to remember that we're actually gliding through the sky—right now.

Jillian holds out her hand. "It's not leaking. Our room has flower misters. It's like we're living in a meadow."

We twirl around the bedchamber, letting the mist sprinkle our faces until we're startled by a voice calling from inside the walls. "*Creativity misting complete.*"

We freeze like statues. "Wait," I say. "Did we just get sprayed with creativity mist?"

"I guess so," Mare replies. "Look." She nods in the direction of a flowery mural slowly appearing above the windows: *With Creativity, Ideas Are Bound to Bloom*

"Wow," I exclaim as I touch the green leaves. "Our room isn't just pretty, it's inspirational!"

Jillian examines a watery droplet on her arm. "I bet one of the past winners of the Piedmont Global Championships invented the creativity mister. I wonder what these drops are made of."

"Do you really think they can boost our creativity, make us think of great ideas?" I ask.

Mare stands in front of a wall of huge drawers. "Who knows, but I found where we keep our clothes."

I tug open the drawer next to hers and it's full of partitions, separating stacks of T-shirts. They're each a different color, but they all say "Team USA" on the back. The messages on the front pockets are all the same, too:

Wonder. Question. Imagine. Soar.

Mare holds one up. "I should have known. More matching shirts."

Jillian calls from the bathroom at the back of the chamber. "Kia, Mare, come in here! The shower controls are shaped like daisies and the sink faucets look like daffodils."

Mare turns the faucet on and off. "Seraphina went overboard with the flowers. I mean I like it, but is she afraid we'll never see flowers again?"

I shrug. "At least they're not all purple."

We're barely out of the bathroom when we see colorful blocks pop out of the wall around the windows. They're scattered, stretching from the floor to the ceiling. I touch one and it wiggles. I touch another one—and it falls into my hand. The words *create the future* light up. I touch another, and it wiggles, too, but not enough to fall off the wall. "Um, Mare and Jillian, can you come here? An inspirational Lego or something just fell into my hand."

The girls rush over and touch the blocks. They shimmy, but none of them fall until Mare reaches for one high above her head. It wiggles like a loose tooth. She catches it and the words *be open to new ideas* shine in her hand. Jillian tugs at one below the window. The words *you're braver than you think* light up, and it falls into her hand, too.

"This is incredible," I exclaim looking as fast as my eyes can focus. "We have our own wall of messages! Let's show the boys." But before we can, they burst through the door.

Ander skids to a halt. "What the—"

Mare spins around. "What? Haven't you seen flowers before?"

"Um, yeah, in a garden. Not a bedroom."

Jillian leans against the window. "Well, I love our bedchamber."

"We have motivational blocks on the walls," I say. "Watch."

I touch a yellow one. It wiggles and falls off in my hand—illuminating another message. The boys tap on them like a piano, but none of them wiggle or light up at all.

Mare shrugs. "I guess they just work for us."

Jillian waves her hand above the triangle bed. "Isn't our flower bed fabulous?"

Ander nods. "Yeah, not bad, but ours is better. You have to see it."

Of course, Ander thinks his room is better. We'll see!

We cross the hall and find a giant hot air balloon sitting in the center of their bedchamber.

Whoa.

An angular, metal basket, attached to ropes, sits on the floor. The ropes lead up to a colorful balloon that touches the ceiling. Jax opens the basket door. "It's like a fort. Look."

I peek inside. Two beds, one on either side, are covered in fluffy, cloud-patterned blankets. The boys crawl in and Ander tugs on a rope. The cloth balloon sections at the top rapidly change colors. *You are the future* lights up, and the beds spin in a circle.

"No way!" I exclaim.

Ander yells to us as he grips the bedpost. "I told you!"

Mare pulls him off the spinning bed, and he lands on the floor with a thud. "You guys would get the spinning beds again."

Jillian heads for the door. "Yeah, your bedchamber is cool, but let's go find chamber eight."

Ander and Jax climb out of the basket, and we walk down the narrow hallway to the last section of the aero-bus. We slide open the door and as we step inside, it feels like we've stepped out into the sky. Chamber eight is painted blue, and a giant window spans the top, the back, and both sides. I can practically see the whole sky from in here! We climb onto the window seat and watch the clouds pass by.

How is this even happening? This aero-bus is like a flying hotel. That's something I never even dreamed was possible. The Piedmont people who built it must be super creative.

As we ride in silence, I wonder what it's going to be like living on this aero-bus all year long. It may be weird. I mean, I love it, but living on a bus for a year? I hope it'll be okay. I hope I like it all the time. I hope it will feel like Gregor said—our airborne home.

My brain suddenly tangles, and I wonder if anything will go wrong while we're on this tour. Things did go wrong at Camp Piedmont *and* at the Piedmont Global Championships. But I know it wasn't the Piedmont people's fault that our first invention got smashed or that Grandma Kitty lied all those years about winning the Piedmont Challenge. It wasn't even their fault that Principal Bermuda was such a jerk to us—and to Gregor and Martina. So, actually, I bet *nothing* will go wrong. *I bet this whole trip will be just like I've been dreaming all along.*

After we unpack our clothes, we meet Seraphina in the dining chamber. Her purple nails tap on the metal table in a familiar rhythm. "I'm glad you all love the aero-bus. I knew you would."

Ander leans back in his chair. "It's a dream, Seraphina. A total dream."

"Ander, it's definitely going to be a dream traveling with you for a whole year."

He grins. "Why, thank you, Seraphina. Thank you very much."

Jillian twists her hair into a bun. "Seraphina, can we see your bedchamber later? I bet it's even better than ours— and ours is the best place I've ever been to."

"Of course! But I guarantee you will not like mine as much as yours. Yours definitely has that magic Piedmont touch."

She's right. It does.

"First, I want to tell you what's happening on the tour. Even though it's wonderful to experience the unexpected, sometimes it helps to know what to expect, too, and this is one of those times. When we land in the morning, we'll be greeted by Master Freeman and Andora Appleonia. I'm sure you remember them, the leaders of the Piedmont Organization. They'll be accompanying us on the tour, traveling in their own aero-buses as we visit each country. We'll also meet up with the teams from France and Switzerland."

I tuck my leg underneath me. "We'll get to see the kids from the French team again!"

"This is going to be so much fun!" Jillian exclaims. "We'll get to hang out with Gwyndol, Danielle, Maëlle— all of them."

"I don't remember the Swiss team. Did we meet them?" asks Jax.

Ander nods. "Their team invented the Thought Translation Box, remember?"

Mare glances at Jillian. "I remember. The boys were *nice*. I hope we get to hang out with them."

"Yes, Mare, you'll have plenty of opportunities to interact with the other teams."

"I knew coming on this tour was a good idea."

"After we meet them for breakfast, we'll travel a short distance to a convention center in São Paulo where groups of Brazilian children will be assembled. There, each of your teams will present your inventions. After that, you'll meet with the children in small groups, answer their questions, give them Swirl and Spark Recall tasks to solve and tips for solving them."

"So, we'll be like teachers?" I ask.

"Yes, you will."

"But after we perform?" asks Jillian.

"That's right. And after that we'll explore the city. We'll be in Brazil for four weeks. Some days you'll have several presentations, and some days you won't have any. It'll give us time to travel around and experience the people, the food, the culture, and the latest inventions of the country. And speaking of food, it's time for dinner."

She taps the spinning food flower, and as I watch it spin, I wait for it to spin right off the table. Soon it slows to a stop, though. The flower petals open, slowly rotate, and our dinner slides onto our plates. We eat quickly, and when we're finished, we place our dishes on the flower petals, and they slide back into the flower.

"No table clearing for us for a whole year?" Ander asks in disbelief. "Now that's a really good perk."

Seraphina places her napkin on the table. "Okay, my Crimson Kids, you're free to practice your lines. But when you're done, make sure you check in with your families, wash up, and get to bed. We have a big day tomorrow."

Later, I lie on my yellow side of our flower bed, thinking of my brother, Ryne. The stars above remind me that he's getting farther away with each passing minute. I knew I was going to miss stuff while I was away this year, like making up random handshakes and watching his baseball games, but I figured I could watch those on the air screens. But after our phone call tonight, I know now air screens won't be enough.

I roll over to see if Mare or Jillian are still awake, but I should have known. Mare is sleeping like a dead person, and Jillian is staring up at the stars. "Guess what happened to my little brother."

Jillian rolls over. "What?"

"He broke his wrist playing baseball tonight."

"Aw, that stinks. I bet he'll like having a cast, though. My brother, Davis, broke his arm playing soccer, and everyone signed it. They treated him like a celebrity."

I pull the blankets up to my chin. "I won't be able to sign Ryne's cast."

"Maybe you can sign it when we meet up with our families."

"That's in December. His cast will be off by then."

She sits up. "We can find a way."

"How? We're like a thousand miles away from him—and his cast."

We sit there in silence for a few minutes until she says, "What if you sign your name on your watch screen and message it to your mom? She can laser it onto the plaster."

I sigh. "I guess that would work." Her idea makes me feel better, but still, it takes me forever to get to sleep. When I finally do, the hum of the creativity mister wakes me up. Plus, the flowers in the flower box next to me smell weird, and it's strange sleeping while we're moving.

I toss around in my bed all night and in the early morning, just as I'm flipping my pillow over again, my watch lights up. Ander's face flashes with a message: *Are you awake?*

I message him back: *Yeah, I can't sleep.*

My watch lights up: *Meet me in chamber eight. Right now.*

THE PLATFORM

I CLIMB OUT of bed and use the light from my watch to find my drawer. The air is cold, so I grab a sweatshirt, slip it on, and quietly sneak out of my bedchamber. When I get to chamber eight, Ander is sitting on the window seat, completely dressed, with his suitcase lying on the floor in front of him.

Oh no!

He looks like a train wreck. "What are you doing?"

"Sorry, KK. I'm going home."

"What? Why? You can't!"

"I have to."

"What do you mean? Did something happen—at home?"

He shakes his head. "No. I thought I could do it, but I can't."

He's definitely about to cry. "Do what?"

"Go on this tour. I thought I could, but I can't be away from my mom and dad for this long—or my sister. I can't do it."

The light of the sun is just starting to shine through the window when he begins to cry. Not calm, sad tears—more like hysterical ones. He starts breathing fast and I run over to him. But then I stop in my tracks. I'm not sure what to do.

"Ander, it's okay. Don't cry."

He covers his face with his elbow.

I think about waking up Seraphina or Gregor, but he would hate me for letting them see him cry. "Ander, it's okay."

"No, it's not! Everyone else is fine. You're not afraid to be here. You're not crying. I'm the only one!"

Um, that's not true. "Ander, you're not the only one. I'm afraid, too."

"No, you're not. You're not afraid of anything."

I nudge him on the shoulder. "Are you serious? Don't you know me at all?"

"You're not freaking out, though. You're not packed up, ready to tell Seraphina and Gregor that you're bailing on the tour."

"And neither are you."

"Yes, I am. As soon as they wake up, I'm telling them both."

I remember my talk with Grandma Kitty. "Ander, you're not the only one freaking out. I freaked out yesterday, when it hit me that I'm going to be away from home for my birthday. That was right before we left my house to meet the aero-bus."

"No, you didn't."

"Yes, I did. I was worried I would be homesick, and I was right. I am."

"You are?"

"Yeah, and we haven't even been gone a whole day yet. That's kind of pathetic, huh?"

He laughs a little. "But you're fine now and I'm not. I've been awake all night."

"I've hardly slept either. Did you notice I was awake when you messaged me?"

He wipes his eyes with his sleeve.

"We can do this, Ander. We can tell each other when we get homesick. Maybe that'll help." I walk to the east side window, hoping he'll follow me, and watch shades of yellow and orange slowly fill up the sky.

It takes a minute, but finally he stands up and leans against the window next to me. "We're probably in Brazil."

"Do you think you can try it for a couple of days? If it's bad after that, you can go home, but at least you'll get to see Brazil first."

He glances at his suitcase, and I see a hint of the Ander I'm used to. "I would like to see Brazil, and I know the kids in Brazil would like to meet Freddy Dinkleweed."

"Uh, yeah."

He picks up his suitcase. "I better put this away before everyone thinks I'm bailing."

"You better."

"Thanks, KK. Sorry I freaked out."

"It's okay. I have a deal for you, though. We're each allowed one freak-out per country and this was yours. Deal?"

"Deal. But KK?"

"Yeah?"

"You better change your clothes—unless you want to meet the French and Swiss kids in your pajamas."

"Ugh!" I reply, racing out of chamber eight.

Later that morning, after we're all dressed in our blue Team USA T-shirts and shorts, we head to the front of the aero-bus. I'm the first one to hop off the steps. I expect to see sunshine and palm trees. I expect to see the beach and feel the blazing heat on my skin. Instead, I see the cloudless sky all around me—and feel air—not hot air or cold air, just air. My teammates and I stand together, confused.

"Where are we?" asks Mare.

Gregor motions to us. "Come this way. We'll show you."

We follow him around to the front of the aero-bus and find ourselves in a giant open-air courtyard. Colorful tables, scattered beneath tall budding trees, rest upon a brick-covered patio. Four other aero-buses are parked along the perimeter—two the size of ours and two smaller ones. They form a circle around the patio, and within a few minutes, the area fills up with kids and their preceptors.

Jillian adjusts her headband. "The other teams are here!"

"Go ahead," Seraphina replies. "Say hello."

Jillian, Ander, and Jax take off while Mare and I search for the French team. We recognize two boys from the

Swiss team and Mare elbows me. "Those are the boys we met in Québec." But before I can answer, Maëlle and Danielle from the French team rush over to us and kiss us on both cheeks.

"I'm so happy to see you," Maëlle exclaims. "It feels like it's been a very long time!"

"It does," I say, noticing the French flag embroidered on her shirt. "I'm so excited you're on this tour with us!"

"Is that your aero-bus over there?" asks Mare. "The white one?"

"Yes," Danielle responds, wearing an identical French team shirt. "It's beyond those trees. It's marked with our country's flag, but I don't think you can see that from here."

"Ours is back over that way. We'll show you later, if we can."

"Oh, yes," Maëlle says in a quiet voice. "We would like that very much."

"Where's Zoe?" I ask.

Danielle points behind her. "She's talking with the girls from Switzerland."

"Oh, yeah, now I see her—with Jillian, too."

"Look," says Maëlle. "The boys from both our teams are near that stage. Shall we go?"

But the six preceptors, two from each of our teams, instruct us to find seats at the courtyard tables. Each tabletop is made of tiny colorful tiles, and each chair is painted blue, red, yellow, or green. Maëlle, Danielle, Mare, and I choose a table together and wait to see what's going to happen next.

Master Freeman emerges from a small, purple aero-bus, smiling and wearing a long, dark coat. Even though we're seeing him in a courtyard this time, instead of in a large stadium, with his snow-white hair, he still looks like the king of the universe.

Andora Appleonia, smaller than I remember, appears from the other purple aero-bus, dressed in a colorful skirt and wearing the same bun she always does on top of her head. She moves majestically like a queen, and I wonder what it's like to be the founder of Piedmont. She must feel very important.

Master Freeman guides her in between and around the tables to a corner where they step onto a miniature stage. Master Freeman waves and the tree trunks all around us light up in purple. "Hello, children, preceptors! Good morning and welcome! We've been anxiously awaiting your arrival. We wish to congratulate you for reaching this pinnacle stage of the Piedmont Challenge. This is a great day for the Piedmont Organization, and we trust that you are as excited as we are to embark on this inaugural Swirl and Spark Creativity Tour! We're pleased that your talented teams have chosen to participate. You have proven to all of Piedmont that you can be innovative problem solvers, which is a much-needed skill in our world today. I am certain that while on this tour, you will inspire the children around the globe with your imaginative works and continue to create new imaginative works as well."

A sea of colorful balloons drops from the sky, reminding me of our first nights at Camp Piedmont and Québec.

Balloon messages! The balloons land in our laps and pop in our hands. It's a symphony of pop, pop, popping all over again. A tiny slip of paper flutters in front of me like confetti, and I reach out to grab it.

The future is yours to decide.

The letters sparkle like moonstones. I say the words over and over, commit them to memory, and tuck the message inside the tiny back cover of my watch.

Master Freeman steps off the stage. "Now, children, as you look around, you may be wondering where you are, thinking this does not look like Brazil, or like the Brazil you have imagined. I assure you, though, we are in the beautiful country of Brazil, in the great city of São Paulo. But to be specific, we are in the sky *above* the great city of São Paulo!"

Wait, what? We're still in the sky?

We shuffle in our seats looking every which way—at the floor our chairs are sitting on, the clouds above the courtyard, the sky beyond the aero-buses—wondering how that's even possible.

He opens his arms wide. "Welcome to the Piedmont Platform! This enclosed Aerogel sky platform will be your home during our time in Brazil. It was designed and built especially for the Swirl and Spark Creativity Tour. We felt it was important for all of us to have a quiet, private place to rejuvenate each day—after the rigors of the tour."

Ander, sitting with Jax, Gregor, and Stephan from France, raises his hand. Master Freeman nods.

"How do we get down on land for the tour?"

"There's a concealed door in the platform floor. Vehicles need only to drive onto it, to be lowered through." Ander turns around and grins.

"Now, allow me to discuss your roles in the Swirl and Spark Creativity Tour. After a summit with the World Government Bureau, we at the Piedmont Organization have decided to tour twelve countries over the next twelve months instead of twenty. During each of those months, you will live in your aero-buses on platforms identical to this one. Your job on the yearlong tour is to inspire the children around the globe to become inventors of the future, to show them how important inventions can be to *all* our futures, and to help them channel their creativity.

You'll spend most days presenting your inventions to these children, but afterward on those same afternoons or evenings you'll be exploring the cities and learning about their cultures.

There will be other days as well, when you will stay here on the platform, solving a task of the utmost importance to you and to those around the world—the final task of the Piedmont Challenge."

I glance at Mare. *Final task?*

"You see, although it is important for you to inspire the children of the world with your creativity, it's equally important for you to continue improving your innovation and teamwork skills. Now more than ever, as citizens of a global community, it's paramount that you prepare yourselves to be inventors of the future—inventors who can work with other people.

If you complete this challenge successfully, then and only then will you achieve the outcomes you desire. Team France will be accepted into L'Académie des inVenteurs de Quimper; Team Switzerland will be accepted into the Institut für Innovation; and Team USA will be accepted into PIPS, the Piedmont Inventor's Prep School."

I gasp. *No! We already got into PIPS.*

"You'll work to achieve a score of excellence. The judging staffs at each of your institutions will then use your score to determine if your team is worthy of acceptance."

That's not fair! They said we already earned our spots at PIPS!

Master Freeman steps aside. "I now present Andora Appleonia, the founder of the Piedmont Organization, who will reveal the final task of this 2071 Piedmont Challenge."

Andora stands up. I swallow hard.

"It's wonderful to see you again, children." She speaks in the same crackling voice I remember. "Master Freeman and I have worked together to create a task that potentially will have ramifications for the entire world."

The entire world?

The task rolls down from an overhead air screen, and she reads it aloud:

Innovation Connects Our World

The final task of the Piedmont Challenge has two parts: Part One begins immediately. Each of your three teams must build an invention. The invention must be useful

36

JACKIE YEAGER

to people all over the world and be developed exclusively with materials found inside your aero-bus.

Part Two will be revealed in March.

On the Day of Creativity in August, you will present both parts to Master Freeman and me and to the international judges from your respective institutions who will be viewing remotely. You will have twelve minutes to present parts one and two.

I bite my thumbnail and swallow the horrible nail butter. We get to invent what we want, but why? I mean, I *want* to create another invention—but *we already earned our spots at PIPS!*

Andora raises her arm and the task disappears. "Any questions concerning the task should be directed toward your preceptors. Now our breakfast experience will begin. Eat well. It's important to constantly replenish your creative energy."

Spinning food flowers pop out of the centers of the tables. The flower at our table spins, the petals open, and eggs, sausage, toast, oatmeal, chocolate croissants, and scrambled apples fly down the chutes and onto our plates. Once the flower halts, a stream of water and a stream of orange juice pour out two spouts and into our glasses.

I quickly taste a spoonful of the peppermint-filled scrambled apples and my insides warm up. Too bad I'm not cold, though. I'm mad—and confused. These scrambled apples can't fix that. *Why did the rules for PIPS change?* Why?

Danielle folds the napkin on her lap. "I wish we had these scrambled apples back home, but I think they're a secret Piedmont recipe."

"Yeah, me, too. They're good and all that," says Mare. "But what's the deal with this new task? We already got into PIPS."

Maëlle shrugs. "It doesn't make sense to me either. I guess we'll be busy this next year."

"Aren't you worried you won't get accepted into your school?" I crumple my napkin and rip off a piece.

Maëlle pauses before she replies. "Well, yes, so I believe we will have to think up a very good invention."

I let out a breath. *I guess we will, too.*

After breakfast, Master Freeman circles our tables again. "As you have learned these last several months, the teams with the greatest bonds create the best inventions. In that spirit, on this first day of the tour, you will spend it together on the platform, solving short Swirl and Spark Recall tasks. But in order to get to know one another better, your teams will be mixed. You'll learn to work with new people, as you will be interacting with one another quite a bit over the next year. These tasks will also show you how to administer similar tasks to the children you meet on tour. I now invite the preceptors to come forward and announce the teams."

Maëlle nudges me. "Perhaps we will be on the same team!"

The preceptors make their way to the small stage, but they're mixed up, too. Mathilde, the French preceptor, stands next to Levin, the Swiss preceptor. "Our team for today will be Ander, Mare, Hannah, Finn, and Zoe."

Gabriel, the preceptor from the French team, stands next to Seraphina and announces, "Our team members are Giulia, Lars, Stephan, Maëlle, and Jillian."

Finally, Elin, the preceptor from Switzerland, stands with Gregor and nods. "Our team will be Jonah, Danielle, Gwyndol, Kia, and Jax. Please take your places with your teams at the far end of the courtyard, and we'll begin the first Swirl and Spark Recall task."

The fifteen of us make our way to the other end of the courtyard and divide into our assigned teams. Danielle and I get to Elin and Gregor before Jonah, Gwyndol, and Jax. Gwyndol is nice, just like I remember from Québec. I don't remember seeing Jonah there, though. He's taller than Jax, which means he's *very* tall. Gwyndol says hello. Jonah doesn't say anything. But I tell him my name anyway because Grandma Kitty says it's important to always be polite, even if the other person isn't.

Elin and Gregor lead us to our Swirl and Spark worktable. As we walk, I ask Gregor in a small voice: "Do you know why we have a new *final* task to solve? At globals in Québec, we earned our places at PIPS. What's going on?"

He stops, looks me straight in the eyes, and whispers: "Life is all about changes, Kia. We would all be wise to keep thinking, keep working, and keep dreaming through all of them."

"I don't understand."

"You understand more than you think you do."

But I don't. I don't understand any of this.

"So that's it. We're not officially in PIPS anymore? We won't get to go there unless we obtain a score of excellence for our final task?"

"That's correct." He squeezes my shoulder, trying to reassure me. "Which you will do. I believe in you, Kia. I believe in all of you."

I feel the tears working their way into my eyes, but I don't let him see that. I won't let any of them see. I'll walk over to our Swirl and Spark Recall table and solve the tasks with my new team. And after that I'll think up another invention—one that gives us a score of excellence. Because we *have to* get into PIPS—and thinking up inventions is my specialty.

We spend the next several hours solving the tasks, taking breaks only for lunch and snacks. We build towers out of floating cards, use pencils to separate paperclips, make up handshakes, memorize them in less than sixty seconds, and create wordless languages. During dinner, my head is still swirling from thinking so much. The food flowers have barely finished scooping up our plates when my teammates and I race out of the dining chamber and hop off the aero-bus.

"Let's check out the platform," Ander suggests. "I need to see the rest of this place."

"Are you sure we're allowed to?" asks Jillian.

Mare races ahead. "Why wouldn't we be? It's not like we're in prison. We can't stay inside the aero-bus all the time."

"Yeah," I say. "Nobody told us we *can't* explore." We stick close to the Aerogel walls, knocking on them as we walk. "It's so weird. It's like we're living in a glass bubble."

Ander laughs. "We *are* living in a glass bubble."

Clusters of colorful trees, growing out of pots, separate each aero-bus. We pass by Team Switzerland's aero-bus first, and the small purple one belonging to Master Freeman after that. Just beyond his, we reach another small purple one belonging to Andora. We're barely beyond hers when we hear her door slide open. I'm not sure why, but we scatter before she can see us and hide inside the tree cluster.

I try not to laugh but a small sound escapes my mouth. Ander elbows me. I stifle another one and peek through the branches. Andora emerges, makes her way down the steps, and pauses. Her skirt billows, probably from an air vent, and she smooths it down with the grace of a queen. She looks far out across the platform and then walks slowly to the back of her aero-bus. She looks over her shoulder, as if she's checking to see if anyone's watching her, but then looks back out toward the sky.

Hmm. I wonder what she's doing.

She disappears through the door, and we hurry away, continuing around the platform.

"That was strange," says Jillian.

"Well, she *is* strange," says Mare. "Maybe that's just how she acts when she's alone."

I start to bite my thumbnail but stop. "Maybe."

We're in front of Team France's aero-bus, when the alarms on our watches ring. "It's almost 9:00 p.m.," says Jax. "We better get inside."

We hurry into the aero-bus and find Gregor and Seraphina waiting for us in the floating chamber. "You're just in time," Gregor says. "Please remember that your curfew while we are on this platform is 9:00 p.m. You must be on the aero-bus by then."

"Got it!" Ander replies. "Let's check out our balloon fort, Jax. Sorry, girls, have fun in your flower room!"

"Oh, we will," I call, as we run down the hall to our bedchambers.

Seraphina yells after us. "Good night, my Crimson Kids. Remember, lights out in a half hour. Tomorrow, you have incredible inventions to show the children!"

My butterflies wake right up. Tomorrow, we're leaving the platform. Tomorrow, we fly down to Brazil.

THE DOORWAY

AFTER BREAKFAST THE next morning, we make our way to the south end of the platform. "An extended aero-car will take us to ground level together," Gregor explains. "We'll spend the day in São Paulo, where you'll demonstrate your inventions to the city's schoolchildren and answer their questions, much like you did at the Showcase Festival at the Piedmont Global Championships. Then, you'll give them Swirl and Spark Recall tasks to solve. After the day of invention inspiration, we'll be free to explore the city. Then, we'll report back to the aero-car by 8:00 p.m. and return to this platform together."

I think of our costumes and our sets and glance at Seraphina. I hope with all my hope that it's all someplace safe. She seems to know what I'm going to ask before I do. "Your costumes and materials have already been sent to the convention center down below."

I let out a breath. "Okay, good."

When everyone has arrived, we pour into the automated purple Piedmont megacar. With three rows behind two front seats, there's enough room for all of us. Master Freeman and Andora ride in the front. The rest of us sit with our teams. The air is so hot inside, though, it makes my legs stick to the leather seat. I shift to unstick them and lean out the window. Maybe I can catch a glimpse of the trapdoor.

Seatbelts fasten around us automatically, and I brace myself as the megacar motor starts and we begin to slowly drop. The patterned walls rise, telling me we're on our way down. It's a strange feeling, like I'm riding on a free-falling amusement park ride—about to bottom out any second. I grip the armrest next to me, imagining that horrible sinking stomach sensation, but it never comes. Instead, the megacar slowly lowers through the floor of the platform and flies in the sky above São Paolo.

The megacar is filled with chatter, everyone talking about what we'll do when we're off the platform—and the task we'll be solving while we're on it. I still don't understand why the rules changed, but I know solving this new task will be fun. If the five of us can create something incredible in just a summer or even a few weeks, imagine what we can think of when we have almost a whole year together.

I stare out the window while we float, thinking about my aero-scooter. My head always swirls with ideas when

I'm riding. But here, my head feels like actual question marks are racing around inside. Overnight we landed on a platform that somehow stretches into the sky. Like what? How is that possible? Wait until Grandma Kitty hears about this!

Jillian leans over and whispers. "Are you thinking what I'm thinking?"

I whisper back. "What are you thinking?"

"We were just sleeping in a sky bubble."

"I know! How unbelievable is that?"

"I think it's like a space age adventure."

The skyline, filled with skyscrapers, comes into view. I don't know what I expected, maybe palm trees and beaches, but not such a big city.

Ander calls out from the end of our row. "Hey, guys, look! We're almost there!" He seems less homesick, and I feel better, too. I'm not scared being so far away from home, even though we're about to step into our first foreign country on this tour—Brazil!

The megacar lands on a parking lot. Our seatbelts unbuckle and the doors open automatically. We pour out of it, into the blazing sunshine, just steps away from São Paolo Expo—a gigantic, shiny building with sharp angles. A bright banner, draped across the sidewalk, is flanked by palm trees and colorful flowers:

Welcome Inventors!
Swirl and Spark Creativity Tour
São Paolo, Brazil

Ander and I look at each other, and for once he's not the only one bouncing on his toes. My whole team looks like they're about to explode. Master Freeman and Andora Appleonia lead us into the Expo where we're surrounded by glass and steel walls that stretch up two stories. Hundreds of people hurry up the stairs, down the halls, and around the first and second floors.

Gregor stops our team in the open atrium. "We'll check in first, and then I believe we'll be escorted to a room where we can make preparations for your presentations."

Seraphina, watching to be sure we stick together, is all business in a straight purple dress with a cape that flairs out the back. Even though she looks like she's about to give a speech, she could pass for a movie star, too. Her platform heels tap the floor until we reach a table where a man and a woman are sitting. They smile widely as we approach them.

"Hello and welcome to Brazil!" the woman says in English, but with an accent. "We are very happy to have you here! I hope you had a wonderful trip."

Seraphina shakes the woman's hand. "Oh, yes, it was very nice."

"I am happy to hear that."

The man shakes Gregor's hand. "As you can tell, we speak English, but that is not the case in most of our country. The majority of people here speak Portuguese. We do not feel that will be a barrier, though. You will have a translator for your presentation today and later when you meet with the children."

"Yes," the woman continues. "The children are very excited to hear all about your inventions. I'm certain you'll have no trouble communicating with them once you get used to working with a translator. Here are your badges. Please place them on the top of your hand for identification while you are here in the Expo." She hands glass-like hologram badges to Gregor, and he passes one to each of us. I hold mine against my left hand, and the circular image appears to stick to my skin.

"Your preparation room is down this hall to the right. It is marked with number 3456. An attendant will collect you at 10:45 a.m. The exhibition will begin at 11:00 a.m.

"Thank you," Seraphina replies with a warm smile. "That gives us just enough time for the team to change and prepare."

We hurry down the hall and into the preparation room. Our props and sets for both our inventions, the Ancestor App and the Satellite Spectacles, are set up in the center of the room. Our costumes are laid out neatly on a table. This is nothing like how it was when we presented to the judges in Québec. No unboxing. No broken pieces. No last-minute panic.

"How did all of our stuff get here? Who set this up for us?" asks Jillian.

Mare examines the piles of costumes. "Yeah, everything is perfectly organized."

"My costume isn't even inside out," adds Ander.

Jillian laughs. "And my feather boa is ready for me to make my grand entrance!"

Jax spins the Ancestor App circle, and I peek inside the Satellite Spectacles box. "The spectacles are in here."

"Of course, silly! Your items were transported here last week. The kind people of São Paolo, the people assisting us here on this first stop on the tour, set them up for you. It looks like they did a spectacular job."

We disappear into our changing rooms and re-emerge dressed in our costumes. I can't stop smiling. When we're dressed like the characters from Crimson Catropolis, I feel energy all around us. The butterflies in my stomach flutter, and I know another big moment for our team is about to happen. Jillian tosses her feather boa over her shoulder. Ander dances a jester's jig. And that's all it takes. I spin around in my pigtails and overalls, ready to take the stage.

Soon three ushers appear in the doorway. Two of them wheel our table of props and sets out of the room. The third escorts our team to a room where the kids from Team France and Team Switzerland are waiting to present. Their inventions are set up on tables just like ours. Before long, Team France is called onto the stage. Mare paces in the corner, rehearsing her lines. Jillian picks at her feather boa. Ander bounces his tennis ball. Jax sits in a corner with his head in his hands, looking like he may throw up.

"Jax, are you okay?"

"I don't feel very good. My stomach hurts."

"Are you nervous? Because you don't have to be. We aren't getting judged or anything."

"I know, but there are so many kids out there."

"So, they're just kids."

"What if they don't understand our skit? Most of them don't speak English."

"I bet they will. But even if they don't, I think they'll like our costumes. I loved playing dress up when I was little."

"What if they laugh at us?"

"I hope they laugh at us! That'll mean they think we're funny."

"I hope so."

"Just say your lines. That's all. I bet once you're out there, you'll feel better."

He nods, but I'm not sure he believes me.

A few minutes later, an usher motions for Team Switzerland to take the stage. They follow her, and Seraphina and Gregor gather us around.

"Okay, my Crimson Kids, you know what to do. You've presented so many times already to judges. But there are no judges here now, only friendly faces who are super excited to see what you have to say. They don't know anything about your presentation, so just go out there and show them how much fun you can have when you create things together."

Gregor nods. "When the speaker announces you, you'll begin your skit right away. You won't even have to wheel your sets out, since they'll already be set up for you. Just like always, Kia will walk out first spinning around wondering where she is. The rest of you will follow."

"And remember," says Seraphina. When you're done with the Ancestor App skit, you'll stop. The speaker will come onto the stage and talk to the audience about your invention. He'll explain it in Portuguese first and then in

English. When he's finished, he'll give you the signal to perform your Satellite Spectacles skit."

Ander hands his tennis ball to Gregor. "That sounds easy."

Gregor looks at his watch. "And after that, the speaker will address the audience again and describe that invention, too."

"So, are you all ready?" asks Seraphina.

"We're ready!" I say.

"Then let's do this! Have fun out there. The kids are going to love it."

The door opens and a man with a headset motions for us to come closer to the doorway. And that's when we hear the speaker announce our team in English. "I now have the pleasure of introducing the team from the United States of America: Kia, Ander, Mare, Jax, and Jillian."

I walk to the door and it takes a second for my mind to tell me what to do. The audience is clapping so loudly it fills the stadium with echoes. There are children *every-where*. So many faces are staring at us. Waiting. The clapping subsides and I hear nothing but silence. Suddenly I'm stuck. I can't move my feet. I don't remember my first line. I don't remember what I'm supposed to do.

Seraphina, standing next to me in the doorway, nods—urging me to begin. But I can't.

Mare's muffled voice whispers behind me. "Go, Kia!"

But how can I go? I don't know what to do.

The crowd of people are staring at us and Seraphina nods again. Ander shakes my shoulder. "KK, they called us. You have to go. Now!"

I look at Seraphina and tears fill my eyes. But she doesn't say anything. Now I've wrecked everything.

She shoulders past me, but I'm not sure what she's doing. She saunters onto the stage with her purple platform heels clicking across the wooden floorboards. Her purple cape flairs behind her as her ponytail swings. She reaches the center of the stage and stands there like a rock star.

"Hello, friends. My name is Seraphina Swing, and I have had the pleasure since the spring to work with these innovative kids from Crimson Elementary School, located in the state of New York. They've worked incredibly hard to create very special things, and they're excited to share those things with all of you. And so now, I welcome you to sit back and enjoy their performance as they transport you to another place and time. I believe they are ready to take you on an adventure to a little-known place called Crimson Catropolis. Isn't that right, team?" She turns and looks at us—she looks at me. I nod quickly.

"Okay, then. Team are you ready?"

And instantly, I remember what I'm supposed to do.

I take a deep breath and together we respond, "Yup dee dup dup dup dup. We're ready to show you our team circle!"

Seraphina scurries off the stage and I spin out slowly, with my arms open wide. "Where am I? Wherever could I be?"

My teammates join me on stage, and as we say our lines and spin the Ancestor App, we transport our audience to Crimson Catropolis. The image of Ander's Great-Great-Grandpa Jim appears on the Golden Light Bulb, and all the while I feel like I always do when we perform this skit—like a star. We sing our finale song and the children jump to their feet. Their faces are so small it reminds me of all the days I wished and wished with my whole heart that I could someday win the Piedmont Challenge. And now I'm standing on this stage in a foreign country, thousands of miles from home, showing young kids our amazing invention.

The speaker takes the stage, and just like Gregor said he would, he explains the Ancestor App to the children. Seraphina is watching from the wings of the stage. She smiles at me and I smile back.

She totally saved me.

Soon, the speaker walks off stage, and we step back into the world of Crimson Catropolis. We perform the Satellite Spectacles skit for the kids, showing them the glasses that can remind them of their soccer practices and homework, notify them when a car is approaching, and take pictures of their friends. I'm not sure what they're thinking. Are they confused? Maybe. But if they are, at least they don't seem bored.

After we're done, the speaker jogs back onto the stage, explains each detail of the Satellite Spectacles invention, and announces to the children that we will be meeting with them in a room someplace else in the building. We're ushered off stage, and I let out a breath I didn't realize I was holding in. My team huddles around me, talking all at once.

"KK, what happened out there? Why didn't you go?"

"I don't know. I panicked. It was like I couldn't remember where to start. My whole mind went blank. It was awful! I'm sorry, I almost wrecked everything!"

Seraphina hugs me. "But you didn't wreck anything. Besides, it gave me a chance to show off my purple shoes to the kind people of Brazil."

"Thanks, Seraphina. You saved me."

"You're entirely welcome. Besides, I should have realized that just standing in the doorway would be an awkward place to start your presentation. Your team always starts with the chant. We shouldn't have left that out."

Ander grins. "Yup dee dup dup dup!"

"Well, we won't forget next time. But in any event, you did so well! I think the kids loved your skits . . . and inventions."

Gregor waves us into the next room. "Yes, nicely done, team. But now we must prepare. You have five minutes before you're set to meet with your first group of children, and we cannot be late."

My butterflies flutter. We're about to meet kids from Brazil!

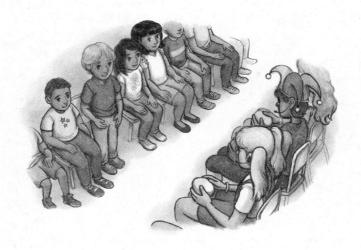

LITTLE INVENTORS

WE'RE ESCORTED INTO a bright meeting room. It's filled with eight- and nine-year-old children sitting in chairs, all of them wide-eyed. We take our places in a row at the front of the room. Seraphina and Gregor sit on the chairs on either end, and the rest of us sit in between them. The children stare and we wait to be introduced.

First, the speaker holds a pile of shiny stones and hands one to each of us. "Friends, I have here microphones to amplify your voices, but they also serve as translators for the children who do not understand English. They are wearing earpieces to hear the translation. Simply hold the stone in your hand and speak as you normally would. It will do all the work for you.

Ander looks his over. "You mean this little thing is really a translator? It can change our words from English to Portuguese?"

"That's right. It's an invention we use regularly when we host international guests in our country. It makes our world feel much smaller and much friendlier because the words they hear in Portuguese sound just like the voices of the people who are actually speaking them."

Gregor takes a stone from the usher. "That's quite an important invention. Impressive."

The usher then hands an earpiece to each of us. "Now, please place these in your ears. The children are holding translator stones, just as you are. The earpieces will help you to understand the children when they speak in Portuguese. You will hear their voices in English, regardless of what language they are speaking."

We place them in our ears, and he continues. "The children have prepared a list of questions for you. But first, it would be helpful to introduce yourselves to them."

"That's a great idea," Seraphina replies. "I'll begin. Hello, everyone. As I mentioned on stage, my name is Seraphina, and I'm one of the preceptors for this American team."

I hold my stone open in my hand. "Hello. My name is Kia."

Ander speaks loudly into his stone. "Hi, I'm Ander.

I look down the row at Jillian. "Hi," she says. "I'm Jillian."

Mare looks up. "I'm Mare."

Jax looks straight ahead with an uneasy expression on his face. "Hello. I'm Jax."

And finally, Gregor says, "Hello, children. My name is Gregor and I'm Team USA's other preceptor."

"Wonderful! Thank you," the speaker replies. "Our children have prepared several very interesting questions for you."

A small girl stands up and speaks into her stone. "Hello, my name is Ana. I would like to know if you are actors. Your play was very good."

We laugh along with the children. I don't think any of us expected that question.

Ander sits up. "Well, we aren't actors, but we thought it would be cool to present our invention to the judges as a play. We thought they'd remember our invention that way."

The little girl smiles and quickly sits back down. A boy jumps up to his feet. "My name is Lucas. Who thought up the Ancestor App? I like that invention. It's seems like you can talk to dead people with it."

The kids break into laughter again. "It is kind of like that," Mare replies. "If there's a person who lived a long time ago but is dead now, you can look up information about them. But we found a way to create an interaction, so you're doing more than just reading about them. You're asking them questions and listening to their answers using the videos that were recorded by them when they were alive."

The boy lets out a breath. "But who made up the Ancestor App?"

The kids laugh again, I think because Mare forgot to answer his first question. "Oh, right. Well, we all did. We thought it up together."

"But how? Five people can't think the same thing at the exact same time."

He has a point! We hesitate for a few seconds, but then I think of a way to explain. "Well, you're right, we didn't actually all think up *all* the parts of the invention at the same time. But one of us thought up a piece of the whole idea, and then another one of us thought up another piece. Eventually we all thought up pieces, put them together like a puzzle, and soon it became a whole invention."

He seems satisfied with that answer and sits back down. Another girl stands up and very loudly announces, "Hello, team from the United States of America. My name is Maria and I would like to be an inventor one day. But I would not like to act in a play like you did. I would rather show the invention and that's all. Why didn't you do that?"

Jillian laughs. "We didn't want to. We thought the play would be more fun."

"Then you didn't have to do a play?"

"No, we didn't have to. Some of us weren't sure if it would be fun. But it turns out we are all happy we did. By doing a play, we learned new things that weren't part of the actual invention itself."

Maria sits down, and a boy stands up. He speaks more softly than Maria. "My name is Chaz. How did you figure out how to make your invention work?"

"We did a lot of the research on the computer," Jax replies.

"Did you all do the research?"

I shake my head. "No, some of us did research. Some of us sewed the costumes. Some of us thought up the story for the script, and some of us figured out how to put it all together into one invention. It took all of us working together, and working very hard, to make it work."

Another girl stands up. "My name is Evelyn. Did you all agree every time?"

That's when *we* laugh into our stones.

Mare looks around at all of us. "I got this one. No, we didn't agree all the time. But we're a team and we had to learn to compromise and collaborate—we had to learn to work together."

"And that part was hard at first, but we got better at it," I add.

The speaker walks to the front of the room. "Thank you for your thoughtful answers. It means so much to our children. Before we finish up with this session, may we ask each of you to share with the children your best tip for creating inventions?"

At first, I'm not sure how to answer. But after a few seconds I think of the best tip I know—the one from Grandma Kitty. And because I think everybody should have Grandma Kitty's voice speaking in their ear, I quickly say, "The best inventions come from taking things you already know and thinking up ways to make them better. The same way scooters were turned into aero-scooters and buses were turned into aero-buses."

I turn to Mare. "Don't be afraid to try something new or something you're afraid of. It may turn out to be fun."

Ander squirms in his seat like he's been waiting hours to talk again. "It's important to brainstorm first. Make a list with all your ideas even if they don't make sense.

Because your idea might make you think of another one, one that's better."

"I think my best tip," says Jillian, "is to imagine something that isn't there, but something that you want to be there. If you wish you had a beautiful travel suitcase made from flower petals, figure out how to make one. The worst thing that can happen is that it won't work. But you won't know unless you try."

"I think it's really important to read about inventions," says Jax. "Because the more you read about what's new, the more ideas you get about what else could be new, too."

Gregor nods. "I feel the best tip for inventors is to push yourself to create something that you think is impossible to create. If you are persistent, you will find a way to do it."

Seraphina crosses her legs. "I have a tip for inventing, too. The best way to create is with other people, and the best way to work with other people is to think of yourselves as a team. That way you'll work to achieve your goal together. Team USA has become known as The Crimson Five and not just because there are five team members from Crimson Elementary School. They have a five-part mantra that they work by as well:

Be Curious. Be Creative. Be Collaborative.
Be Colorful. Be Courageous.

"That is what The Crimson Five really means. This mantra has helped our team work together to create amazing things. And if you do the same, you will be able to create amazing things, too."

"Magnificent!" the speaker says and motions for the children to stand up. They jump to their feet and fill the room with their applause and smiling faces. "Thank you for inspiring our children with your words of wisdom. This is an experience they will not soon forget!"

They leave and the room is transformed. Ushers scurry around, setting up the Swirl and Spark Recall tasks at tables of six or seven. Once the room is ready, we each take a table and review the materials and instructions in front of us. The children re-enter, and we read our tasks to them. I watch wide-eyed as the children work together to solve them.

Hours later, after two more sessions like it, we're starving. The speaker seems to already know that and gathers us around. "Thank you very much for what you have done to inspire the children of Brazil today. But now you must be hungry. We've made a lunch reservation for you at a wonderful place not far from here, and today is Monday so you will want to experience a traditional São Paulo dish: a *virado à paulista!*"

"What does it matter that it's Monday?" I ask.

"In São Paulo's popular lunch restaurants, there's a set menu of lunch dishes for each day of the week, often followed to the letter by the locals. The *virado à paulista* is Monday's special dish."

"What is it?" Ander asks, with a skeptical expression on his face.

"Before I tell you that, you should know that in Brazil, lunch is a very large meal. With breakfast being little more than a cup of coffee and a slice of toast, and dinner usually served too late to be anything rich and heavy, lunch is what Brazilians consider to be the most important meal of the day."

"That sounds good to me," Mare says with enthusiasm. "I like large meals."

"Well, you're in luck, then, because Brazilian lunches are hearty, sit-down affairs with generous portions, featuring large helpings of rice and beans. Brazilians do not consider eating a sandwich or a bowl of soup as a real lunch."

"So, lunch is rice and beans?" Ander asks.

"I suggest you see for yourself what the *virado à paulista* is."

Gregor shakes his hand. "I'm sure it will be wonderful. Thank you for the suggestion and for your warm hospitality."

"Enjoy your time in our country. I believe you most certainly will!"

"Thanks," says Ander. "I am starving!"

"Me, too," I say, and we quickly head back to our room. When we've finished changing out of our costumes, we walk outside the Expo and into the Brazilian heat. The sun is bright and feels warm on my skin as we amble through the colorful streets of São Paulo.

Before long, we arrive at the restaurant where beautiful music is playing. We're seated at a table outside on a covered patio and do our best to decode the menu. Gregor and Seraphina insist that we try the Monday dish, and we wait as patiently as we can for it to arrive.

"Where are the other teams?" asks Jillian.

Gregor glances at his watch. "They had their breaks earlier and now they're answering questions from the children, just like you did. We may run into them later as we're exploring, or perhaps at dinner."

"Seraphina, how do you think we did at giving the tasks to the kids?" I ask.

"You did a fabulous job. You would think you've been teachers for years!"

"It was fun."

Jillian folds her napkin and places it in her lap. "I was so nervous answering their questions at first, but their questions were easy. That one girl actually asked us if we were actors!"

"I liked hanging out with the kids," says Ander. "Some of them reminded me of me when I was nine."

"That speaker was nice, too," I say.

"All the people here have been very friendly," says Seraphina. "And I can't wait for us to meet more."

Mare refolds her napkin. "What are we doing after lunch?"

"Well, I thought we could walk around and explore the neighborhoods. There's a place called Beco do Batman, which means Batman's Alley, where we can see amazing examples of local art. São Paulo has a very vibrant street-art scene, from what I understand. What do you think? I'll take pictures so you can send them back to your families."

"Yeah, my mom would like that," I say. "Grandma Kitty would, too."

The waiter brings our lunches, and we stare at the huge piles in front of us.

He laughs in a kind way. "You should know the history of this dish—and what's in it. Dating back to the fourteenth century, traditional *virado à paulista* is made of *tutu de feijão*, which is refried beans thickened with manioc flour, a pork chop, a sausage, a deep-fried banana, a fried egg, sautéed kale, pork cracklings, and a generous portion of white rice."

Mare pulls her hair into a ponytail. "It looks good!"

And she's right. We taste every bit of the Monday dish, and it is good! When we can't manage to eat any more, we leave the café feeling stuffed and re-enter the streets of São Paulo. Although we're thousands of miles from home, the people don't seem to care that we aren't from here. They're friendly and very happy to say hello.

A man with a cart offers to show us the items he's selling. Seraphina buys a beautiful purple scarf and ties it around her purse. We spend the rest of the day touring the art-filled streets, and later we eat dinner in a brightly colored restaurant with Andora, Master Freeman, Team Switzerland, and Team France.

The purple megacar is waiting for us when we arrive back at the Expo. The passenger door opens for us automatically, our three teams pile in, and our safety straps wrap around us. Seconds later, I feel us taking off. The night is quiet and even though I'm not sitting on the end, I stare out the window. It's an incredible sight flying at night. It's not much different than flying in our aero-car, but we never fly this high. We barely fly higher than the treetops. This is cool. I wish we could hover here all night and count the stars.

When we enter the platform through the trapdoor, I remember again that our home for the next month is in the sky, over the city of São Paulo. It's so strange! It's like we're in a treehouse, only there are no trees and we're like a billion feet higher.

Once the motor turns off, we say goodnight to the other teams and make our way through the courtyard to our aero-bus. Once we're inside, Seraphina turns in to her bedchamber as we turn in to ours. "Good night, my Crimson Kids. Don't forget to call your families!"

The girls and I open our door, and we're greeted by the flowery mural as it magically reappears over the windows:

With Creativity, Ideas Are Bound to Bloom!

The misters turn on, the flowers perk up, and I'm way more awake than I was in the megacar.

Jillian flops onto her flower bed. "I still can't believe this room is in the sky."

"Me either! I'm going to call my mom before I get ready for bed."

Mare crawls under her blankets. "I'm going to relax right here first."

I push the buttons on my watch to call home. But I'm watching the small square so intently, I don't notice the hologram image in the center of the room. Not until I hear voices calling my name.

"Kia!"

I'm startled, because right there in the middle of our bedchamber is my mom, my dad, Malin, and Ryne! They aren't *really* there, but they are! It's them but they look more like silvery, wiggly ghosts. I've seen holograms on TV before, but never in real life.

"Is that *really* you?" I ask my family. They look just as shocked as me.

Dad jumps to his feet. "It's us!" His grin is so big, I wouldn't mistake it for anything.

Mom stands up and gasps: "Oh, Baby Girl. How are you? We can actually see you right there in your room."

"And I can see you all right in the living room!"

"This is so cool," Ryne exclaims. "Kia, look at my cast. Everyone signed it. But I saved a spot for you."

"Jillian thought of a way I can sign it. I'll send my signature to Mom, okay?"

"Cool!"

Malin flops down on our living room couch. "Kia, your room is awesome."

"I know! Can you see Mare and Jillian? They're lying on our flower bed."

Jillian waves. "Hi!"

Mom pushes her glasses onto her head. "Hi, girls. Your room is adorable."

"Wait until you hear the best part. Our bedchamber is *inside* our aero-bus and guess where the aero-bus is parked?"

"Where?" asks Dad.

"On a sky platform."

Mom looks confused. "What's a sky platform?"

"It's like a bubble in the sky. All our aero-buses are parked on it. It's where we stay when we aren't showing our inventions or talking to the kids or exploring Brazil."

"I can't believe it," Dad replies. "I read something about sky platforms in the news last year, but I didn't think any had been built yet. Apparently, they were developed by inventors in Rochester, New York. Leave it to the Piedmont Organization to be the first to use them."

"It's really weird. I like it, but it's really weird."

Mom smiles like she understands what I mean. "How was your first day?"

"It was good. The kids asked us easy questions."

"Well, that's great. I'm just so happy we can talk this way. It's so much better than just seeing your face. I feel like I'm right in your bedroom with you."

"You mean *bedchamber*!"

"Oh, yes. Bedchamber."

"And I feel like I'm right at home in our living room."

"I knew the Piedmont organizers had something planned so that you wouldn't feel homesick. I had no idea it would be like this."

"Well, I'm glad today was fun, Little Bear. You get some sleep now. I know it's later there in Brazil than it is here in New York."

"I will. I'll call you again tomorrow. Tell Grandma Kitty I said, 'Hi.'"

"We will, Baby Girl. Sweet dreams!"

I press a button on my watch and my living room disappears. I look at Jillian and her mouth is open in disbelief. "Wow!"

Mare throws off her blankets. "Me next!"

"Okay, then I'm getting ready for bed," says Jillian. "I'll call after."

Jillian and I brush our teeth at the daffodil sink, and before long, after Jillian and Mare have seen their families, we're all in bed. The floral scent fills the room, and as I drift to sleep, I stare at the mash up of petals. I think daisies are the happiest flower grown any place, and now, I'm the happiest person any place, too. Today was a good day, and we get to have even more days like this in Brazil. I don't know why I was even worried about being so far away from home. After talking to my family tonight, I feel like my living room at home is right down the hall from this bedchamber.

MAGIC IN THE MARKET

WEEKS LATER, I am lying awake, staring at the stars shining over my flower bed. My brain swirls in overdrive, and I'm not one bit tired. I roll over and look at the time, 9:35 p.m., and the date, October 24. In less than two and a half hours, it will be my birthday. It'll be October 25. I'll be twelve years old—and I'll be a million miles away from my family.

Birthdays are a big deal at my house. We wake up extra early in the morning and meet in the living room. A colorful *Happy Birthday* sign that my mom made hangs on the fireplace. A few gifts are sitting under the sign all wrapped in the same bright paper. We eat cinnamon rolls and orange juice and then open them all up.

This birthday will be different. I won't wake up hearing my mom's voice singing "Happy Birthday, Sweet Girl!" I won't have a birthday sign. I won't have gifts or cinnamon rolls. I won't see my family.

I pull the blankets up to my chin and blink the tears from my eyes. I don't think I want my birthday to come. Who cares about turning twelve anyway? It's not an important year. It's not like I'm a teenager. It's not like it's *anything*. I wish I could just skip it. I'll pretend tomorrow is not October 25. It won't be the same this year anyway.

Hours later, I'm sure I'm dreaming, because I hear singing. The tune is familiar. The *song* is familiar and it's coming from someplace close. I hear my mom's voice getting louder and louder. *Wait, it's Mom!* She's singing!

"Happy birthday, Sweet Girl!"

I hear a second voice. "There she is! Hey, Little Bear, happy birthday!"

My dad's voice sounds so real, but I know it's not.

I roll over and slowly open my eyes. Images of my family come into focus and maybe I'm not dreaming. *Is this for real?* My whole family, sitting in my real living room, is projected like a hologram into my bedchamber!

I jump out of bed.

"Kia!" Ryne shouts.

"What? You're here?"

Grandma Kitty stands in the center of the room waving, her bracelets jingling around her wrist. "Of course, we are! You know how clever the people of Piedmont are with their inventions. Happy birthday, Sugar Plum!"

"Grandma Kitty! You're here, too?"

"I wouldn't miss your twelfth birthday for anything in the world."

Mom grins. "Happy birthday, Sweetie!"

Malin yawns. "Happy birthday, Kia. It's your last year before you're a teenager—the important year."

I rub the sleep from my eyes. "Twelve is important, too, you know."

Grandma Kitty nods. "Absolutely. Twelve is the beginning of everything. It's a number that begins with one, then two and then everything to come after, everything that will make your life your own."

I smile. Maybe twelve *is* the beginning of everything.

Jillian jumps out of her flower bed. "Happy birthday, Kia!"

Mare drags herself out, too. "Yeah, what she said."

"Thanks! Come see my family!" They sit on the floor next to me and we huddle together. "Isn't this incredible? It's like my family's right here. Look at my birthday sign!" It hangs on the fireplace just above a bunch of gifts. "I like it, Mom."

"I'll always make you a birthday sign, no matter where your adventures take you."

"I wish I could open my presents. Could you bring them with you when you meet us in Norway?"

Dad shakes his head. "Nah, there's no need for that."

"What do you mean?"

"Well, open your door and find out."

"Why?" I walk to the door to find Ander, Jax, Gregor, and Seraphina standing there, like they've been waiting the whole time. Gregor's arms are full of gifts—all wrapped like the ones under the fireplace. Seraphina swoops in, holding a plate full of cinnamon rolls. "Happy birthday, Kia!"

"No way!"

"Yeah, Happy birthday, KK."

"We heard you couldn't have a birthday without cinnamon rolls, so your mom gave me the recipe and I made them myself."

"Thanks! But wait, are these my birthday presents—or are those?" I look at both sets of gifts and I'm so confused.

Ryne grins. "The ones here with us are empty boxes. We gave Seraphina your presents before you left for Brazil."

"Seriously? Ryne, you're terrible at keeping secrets. How did you keep this one?"

"Whatever, Kia," Malin replies. "Open them up. You know we can't eat our cinnamon rolls until you do."

"Okay, I will!" I unwrap the gifts while my family looks on, and then we eat the cinnamon rolls together like we really are all in the same room. It's like I'm not millions of miles away from home and I didn't need to skip my birthday this year after all.

Before my family fades away from the bedchamber, though, Seraphina pulls me aside. "I have a gift for you, Kia."

"You do?"

"Yes, birthdays are a big deal in my house, too, and so I wanted each of your birthdays to feel special on the tour as well."

"Mine does, for sure."

"Maybe this will make it feel extra special." She hands me a small box wrapped with a purple bow. I unwrap it to find a chain inside—a chain with a rectangular plate that reads:

Shine like the twinkle star!

"I thought you could wrap it on your backpack strap. That way, wherever you go, you'll think of your adventure on the tour and remember to shine brightly—as only you can. Each star is different, you know, and each one twinkles in its own way. I want you to always remember that." She hugs me and I look again at the sparkly chain.

"I love it, Seraphina. Thanks. I'll put it on my backpack right away."

"Yay, I'm glad you like it! Now I think you'd better tell your family you'll talk to them later because we have a fun beach day planned in Brazil."

"What, really? Okay!" I say goodbye to my family, and even though I can't see them in person, this was practically perfect. And now we're going off the platform to a beach in Brazil. I guess Grandma Kitty was right. Twelve is a birthday I'll never forget.

THE WATER IN Brazil is blue, blue, blue, as far as I can see. We walk with Seraphina and Gregor across the hot sand, carrying our beach bags and towels. The sun is so bright I shield my eyes and search inside my bag for sunglasses.

When I stand in the water, I can see my toes. Small colorful fish swim their way around me, and part of me wants to freak out as they glide by, but part of me thinks it's so cool that I can see them so clearly. They swim in their little schools, and it makes me think of my under-water bubble bike. One day I *will* build it. I just need to think up one more invention for this competition, so I can someday build it at PIPS.

After spending the day snorkeling with my team, swimming by coral like I've only ever seen in books, we lie on our towels, close our eyes, and dry off in the sun. I thought today would be the worst birthday I had ever had. But lying here in Brazil with my team—my friends—I know I was wrong. Twelve may be my best year yet—like Grandma Kitty said, the beginning of everything.

A FEW DAYS later, after our last session with the kids in Brazil, we're back up on the platform. We board our aero-bus, Gregor excuses himself to go to the driving chamber, and Seraphina gathers us in the floating chamber. We hop onto the couches while she floats on a chair with her legs crossed in front of her, swinging her purple platform heels. I wonder if she's always loved purple or if it's a color she likes because she's a Piedmont person now. I bet she's always liked it, because the other preceptors don't wear purple. Just Seraphina.

"Okay, my Crimson Kids, Brazil has been a blast but now that it's almost November, we're off to our second tour stop. Later tonight, we'll land on the Moroccan plat-form high above the city of Marrakesh!"

"I've never heard of that city," Ander replies. "And I've heard of most cities. What's it like?"

"Well, Ander, I'm so glad you asked. Marrakesh is at the foot of the Atlas Mountains. I've read that it's noisy and full of history. There's a lot to see and do, like sample traditional Moroccan street food at the nightly market, shop for spices and artisanal jewelry, and visit places like the Saadian Tombs and El Badi Palace."

"Ooh, artisanal jewelry!" Jillian exclaims. "Can we shop for that?"

"And a palace?" I ask. "Can we see that, too?"

"I'm sure we can."

"I want to check out the tombs," says Jax.

Ander jumps off the couch. "Me, too."

"We're there for a while, so I hope we'll have time to do all of that."

Mare rolls over and props herself up on her elbow. "When will we get there?"

"Around 3:00 a.m. We'll be parked around the court-yard when you wake up."

"There's a courtyard on that platform, too?" I ask.

"Yes. I think you're going to see that the Moroccan platform is practically identical to the one in Brazil. They all are. They're designed that way so that they'll feel famil-iar even though you're in a new place."

The next morning, we burst out of the aero-bus and head straight for the courtyard. With its transparent walls separating us from the clouds, it feels like we're back in Brazil, right where we were yesterday. The platform in Morocco holds the same brick courtyard with the same tiled tables and colorful chairs. The lampposts are scattered around in the same places. The benches rest in the same corners. Potted tree clusters are situated between our aero-buses, and even those are parked in the same manner around the platform circle. I guess Seraphina is right—it does feel familiar. It feels like we've been here the whole time.

Later that day, the megacar, carrying all of us, lands in Marrakesh and I am mesmerized. It looks like a movie set in the middle of a desert with sand-colored buildings and palm trees. I'm anxious to explore and see it all, but first we must do what we came here to do: inspire the children. Our time in the convention center goes by fast, and after performing our skits for the kids, answering their questions, and giving them tasks to solve, we finally can explore.

An usher gives us directions and soon we find ourselves at the main square in the center of the city—a place called Jemaa el Fna, where traditional entertainers perform for small crowds in a magical open area. We wander from one area to another and finally watch wide-eyed as a snake charmer entrances dancing snakes and the onlookers.

The square becomes a busier place in the late afternoon, so we stick close together because we don't want to get lost. Soon, it becomes a carnival of acrobats, musicians, storytellers, and other entertainers—and I don't know where to look first. Dancers entertain the people who stop to watch their movements. Music fills the air, making it feel like a million parties going on at the same time.

Behind the square is the souk, or *sūq,* which we learn is Arabic for market. There we find hundreds of little shops and stalls around every corner. The narrow, busy streets are filled with smaller souks, too, like the spice souk, the meat souk, the clothing souk, and more. With so many sights, it's impossible to glimpse it all. The last souk we pass is the carpet souk, filled with piles and piles of hand-made Moroccan carpets and rugs. No two are the same, and if I could bring one home to Grandma Kitty, I would.

A woman in a flowy dress makes eye contact with me. "There is so much to see in the souk. Have you looked through the Virtual Market Box?"

"What is that?"

The woman reaches under a table and places a glass box on top of it. "It will show you all the souks in the market and all of the items in each one. Please, have a look."

Seraphina and Jillian step up to the counter, too, and I carefully open the top of the box. A golden map rises out of it. The names of the souks blink, and she nods, telling me that it's okay to choose one. I touch the one that says *Spices*, and the number 17 flashes, instructing me where to find the souk. The number disappears and an accordion-like list emerges, listing the many spices found there.

I look up at the woman in awe. "Wow!"

As dusk falls, we wind our way through the souks, speaking with the local vendors. The women wear beautiful robes. The men wear colorful shirts. Before long, though, we find ourselves back at the main square and see that Jemaa el Fna has become an open-air dining place packed with stalls lit by floating lanterns. The cooking fills the area with strong aromas, and my stomach growls loudly.

"Can we eat here?" Ander asks. "It smells good."

Seraphina looks at Gregor. "What do you think? I'm up for it if you are."

"I am," he replies with enthusiasm. "These stalls appear to be filled with local cuisine. But how do we choose?"

"Let's pick a spot with other children in line. If they like the food, I bet we will, too." So we find a stall where several families are eating and order couscous, *pastilla*, sausage, and soup. When it's ready, we find a table that looks just like the colorful ones up on the platform courtyard.

Jillian looks around the square. "It's like another world here. I never knew a place like this existed."

"I love it here, too," Seraphina replies. "That market was amazing."

"How about those snake charmers?" Ander asks. "Those were cool—and creepy."

I picture the hissing snakes and shudder. "I liked the Virtual Market Box the best. That was a great invention."

When Gregor sees that we've finished eating, he urges us to clear our plates. "We better get back to the megacar now. We don't want to keep the others waiting."

We do as he asks. As we hurry away from Jemaa El Fna, I try to memorize the lights, the colors, the scents, and the sounds. It's the most magical place I've ever been to and I hate to leave it. I just wish our team could invent a teleporter. Then we could come back whenever we want. Now *that* would be an incredible invention.

THE POONCHA TREE

A FEW WEEKS later, Seraphina and Gregor are waiting for us in the courtyard. They're sitting at the colorful tiled tables with Mathilde and Gabriel, the preceptors for Team France, and Elin and Levin, the preceptors for Team Switzerland. Team France and Team Switzerland step out of their aero-buses, too, and soon we're all gathered together underneath a canopy of trees.

Benches, arranged in a semicircle, await us and Levin motions for us to sit down. We scurry to take our places. "You each have the same mission, task, and goals on this tour. As you know, your mission is to inspire and educate the children of the world with your inventions. Your task is to create new inventions, and your goal is to gain placement into your elite inventor schools of choice. Today, the task-solving portion of the tour officially begins."

We shuffle in our seats and my butterflies wake up.

"You've reached the pinnacle stage of the Piedmont Challenge, but in order to secure a spot in your desired institutions back home, you must complete one last task. And even though you'll create your inventions separately and be evaluated separately, you must climb this one mountain together."

We glance at one another. It suddenly feels awkward sitting here with all of them, knowing we're all working toward the same goal. "It is up to each team to work on the platform where they wish, beginning today. If you need our assistance, we will be easily accessible."

"Do you have questions?" Seraphina asks.

We shake our heads.

"Okay, then, time to brainstorm! We can't wait to see what fabulous things your teams create!" The other preceptors wish us luck and one by one exit the courtyard.

Zoe pulls her sleeve over her knuckle. "I didn't think to ask before, but Seraphina mentioned the word *brainstorm*. What does that mean?"

I tuck my foot underneath me. "Brainstorming is where we all say ideas of how to solve the task aloud. We may not use any of the ideas, but one of them may lead to someone thinking up another idea."

"And it doesn't matter who suggests the idea," Ander replies. "It just matters that we have a lot of ideas to think about."

"That sounds good," says Hannah. "I think our team should do that, too."

"But first you should read the task," says Ander. "We all should, so we know exactly what we're trying to solve."

I watch Ander for a second. He's not asking to take a break. He's not saying that reading the task is boring, like he usually does. He's . . . being a leader.

"That's a good idea," says Maëlle. "I think our team should try that, too."

Ander tilts the air screen toward all of us. "Why don't we do that now? Stephan, can you search for our task on the air screen so we can read it together?"

Stephan walks over to it and presses buttons on the barely visible keyboard. Within a few seconds, the task appears in large blue letters.

"Do you guys mind if I read it?" Jillian asks. No one objects, and so she stands up like she's about to take the stage.

Innovation Connects Our World

The final task of the Piedmont Challenge has two parts: Part One begins immediately. Each of your three teams must build an invention. The invention must be useful to people all over the world and be developed exclusively with materials found inside your aero-bus.

"This seems easy," says Finn.

"Yeah, not as hard as our other tasks," Ander replies. "Because we totally get to pick what we want to make."

"Do we have red boards to use?" asks Jax. "That would help us get started."

"What's a red board?" asks Giulia.

"It hears ideas as you say them and makes them appear on the screen. No one has to write or type at all."

"That's fabulous," says Gwyndol. "Where do we find one of those?"

Before we can even search, Jax has already found three of them on a nearby table.

"Nice job, big guy!" says Ander. Jax's face turns as red as a cherry. The other kids hardly notice, but I do. I don't think Jax likes it when people are staring at him.

Jonah stands up. "We better separate into our own teams now. Our team will work on our aero-bus. I want to make sure no one steals our ideas."

Hannah rolls her eyes. "No one's going to steal our ideas, Jonah. We don't have any ideas for them to steal yet anyway." But her team stands up and follows him out of the courtyard. "I guess we'll see you guys later," she calls to us.

I wave to Hannah as Zoe stands up. "I like being outside in this courtyard. What if our team works over there at the other end and your team can work right here? We won't be able to hear each other talking."

"Okay," says Jillian. "Good luck brainstorming!"

"You, too," Maëlle replies, and together the French team jogs to the other side.

Ander walks around the table. "Okay, let's call out our ideas and see what sticks."

Jax's hand shoots up. "Let's make a boat-type invention." The word *boat* appears on the red board.

Jillian folds her hands together. "I think we should make an invention for artists that would clean all their paint brushes so they wouldn't have to wash them by hand." *Paint brush cleaner* appears on the red board.

Mare yawns. "Remember, we can only use items we find inside the aero-buses."

"How about a new sport?" asks Ander. "One that could be used by people all over the world." The word *sport* appears on the red board.

I try to think of an idea. What's an incredible invention that people all over the world would like? I try to think of something, but all I can do is think about how unfair it is that we're solving another task—again!

The French team is huddled together. It's a little distracting. They're just close enough where we can see them, but not close enough to hear what they're saying or see what's appearing on their red board. But I know they're there, thinking up great stuff, and it makes my brain tangle.

"Okay, guys, what else?" asks Ander.

We sit there together at the colorful tables for a long while, calling out idea after idea and watching them appear on our red board. The clouds roll by while we think, and all I know for sure so far is that I don't like any of the ideas. But I also know, from the tasks we've solved before, that it might take us awhile to figure this out. We need to think of something incredible, or none of us will be going to the schools we want. I won't get to go to PIPS, and I'll never get to build my sixty-seven inventions. And even though this whole new task situation is *so unfair*, complaining, even to myself, won't help. I need to follow the rules and create an excellent invention with my team—or I'll be sent back to Crimson for good.

Hmm. Wait a minute. That's it. Maybe we could build one of my sixty-seven invention ideas—the ones I keep in my Someday Box! "Hey, how about an underwater bubble bike?" I suggest. "I've been dreaming of building one for a really long time."

The red board records, *underwater bubble bike.*

"That would be cool, KK, except we can only use materials found on the aero-buses. I'm not sure we'd find everything we need to build that."

"Yeah, maybe not." I wonder if any of my other sixty-seven ideas could be built here, with stuff we can find on the aero-bus. But my brain is covered in fog. I think everyone else's is, too, because we sit in the courtyard without talking. Ander bounces a tennis ball. Mare leans her chin on the table.

"I can't think of anything," says Jax.

"I can't either," I say.

"Wait a minute," says Mare. "I think we're approaching this task backward."

"What do you mean?" Jillian asks.

"If we must use materials found on our aero-bus, maybe we should start there. Let's see what stuff we can find and then think up an invention afterward."

"That could work," I say, and together we race to the aero-bus.

"Let's check the floating room," Ander suggests. "I bet there's something good inside."

We check the shelves, and we check behind the furniture. We don't have to look under it because it's seriously floating in the air. We scan the tables, and we look under the cushions. But we don't find anything that inspires us for an invention. We check the dining chamber and our bedchambers after that. But we don't find anything. Maybe this task is going to be harder than we thought.

After dinner, Seraphina tells us we're free to hang out with the other kids, so we wander to the courtyard to see if any of them are there. Jonah from Switzerland pulls a chair out, turns it backward, and swings one leg over the seat to sit down. He rests his arms on the back of the chair and shakes his head. "What took you so long, America? We've been waiting here for hours, ready to be social."

We get to his table and Hannah sighs: "Don't listen to him. We just got here, too." Jonah doesn't seem bothered by her, though. He just sits there with a smirk on his face.

Maëlle and Danielle arrive, talking about our task. "Hi, everyone. Have you figured out an invention yet?"

"Invention?" Finn replies. "No, we don't have an invention yet."

"We don't either," says Zoe. "Not yet anyway."

Ander pulls out a chair. "We don't either, but we will soon. I can feel a great one coming to me."

I shake my head. I know Ander doesn't have any great invention coming to him. He might eventually, but he doesn't now. Jonah folds his arms across his chest. "Well, we will certainly create something top-notch. We did think up the Thought Translation Box, so inventing something else can't be too difficult." He rocks back and forth in his chair, trying to look like a preceptor, but it's not working.

After the other teams head back to their aero-buses, we wander around the platform, where we stumble upon a new tree cluster near our own aero-bus, one that wasn't there before. It looks different than the others with one unusual tree in the center. It's full of colorful objects and silver cups. The longer we stare, the more cups appear. Ander reaches out to grab one but pulls his hand away. "It's cold!" I touch it, too, and my fingers almost stick to the cup.

Mare rises up on her tiptoes. "It looks like some kind of drink."

Jillian crouches next to a metal plate below the tree.

Here lies the Pooncha Tree, where the
Piedmont problem-solving elixir grows.

Help yourself, but to protect your hands from
the icy cold, wrap your cup with a Pooncha cloth.

Enjoy . . . and soon your
tangled mind will swirl once more.

"That's cool!" Ander exclaims. "I mean, literally cool."

I grab a soft, colorful piece of fabric and pull it from a branch. "These must be the Pooncha cloths." I slip it onto a cup, tug the cup from its branch, and hold it with both hands. My teammates watch me, waiting for me to try it. I quickly take a small sip. "It tastes like bananas and pineapple."

"This place is so strange," says Mare. "We literally have a drink tree just steps from our aero-bus."

We lean up against the platform windows, drinking our elixir from the Pooncha Tree as brilliant shades of orange and yellow fall like a curtain. The platform grows dim, and one by one, the lampposts turn on, illuminating the courtyard. I stare at the Pooncha Tree and wonder, could it really work? Could this drink really help untangle our thoughts, help us to think up another incredible invention? I bet it can. I bet it's an invention created by one of the winners of the Piedmont Global Championships. That's exactly why we need to keep trying. Our next invention needs to be even better than the others. That's the only way future teams will know that our team has made incredible stuff. Tomorrow we'll think of something. I know we will.

THE ICE POND

THE CALENDAR FLIPS to December, and we're on our way to Norway, our third tour stop. Soon, I'll get to see my family. Even though they won't be arriving for a few weeks, just knowing they'll be here soon makes my butterflies dance. I have a lot to show them, like this bedchamber. I lie in my flower bed staring at the daisies and marigolds, running my hand over the petals. Every once in a while, the creativity misters turn on and I let the droplets sprinkle my face. I would definitely like a sprinkle of creativity tonight. We need to think up another incredible invention—and soon. If we don't, we'll never get into PIPS—for real this time.

The next morning, we run through our lines in chamber eight. When we're finished, we pour into the megacar with the other teams, drop through the platform floor, and fly down to the city of Bergen, located on the west coast of Norway.

I stare out the window. As we drop into the city, I feel like we've entered a land of colorful dollhouses—some red, some blue, some yellow, some grey—lined up against a backdrop of mountains. The whole scene looks like a page torn out of a picture book. As the megacar nears the ground, the Grieghallen Convention Center, a strangely shaped building that sits on stilts in the middle of the city, grows bigger and bigger.

We pile out of the megacar and step onto the ground of Norway for the first time. Teams France and Switzerland follow their preceptors inside, while Gregor and Seraphina gather us together near the street. The air bites at my cheeks, so I zip up my parka and tuck my chin inside.

Seraphina pulls her fluffy purple hood over her head and shivers. "Okay, my Crimson Kids, welcome to Bergen, the second largest city in Norway, known as the gateway to the majestic fjords!"

"What are fjords?" asks Jillian.

Gregor pushes a button on the megacar, and a heated canopy extends over us. "Well, fjords are quite spectacular and must be seen to be believed. Essentially, though, they are long, narrow sections of the sea surrounded by steep cliffs. They're very deep, some more than thirteen hundred yards, and were formed by glaciers eroding the mountains in their path. There are one thousand fjords in Norway."

"Yikes, can we see one?" Ander asks.

"Yes, but not until your families arrive. Do you remember when we went sightseeing in Canada during the

Piedmont Global Championships? We rode on the funicular in Québec to get to the top of the Breakneck Stairs? We'll do the same here. We'll take the Fløibanen funicular to the top of Mount Fløyen for an overhead view of the city and a fjord. We may even take a day trip to see one closer than that."

We look at each other and smile. *That's so cool!*

"But today, we meet the children of Norway," Seraphina exclaims. "Let's go!"

We enter the building that's triangular on one side, with windows that stretch up to the ceiling. It's enormous! A woman standing in a glass case stops us before we can go further. She tilts her head and smiles. "Welcome to the Grieghallen. Please place your hand on the screen in front of you. Then step onto the circle marking on the floor so that you may be scanned and directed to your destination."

Ander leans over and whispers. "Wait, is she a robot?"

The woman folds her hands in front of her. "I am a hologram. My name is Britta. I am here to guide you. Please do as instructed."

One by one, we follow her directions. The glass case lights up, and she waves her hand like a talk show host. "So wonderful to meet you, Team USA. The children of Bergen are quite excited to meet you. Please follow the green arrow. It will guide you to your destinations throughout the day. Enjoy your stay at the Grieghallen."

A laser-looking green arrow appears in the air in front of us. The words *Tap to Go* blink until Gregor touches it. Once he does, it slowly floats along the hallway and we follow behind. It ushers us into an auditorium with a large stage, many lights, and many, many chairs set up in a semicircle. I guess it wants to show us where we'll be presenting. Next, we're led into a small room with a partition dividing it in half. The arrow stops at the door and attaches itself to the wall.

Gregor points to the two areas. "It looks like this is our room. Your costumes are set out for you. Girls on this side. Boys on that side. Go ahead and change. Seraphina and I will wait for you out here."

Mare, Jillian, and I enter the left side and find our costumes laying in neat piles. I change out of my clothes, slip on my overall shorts and T-shirt, and brush my hair into pigtails. When Mare and Jillian are dressed, too, we check ourselves in the mirror and make our way back to Seraphina and Gregor. Ander hops out the other side, wearing his Jester hat. Jax, wearing his black cape, follows close behind.

"Freddie Dinkleweed, at your service!"

Mare rolls her eyes. "Are you going to say that every single time you put on that costume?"

He grins. "Yup, that's the plan."

Seraphina gathers us together. "You all look fantastic. Are you ready?"

"We're ready," I say. "But don't forget to start us, okay?"

"I'm on it, Kia." After all these times, Seraphina knows we need someone to get us going. So now, every time after Master Freeman talks about the Piedmont Organization and introduces us, she says hello to the crowd and asks us if we're ready. "But, Gregor, do you want to do it this time? I don't have to be the one every time."

"Oh, no. I do not wish to address the crowd. They always seem to like you, anyway. I am happy to stand with the team and watch from backstage."

She smiles and seems to know that he does not want to talk in front of hundreds of people, even if most of them are kids. Soon, an usher leads us backstage where Team Switzerland is almost done presenting their inventions. By now we can practically recite their presentation, and Team France's presentation also. I bet by next summer, we'll be able to explain *one another's* inventions, too.

We take our places on stage, and the crowd goes quiet. But the silence doesn't bother me anymore. As I look out at the faces in the first few rows, I feel like a rock star. Performing for the kids is the best feeling in the universe. We tell the stories of Crimson Catropolis and demonstrate the Ancestor App and the Satellite Spectacles. They gasp at some parts of our skits, clap at others, and jump to their feet cheering when we're done.

When we're finished, the usher leads us into a small classroom, almost like the ones in Brazil and Morocco. The kids of Norway ask a lot of questions. Not all of them are about our inventions, though. Some of them are about us—like, are we homesick, and what do we like to do when we're not inventing things. That first question was easy. I'm not homesick. But . . . I really can't wait to see my family again. The second question was harder. I love to fly my aero-scooter, but besides that, my favorite thing to do is think up inventions.

Before long, we're back in the megacar and up on the platform again. Inside our bedchamber, the girls and I sit on our flower bed. Mare pulls her pillow onto her lap and sighs. "How many more days until our families get here?"

"Fifteen, I think," says Jillian. "I can't wait."

I look at the calendar on my watch. "Me, too, but don't forget. We have another big celebration tomorrow. It's December 2—Ander's birthday."

"Oh, right," says Jillian. "We're getting up early to sing to him."

"Ugh," says Mare. "Can't we sing to him at noon?"

"Mare, it's our new tradition. You guys sang to me first thing in the morning on my birthday, so we need to sing to him, too."

"You better not wake me up on my birthday." She throws her pillow over her head, and that's that. She'll probably be asleep in three minutes.

I face the flowers and try to drift off to sleep. Their scent doesn't distract me anymore. It's like they're not even there. Even the hyacinth and jasmine.

Early the next morning, the misters turn on and sprinkle our faces. I jump out of bed, but Jillian and Mare don't budge. "Guys! It's Ander's birthday. We have to wake him up!"

"Ander wants to sleep on his birthday," groans Mare.

"No, he doesn't! He wants to hear his friends sing 'Happy Birthday.'"

Jillian rolls out of bed. "Is Seraphina bringing the cinnamon rolls?"

"She said she is."

"Okay, fine," says Mare. "I'll get up for the cinnamon rolls."

We step across the hall and I raise my hand to knock on the door, but Jax opens it just as I do. We sneak in and open the basket to their giant balloon. Ander is buried underneath his blankets. But not for long! We shake him, and he slowly rolls over.

"Happy birthday!" I yell.

He sits up and blinks his eyes. "Thanks, guys," he answers in the quietest voice he's ever spoken in. I almost feel bad for waking him up, but then he throws off his blankets, jumps out of bed, and shouts: "I'm twelve! I'm twelve! Happy birthday to me!"

I should have known. Ander would never sleep away his birthday.

Seraphina swings open the door carrying the tray of cinnamon rolls. "Happy birthday, Ander!" She peeks inside the basket and sees the five of us inside. "Well, aren't you guys all cozy? Scooch over. Make room for me!"

Gregor looks inside with hesitation. "Happy birthday, Ander. Perhaps now that you're twelve, you will act like an adult."

"But twelve isn't an adult. I'm not even a teenager yet."

"You're right. That was just wishful thinking on my part."

Seraphina grabs a pillow and throws it at him. "Be nice to the birthday boy or no cinnamon rolls for you."

"Fine. Ander, may you become the best version of yourself this year."

"Why, thank you, Gregor. I appreciate that very much, kind sir."

I don't think twelve will change Ander one bit.

After we eat our cinnamon rolls, Ander crawls out of the balloon to talk to his family. Their hologram images appear just outside the basket, so we stay inside eating the rest of the rolls left on Seraphina's tray. Once he's done, we get dressed and join the others in the megacar. I think Ander will like his birthday celebration in Norway. He'll get to play Freddie Dinkleweed *and* do something he hasn't done in a while. Wait until he hears what it is!

WE LEAVE THE Grieghallen, and the megacar drives Gregor, Seraphina, and our team through the streets of Bergen. The other teams are not with us because this adventure is just for Ander—well, and for us, too. Not far from the convention center is a pond, completely frozen over. We hop out and Gregor opens the trunk of the car. He pulls out several giant bags, and Ander's eyes get bigger than baseballs. "Why do you have hockey bags in there—my hockey bag?"

"Apparently you're a hockey player. We thought we might like to play a game."

"Yeah," says Seraphina. "You can teach us how to play."

"And," I say. "You can show us all those hockey moves we've heard so much about."

Ander practically dives into his hockey bag. "No way! Let's go!"

We open the bags, and Ander shows us how to put on all the gear. "Now, listen, no checking allowed. You guys don't know what you're doing."

"What's checking?" asks Jillian.

"See what I mean. Checking is when you hit someone to get the puck."

Gregor nods. "It's used to separate an opponent from the puck."

"You know hockey?" Ander asks.

"I know many things, young Ander. When will you realize that?"

"All right," says Ander. "Let's see whatcha got!"

When we finish dressing in the thick hockey pants, shoulder pads, elbow pads, jerseys, and neck guards, we tie our skates and put on our helmets and gloves. "This is going to be awesome," says Ander, "but I'll warn you. The hardest part of hockey is skating. If you can't skate, you won't have a chance with anything else."

But Ander doesn't realize that I know how to skate and so does Mare. Jillian, Jax, and Seraphina, well, not so much. While they struggle to stay on their feet, the rest of us take our sticks and a puck and play a game of two-on-two. Ander and Gregor skate, pass, and shoot the puck. Mare and I have no idea what we're doing, but we skate around with our sticks and pretend we do.

"It's so cold out here!" Jillian wails from the edge of the pond. The air is bitter cold, and I can see my breath in front of me. The tips of my ears sting and my whole head is throbbing. But I want this day to be everything Ander hopes it will be, so while everyone else is taking off their equipment, Ander and I take one more skate around the pond.

"I can't believe I got to play hockey on my birthday—in Norway! I wonder how Gregor and Seraphina knew I would want to?"

"Well, they know you love hockey."

"Yeah, so."

I shrug. "I may have asked them if there was a place you could play. Gregor took care of the details."

His face is cherry red, frozen from the cold, but he manages to smile anyway. "Thanks, KK. This was so cool. Race you back!" He takes off for the other side of the pond and it's so not fair. I can't skate as fast as I run. But I race him anyway, and he beats me by a mile. We quickly slip off our gear, climb into the megacar, and drive away from the iced-over pond. By the time we get back to the Grieghallen, we've warmed up and the other two teams are waiting for us.

"Are we going back to the platform now?" asks Ander.

"Not quite," Seraphina responds. "I've heard there's a good restaurant nearby. They probably even serve birthday cake."

His face lights up, and I'm happy that Ander's happy on his birthday. I know how homesick he was at first. But I don't think he's homesick anymore—even today.

On the drive up to the platform, I think about the great day we had. But I think about our invention, too—the one that we haven't thought up yet. Maybe once I'm back inside our bedchamber and the creativity mister sprinkles over me, I'll have a great idea. Maybe I'll figure out exactly what invention we need to create to finally get us into PIPS.

THE BALANCE BLOCKS

AFTER MORE THAN a week of presenting our inventions to the children of Norway and giving them Swirl and Spark Recall tasks to solve, we still haven't thought up an invention. "This is so hard!" I say, tossing my pillow onto my flower bed. "Our other tasks were easier. They had more rules, more steps to follow."

"Yeah, now that we can invent anything we want, we can't think of anything at all," Mare laments, as she refolds the clothes in her drawer. "What's wrong with us?"

"Nothing's wrong with us," Jillian replies. She crams her clothes into her drawer and shoves it closed. "I think we're thinking too much. Maybe we should just hang out for a while."

"You mean take a nap."

Jillian twists her hair into a bun. "No. Doesn't Seraphina always say that playing like we did when we were little kids is a great way to find your creativity—or something like that?"

"Yeah, something like that."

"So maybe we should pretend we're kids . . . walk around the room pretending that we're toddlers. I have a little cousin who's three. She touches everything she sees—and asks lots of questions." Jillian kneels on the floor and points to the flower bed. "What's that? Why are there flowers in that bed?"

I stare at her for a second, but then I reply. "That's our flower bed."

Mare crouches down next to her, pretending, too. "Don't you roll into the daisies when you're sleeping?"

"No," I say. "Our beds are big enough."

Jillian crawls over to the wall. "What are those?"

"Those are blocks," I reply in my most grown-up voice.

I stand up and place my hands on my hips. "Well, they're stuck to the wall. They fall off sometimes, but there aren't enough for us to play with."

Jillian looks up at me and replies in a babyish voice: "Then, let's go search for toys. Come on!"

I sit on the bed. I'm not sure how Jillian's game is going to help us. "Three-year-old children don't crawl, you know."

"But crawling is fun," she reminds me. "Come on!"

"Okay, we can look for things to use to solve our task." I kneel on the floor and follow them around the room. We sing songs that we sang when we were little. We look in drawers, under the bed, and in the bathroom. Then we take our search into the hallway where the boys are watching from their doorway. Jax stares, but Ander doesn't seem surprised at all that we're crawling.

"Come on!" I say. "We're looking for stuff to invent with."

Ander and Jax jump into the back of the line. They sing our song and soon the five of us are marching instead of crawling, on the hunt for something—anything that we can build an invention with. We search the boys' bedchamber, both inside and outside of their hot air balloon, but we don't find anything useful. We enter chamber eight next, and we're barely inside the room when the closet door bursts open and a mountain of colorful blocks, like the ones on our wall, spills out the door.

Ander slowly enters the chamber. "What the heck?"

We crowd around the door, wondering how it opened on its own.

"These are like the blocks on our bedchamber wall!" Jillian exclaims.

I pick up a yellow block. "These are heavier than the ones on our wall, though."

Jax kneels next to the pile. "Some of them are magnetic. Watch."

He holds two together. They attach almost like magic and light up for a split second. They don't give off a message like the ones in our bedchamber, but when they connect, it's like they're meant to be attached.

"Wait a second," I say. "Maybe we could use these for our invention."

"Like how?" asks Mare.

"I don't know yet, but I bet we can think of something."

Ander opens the closet door wider. "Let's bring the rest out here. Maybe an idea will come to us."

We form a chain and take the blocks, one by one, from the colorful mountain and pass them to one another until they're lying all over the chamber eight floor. Then we scatter around the room, playing with them the way little kids would. There are so many, we stack them like towers, line them up like dominoes, connect them like Legos, and build a fortress with bridges.

I set two blocks side by side and examine them, trying to figure out what else they could be used for. I move them around so that they're touching the long way and they connect like magnets. My brain swirls until I imagine a balance beam. But not just a regular gymnastic beam, a longer, more elaborate one. "I wonder if we could walk on them."

"What for?" Jax asks.

"I don't know. Maybe to see if we can balance on them?"

"Why?" asks Mare.

I stand up to get a different perspective. "I'm not sure. Maybe we could make a whole block system."

Jillian leans back against the window seat. "That would be fun."

Mare shrugs. "But what would the point be?"

"I don't know yet. Maybe if we connect them, we'll think of something."

"There are so many blocks," Jax replies with a thoughtful expression on his face. "I'm not sure we'll have enough room to use them all."

He's right. "Let's just use as many as we can fit, I guess."

Mare presses down on a light blue block. "We need to figure out how strong they are first, how much weight they can hold, and how we can connect them. Some of them seem to connect like magnets already, but some of them repel each other."

Jillian scoops up a bunch. "Okay, then, let's put as many as we can together and see what kind of beam we end up with. Then we can decide the rest."

Before we know it, we've spent the afternoon spread out all over chamber eight, connecting the blocks. Some *want* to connect, and others don't. Our multicolored beam expands from just a few feet long to more than twenty, winding across the floor. I stand up on the window seat to get a better look. "It looks like a colorful snake."

Ander picks up two leftover blocks. "Hey, we forgot about these. He inches them closer to each other, but before they magnetically connect, they pop out of his hands! They don't fall to the ground, though. They push back up like reverse gravity. "What the heck?"

He tries to grab them as they float midair, to move them, but they won't budge. We crowd around him to get a closer look, and the same thing happens with the blocks Mare is holding. She tries to control hers, too, but they move over to Ander's blocks until all four are connected about three feet above the ground.

Mare stares them down. "What's happening?" They hover in front of us, refusing to budge. Jillian selects two from a different pile, but when she tries to connect them to each other, they drop out of her hand. A nearby purple block slides over and connects itself to them.

"This is weird," Mare says, walking around the other side of the blocks. "It's like they know where they want to go."

Ander bounces on his toes, with a huge grin on his face. "And have minds of their own!"

I step off the window seat and crouch down next to them. "It's like they're magical."

Jax shakes his head. "There's no such thing as magic. Only science and technology could be responsible for what's happening."

Ander shrugs, like watching blocks move like magic is the most normal thing in the world. "Well, whatever it is, it's cool."

"Let's move them around some more and see what happens," Mare suggests. She rolls up her sleeves and pulls two that are already connected from the colorful structure. We soon realize that some have no energy to them at all, and we place them where we want. But some are forceful and decide where to go on their own. They arrange and rearrange themselves, and by the time all the blocks are connected, a four-foot-tall, rollercoaster-type structure is taking over the chamber.

The hills and valleys of our structure cross over each other, with parts of it measuring two or three feet off the ground. Some pieces lie on the ground, inviting us to step on them. We walk around examining the structure, touching it, testing its strength. The blocks don't light up like the ones on our bedchamber wall, though, and we aren't sure why. We also don't know why the different blocks connect the way they do. All we know is that the blocks we've discovered—or that discovered us—are nothing like we've ever seen before.

Mare leans back on her elbows. "The structure looks strong, and it doesn't seem like any of the blocks want to break apart."

"This could be an incredible invention," I say. "If we can decide what it *is* exactly."

Ander points to a purple block. "This looks like the starting point, and did you guys notice there's more than one path from the starting point to the end point way over there?"

Jax stands at the other end of the chamber. "It looks like this is where the beam ends."

Ander grins. "Can I try? To test it, I mean."

"Are you good at balancing?" asks Jillian.

"Yeah, probably," he says with hesitation.

"I'll do it then." She nudges him out of the way and steps onto the purple block. She balances on one foot for a second before she attempts to step onto the next blue one. It's attached to a yellow one and she steps on both with ease. She walks across several more, crossing the level section, with her arms parallel to the floor. After she crosses about fifteen blocks, she reaches the first hill. The incline is gradual and she handles it with no problem. Just as she's about to reach the top, she spins around and heads back in the direction she started from. The next block flashes *stay strong*.

What? "Did you guys see that? The block gave her a message!"

Ander hops onto the beam. "Me next!" He crosses the structure, but much less gracefully than Jillian. He stops also before the incline blocks take him upward. Instead of continuing, he turns and the next block flashes *find your next gear.* "That's so cool!"

Mare hops on and is careful, measured, like she's analyzing every block as she steps on it. She reaches the incline but keeps going. Before long, she's four feet above the ground and comes to a split in the beam. She steps onto a red block that would take her along the path on the right, and after five blocks, the structure declines, taking her closer to the ground. Soon she reaches the end of the beam and she hops off. The last block flashes *well done,* and she flashes a smile.

"Okay, we need to talk about this," I say. "This could definitely be an amazing invention."

We form a circle on the floor near the east side windows. I cross my legs under me. Mare pulls her hair into a ponytail. "What is it, exactly?" she asks.

Ander rolls a tennis ball in front of him. Back and forth. Back and forth. "Well, it is a test of balance. What if we invent a game called Balance Blocks? It could be for grown-ups. They always want to play kid games."

"How would it work?" Jax asks.

"The objective would be to walk across as many blocks as possible in a certain amount of time. So, if you have five people on each team, each person walks across the blocks trying to get as many points as they can for the team. At the end, the team with the most points wins."

"And we could assign points based on color," suggests Jillian. "Let's say green is worth the most points. The more green blocks you touch as you walk across the structure, the more points you'll get."

Mare nods. "That sounds good."

"What about scoring the game?" I ask. "Like, how do we add the numbers?"

"We could add them up ourselves," says Ander.

"We could," Jax replies. "We could each choose a color and calculate the points at the end."

I bite my ring-finger nail. "But I think we need something more technological than that. Remember, this invention is what's going to decide if we get into PIPS."

"Yeah," says Mare. "This game idea is good; a great scoring system would make it better."

"Okay," says Ander. "Let's figure out a system." He pulls down an air screen and we crowd around it. We research scoring methods but can't find exactly what we're looking for.

Jax stands up. "What if we set it up to keep score automatically? We could write a program for it, based on color and the point values for each block."

"How do we make the blocks communicate with the computer, so that when someone touches a block, the point is sent to the computer?" Jillian asks.

"Easy. We need to add something to each block."

"You mean like a sensor?" I ask.

Ander hops up on the window seat. "Yes! Just like the ones used in Nacho Cheese Ball, the game we played at Camp Piedmont. In that game, players throw scoops of cheese at each other and at targets. The suits and targets have sensors. Each time one is hit with cheese, the point total appears on the score board."

"That would definitely make the game work better," says Mare.

"I think so, too," I say. "How many colors do we have in total?"

"Let's see," says Jillian. "Red, green, blue, light blue, purple, yellow, orange, pink, white, and black. That's ten."

"Let's make white worth ten and black worth one," suggests Ander.

In the end, we decide on white, ten; red, nine; green, eight; blue, seven; light blue, six; purple, five; yellow, four; orange, three; pink, two; black, one.

"So, what's the time limit?" I ask.

"How about one minute?" Mare suggests. "The object is to touch as many blocks as possible before time is up."

While we call out ideas, Jax enters the information onto the air screen. Before long, we have most of our game details figured out, all stored in front of us. The colorful structure stands next to us, and I can't help but smile. "This is going to be a great invention."

"And it's something everyone can use," says Ander. "No matter how old they are, where they live, or what language they speak."

As we high five one another, we hear a clicking noise along the hallway floor and then a knock on the door. We open it to find Seraphina standing there. When she sees our colorful structure, her eyes open wide. "What is this incredible contraption?"

"It's our invention," I say. "We finally have an idea."

"It looks amazing. Care to share any details yet?"

"No, not yet. We still have some things to figure out."

"Well, it looks fantastic, whatever it is. But now it's time for a break. I've left chocolate cream puffs for all of you in the courtyard."

"Yes!" Ander jumps to his feet and races for the treats. I close the door to chamber eight and follow the rest of my team to the courtyard. When we get to the table, we see more than chocolate cream puffs. There are platters full of cheese, apples, and strawberries, too.

We hang out with the other kids until we've had our fill of snacks. When we've finished, we race back to chamber eight and make our plan to write the scoring program. After hours of research, we're forced to stop for dinner. It's fine, though, my brain feels like it's buried in cement. At least we have an invention. Now all we have to do is finish it.

THE CABLE CAR

WE'VE SPENT PRACTICALLY every day the last couple of weeks presenting to the children in Norway, with hardly any time at all to work on the rest of our invention or even think about it. Our schedule has been packed to make time for the tour break with our families. We've haven't seen much of the country either, aside from the ice pond on Ander's birthday. But Seraphina says that's all about to change, because today our families arrive, and we'll be able to explore together.

My hands feel sweaty as I sit in the megacar. I unzip my coat and shift in my seat. It's hard to sit still with the butterflies pushing against my stomach. They seem to know that my family is close by, that I haven't seen Mom, Dad, Malin, Ryne, and Grandma Kitty since October.

Bergen—the city of tiny houses—eases into view, and I just wish the megacar would land already. When it finally does, we step out into the crisp Norwegian air, but it instantly bites at my face. Our families crowd around the megacar, and within seconds mine has squished me like a bug. Surrounded by the chaos, I stay wrapped inside their arms, warm even in the frigid air.

Mom is the last to let go, and when she finally does, she's beaming like a ray from the sun. "I've missed you so much, Baby Girl!"

"Little Bear!" Dad says with a smile. "I think you're about eighteen inches taller."

I laugh, because even if I have gotten taller, I'm the smallest one on my team, and still taller only than Ryne. So I'm sure he's only kidding.

We stand beside the megacar talking with our teeth chattering, until Seraphina and Gregor lead us to a special Team USA bus, and we gladly climb inside with our families. Soon it's too loud to hear what anyone is saying, so Seraphina clicks on a microphone. "We have a fun day planned for all of you!" she announces. "First, we'll be taking the Ulriken cable car up to the highest point of Bergen, Norway's seven mountains. We'll be sightseeing the entire area.

"Do you mean more shopping?" Ander asks.

"More wandering!" she replies. "And don't worry, Ander. I have a feeling you're going to love the cable car ride. We all will. Plus, from the summit, we'll see the mountains, the islands, the fjords, and the sea. I suspect it will be breathtaking!"

The bus reaches our destination, and we climb into several red and yellow cable cars with cartoon children painted on the sides. My whole family rides together, and we stand at the windows looking out at the amazing view. Seraphina was right. The city and mountains look like they jumped out of a movie. But best of all, I'm seeing it with my family.

We sit down on the benches, and I wedge myself between my parents. Grandma Kitty sits across from me with Malin and Ryne on either side of her. We talk about Norway. We talk about baseball. We talk about Malin's new boyfriend. And we talk about the platform.

"I can't believe you're living in a sky bubble!" says Ryne. "Can you see outer space?"

"It's not that high, but it is incredible."

The clouds roll by our window, and we stare at the mountains and the fjords below. When we reach the very top, we step out of the cable car where it feels like we're on the top of the world. We explore the area, just like Seraphina said we would, and walk in and out of shops nearby, too. We stop at a small restaurant for an early dinner of boiled potatoes, vegetables, and smoked herring. I've never tried herring before, but Gregor says it's a dish the people of Norway eat all the time. Besides, Seraphina says it's good to try new things, so I do.

After our Norwegian dinner, we take the cable car back down the mountain. On the ride down, I lean my head on my dad's shoulder and close my eyes. My family will be here with me for more than two weeks! We'll celebrate Christmas together and see all kinds of things in Norway.

I'll get to tell them all about our new task, the other kids, and our invention. But not now. Maybe tomorrow. My eyes are heavy, and I just want to drift off to sleep.

A FEW DAYS before Christmas, Jillian and I set our watches for 7:00 a.m. Ander and Jax do the same. We know that Mare says she wants to sleep late on her birthday, but we know better. If we don't surprise her by singing "Happy Birthday," she'll be sad—even if she won't admit it.

Jillian and I are ready when Ander and Jax knock quietly at the door. We sneak them in, but I don't know why we're trying to stay silent. Nothing wakes Mare up. Nothing. When we're all standing around her bed, I count to three in a whisper and we sing out, "Happy birthday, Mare!"

She doesn't move.

I shake her shoulder. Still nothing.

"Mare, wake up," Jillian whispers. "It's your birthday!"

"Happy birthday, Mare!" Ander shouts in a booming voice.

Slowly, her arm moves. She grabs her pillow and flings it at us without a sound.

I try to stifle a laugh, but she throws another one at me. I can't help it. Even on her birthday, Mare is Mare!

Seraphina and Gregor walk through the door carrying gifts from her family and the tray of cinnamon rolls. That's when Mare sits up and rubs her eyes.

"I love my birthday. But I hate all of you."

Seraphina smiles. "We love you, though, Mare. Happy birthday. Eat up! We're meeting your families down in Bergen for more Norwegian fun today. Guess what? We're going dogsledding."

"Yes!" Ander high fives Jax. "This will be almost as good as playing pond hockey."

Mare smiles. "Okay, that's worth getting up early for."

ON THE FIRST day of January, after celebrating New Year's Eve with the other teams in a large room at the Grieghallen, I stand outside a café with Grandma Kitty. Our megacar is parked a few feet away and, in fifteen minutes, it will take us back up to the platform, and my family will leave for the airport. I'm trying hard to stay happy, because we've spent over two weeks together, and because I don't *want* to feel sad. But I already miss them, and they haven't even left yet.

"Buttercup, you haven't said much about your invention. This whole time, your lips have been sealed. Is that because it's top secret?"

"No, it's not top secret. It's just, well, oh, I don't know."

"I know that look on your face. Something's wrong. Is the invention giving you trouble?"

"No, it's not really giving us trouble. I just wish I knew if it was spectacular enough to get us into PIPS."

"Ah, I see. You don't think it's good enough."

"Well, it *is* an amazing game. I'm just not sure it's enough."

"Have you asked yourself how you can make it enough?"

"Sort of."

"Maybe you need to think of something else for a bit."

"I thought that after this break something would come to me, but nothing has."

Grandma Kitty laughs. "Your break isn't even over! I have a strong feeling that once you get back up on that platform and start working together, the ideas will pour out like water from a faucet."

"But it's not just that. After this break we learn what the second part of our task is."

"Well, there you go. Maybe that will help you see things in a new way."

"I guess."

"You can do it, Smartie Girl. Mark my words. Now that your break is over, you and your team have a chance for a new beginning—a fresh start. There's no telling what you can accomplish up there on that platform together."

"You're right. Thanks, Grandma. I'm happy we got to hang out in Norway together."

"Me, too, Buttercup. Me, too."

My family emerges from the café, and I decide as soon as I see them that I'm going to say goodbye real fast and jump right into the megacar. And then I'm definitely not going to watch them get smaller as we fly away. So, I don't. I lean back in the seat and bite my ring-finger nail. Grandma Kitty is right. We're going to make our game of Balance Blocks even more incredible as soon as we land on the platform. The judges will love it—and then they'll have to let us enroll in PIPS!

FINDING MABEL

THE AERO-BUS LOWERS through the platform, and just like that our time in Norway is over and we're headed to our fourth tour stop—China, ready to start the new year. I try not to think about my family or that the next time I'll see them will be in May, when we're stationed in Italy. It only makes me miss them, and I don't want to miss them. Instead, I think about our invention, because unless we improve our Balance Blocks with a spectacular scoring system and impress the judges at PIPS in August, we'll be headed back to Crimson—and I'll be programmed into Math.

This ride to China will take several hours, so we decide to make the most of it. After doing our research this morning on writing the scoring program, we're ready to move to the next step: adding the scoring sensors to the blocks.

"We have to find materials," I say.

"All right," says Jax. "We need wire, stuff to make a circuit board, and something to stick on each block."

"Made out of cloth or something?" asks Jillian.

"I don't know. Maybe."

Jillian leads the way to the dining chamber. "This was much easier when we could just choose what we needed from the Piedmont Pantry at Camp Piedmont."

We enter the dining chamber through the pocket door and scatter. I start with the bottom cupboards. Jax starts with the top. Mare searches the drawers, and Ander and Jillian explore the area behind the snack counter.

Ander hops on the counter stool. "As long as we're in here, maybe we should order a snack." Before any of us can argue—or agree—he presses a bunch of buttons and a tray of colorful cupcakes pops out of the countertop.

"Good choice!" I say, picking up one labeled "tropical breeze."

"Oooh," Jillian squeals. "I'll take this cherry cheesecake one."

Jax chooses chocolate smores, Ander takes Boston cream pie, and Mare picks red velvet celebration. They almost look too good to eat, but cupcakes should always be eaten, and within minutes, it's like they were never even there. The tray disappears back into the counter, and we're left wiping the crumbs off our faces.

"Okay, let's get back to our search," says Ander. "I'll check up here." He climbs onto the counter to look through the shelves.

I don't find anything at all in my cupboard except cookbooks. Cookbooks? It's so weird. No one really cooks on this aero-bus, so why would there be so many cookbooks? But then I remember that Seraphina has made birthday cinnamon rolls for Ander, Mare, and me so maybe they're for her. I move to the next cupboard, hoping to find something perfect to use for the sensors. But all I see are pots and pans. I guess if we want to cook some blocks, these will help.

"I found some wire up here." Ander tosses a roll to Jax.

"Thanks, that might work."

"I found a first-aid kit," says Mare. "There might be something in here."

While she searches, Jillian places a tub of glue or something on the counter. "Maybe we can use this."

"I found bandages and tape," says Mare. "We could use them to attach the sensors."

I open the next cupboard and see a metal object. I lean in to get a closer look and gasp. "Mabel!"

"What?" Mare asks.

"I found Mabel. Our robotic monkey assistant!"

I push a button on the side of her ear, and she lights up. Her eyelids open and she unfolds from her sleeping position. When I open the cupboard door wide, she rolls out onto the dining chamber floor.

My teammates gather around her, and I say, "Hi, Mabel! You're here!"

"Yes, I am here. I have been resting in this cupboard since take off from Piedmont University in Maryland on October 1, 2071."

I pat her robotic head. "Aw, I'm sorry it took us so long to find you."

"That is all right. I am here to assist you."

My teammates and I exchange glances. "Okay. Can you find objects that will help us add scoring sensors to a large set of blocks?"

Mabel stands still for a moment. Her lights flash randomly in a bunch of colors, and she scurries away on her wheels. She stops at the counter. Her lights flash a few more times, and a small secret door opens. She disappears into the opening, and the door closes behind her.

Ander laughs. "Where did she go?"

"I don't know," I say. "Maybe she didn't understand my question."

"I bet she did," says Jax. "If she didn't, she would have asked you to repeat it."

Jax is right. A few minutes later, the secret door opens, and she rolls out pulling a cart behind her. "As you requested, objects to help you add scoring sensors to a large set of blocks."

Mare's eyes open wide. "No way."

I pat her head again. "Thanks, Mabel."

She blinks and yawns. "You are welcome."

I push a button on her arm, and she rolls back into the cupboard.

Jax shrugs. "I guess we should have searched in here sooner. Let's bring this cart to chamber eight and see what's here."

When we get there, we dump it all out on the floor, a few feet away from our block structure. There's copper foil, wires, LEDs, circuit boards, and a bunch of other shiny pieces. While the rest of us examine the pieces, Mare organizes them into piles.

Jax picks up a circuit board. "This is good. We can create touch sensors. They'll detect changes in the capacitance between the onboard electrodes and the object making contact."

Jillian turns toward him. "Excuse me?"

"The sensors will be able to tell when a person steps on the block. Basically, it will be an open circuit when the block is not touched and a short circuit when the block is stepped on. But the signal that's measured will be directly converted into a digital signal output, and this digital signal will be transmitted through a cable digitally."

"If you say so," Ander replies. "You might have to explain it as we make them."

"This is going to take some time," Jax replies.

"Then we better get going." I run to my bedchamber and grab a notebook and pencils. Jax draws us a picture of the sensors we're trying to make. We brainstorm, trying to determine how to attach them to each block and eventually decide on duct tape.

"Duct tape will work, and we have some here on the aero-bus, so it's perfect!" Jillian replies. "We can attach one underneath each block, right? That way all the wires will be hidden."

"Sounds good," says Mare. "Let's do it."

We spend the rest of the day and night building our touch sensors. We need a lot of them and eventually we run out of materials. But we bring Mabel out of her cupboard and ask her to bring us more. She does and before long, half the sensors are done.

When it feels like we can't look at one more sensor piece, Mare crawls up onto the window seat. "I'm so tired. Can we finish the rest of these tomorrow?"

"Yeah," says Jax. "I bet we can finish by dinnertime."

Just as we're closing the chamber door, though, Gregor appears in the hallway. "Change of plans, young team. Meet Seraphina and me in the floating chamber tomorrow at 7:00 a.m. We're not spending the day on the platform like we thought. We have something different planned."

THE BIG BUDDHA

WHEN I WAKE up the next morning, I'm still thinking about the Balance Blocks. But I don't have time to think about them right now, because today we're not staying on the platform like I thought we were. We're headed down to China for the very first time!

Jillian flies out of the bathroom and races toward her giant drawer. She pulls out one shirt after the other, throwing them over her head, searching for something. The clothes fly everywhere, and Mare stands next to her staring.

"What are you looking for?"

"My red team shirt. That's the one we need to wear today, and I can't find it."

I look at my watch. "Jillian, come on! We need to meet in the floating room in two minutes."

"I'm hurrying. I was sure it was rolled up in a pile under my blue one."

Mare sighs. "That's a real efficient system." She points to Jillian's flower bed. "You left it on the floor. I folded it and put it on your bed."

"Oh, good. Thanks, Mare!"

She wriggles into it, I grab her backpack, and we run down the hall. The boys are waiting and so are Gregor and Seraphina.

"You were almost late," says Ander. "But you made it. I entertained everyone with my juggling skills while we were waiting."

I shake my head. "Oh, I bet."

"Okay, my Crimson Kids, are you ready for China? I can't tell you how excited I am to see it. It's home to one of the oldest cities in the world! The country is referred to as the People's Republic of China, and Beijing is the capital. It's located in Northern China and is more than three thousand years old."

"So, we're going to Beijing?" I ask.

"Later this month we will be presenting there and seeing the Great Wall of China."

"It's actually a series of four walls," Ander explains. "And it's more than two thousand years old. Did you know that?"

"I didn't know that," Seraphina replies. "But thank you. Now I do. Today, though, we're off to another city, which is on a peninsula that juts out from mainland China plus two major islands. Any guesses where it is?"

Ander beams. "Hong Kong!"

"That's right. And the peninsula is separated from the two islands by Victoria Harbor. We'll be visiting both islands today."

We jump off the aero-bus and race for the platform window. I expect to see something, anything that will tell me we're in a different country, but just like all the other times, it feels like we're still in the same place. I guess the sky looks the same all around the world.

Team France is already inside the megacar when we climb inside. Team Switzerland arrives a few minutes later, and we make our way down to Hong Kong.

"KK, did you know that people speak Cantonese in Hong Kong but Mandarin in mainland China?"

"No, I thought the language they spoke everywhere in China was called Chinese."

"Nope. But now you know. And you should also know that tons of people in Hong Kong speak English, too." He takes a deep breath and keeps going. "Did you also know that the number four is bad luck?"

"No."

"It is. It's bad luck because the way they pronounce it is similar to the way they pronounce the word for death. So, yeah, four is bad."

"What else?" I ask.

"Never leave your chopsticks stuck in a rounded bowl of rice. It's bad manners."

"Okay, I won't."

"We might see street signs or places with royal names, like Queen Elizabeth Sports Stadium."

"Why?"

"Because Hong Kong was a British province until the year 1997. The government was British and so was the school system. That's why many people still speak English."

"Then maybe we won't need translators while we're here."

We land on Hong Kong Island, right in front of the Hong Kong Convention Center where we'll be presenting later in the week. All of the convention centers have been really cool, but this is amazing. Victoria Harbor flows in the front of it, and all these high-tech buildings sit behind it. We walk around the back to look at them, and I need to look twice. A giant golden statue towers before us—looking just like a Golden Light Bulb! But this one isn't a light bulb at all. It's a statue of a golden flower.

"This, my Crimson Kids, is the Golden Bauhinia statue—the Hong Kong Orchid Tree, the symbol of Hong Kong itself."

Jax looks up. "Look at how big it is."

"If you think this is impressive, wait until you see what's next," Gregor replies. "We're heading to Lantau Island."

Later, we land on the island at the base of a mountain. Gregor gathers us around. "We're going to see a monastery."

"Where monks live?" asks Mare.

"Yes, and work. This is a working monastery, so you will certainly see them walking around. Follow me."

We turn the corner and see an enormous cable car system. "The Ngong Ping 360 will take us to the top of the mountain. But this cable car is different than the one in Norway. It has a glass bottom floor. We'll be able to see the harbor below us as we ride up."

We step inside, onto a floor that doesn't look like a floor at all, and it feels like we're going to fall right to the ground below. I can't look away, though. Soon, we're moving up and over the water.

The ride takes about twenty minutes and when we step out of the cable car, we still haven't reached the top of the mountain. "Come on!" says Seraphina. "Let's go up."

We stand at the bottom of a vast staircase and look up . . . way up. It looks like a giant is sitting at the very top. "How many steps are there?" asks Mare.

"Two hundred and sixty-eight," Gregor replies. "I hope you're ready for a workout."

Seraphina leads the way, and we fall into place behind her. When we finally reach the top, we find ourselves out of breath and at the base of an enormous statue—one a million times bigger than the flower statue.

"This young team, is the Tian Tan Buddha!"

I look up and up and up at a humongous bronze statue of a Buddha.

"Although the Po Lin Monastery has been in existence since the 1930s, the statue was completed in 1993 and symbolizes the harmonious relationship between man and nature, people and faith."

Ander looks at Gregor in amazement. "That's one big Buddha!"

Gregor laughs. "One hundred and twelve feet to be exact."

"Look at his face," I say. "He looks all knowing . . . wise."

"I feel like we're on top of the world up here!" Jillian exclaims.

Seraphina spins around. "Isn't it breathtaking?"

We wander, looking at the water, the mountain, and the buildings. Some are ancient, some are modern, but all of them remind me of just how far away I am from home. I wish my family could see it. Mom and Grandma Kitty would love this view, and Ryne would love the Buddha.

After taking the Ngong Ping 360 back down the side of the mountain, Gregor and Seraphina usher us through the busy streets into a glass structure connected to the curb. The door slides open, and we step onto a slow-moving, tube-like surface. "What is this?" Ander asks.

"This, young team, is a Hyper Speed Tube Lane. Hang on!"

We grab the side railings, and I feel myself moving, but not quickly. But when I look through the glass wall, out into the streets of Hong Kong, I see flashes of double-decker buses, bridges, and even water whizzing by! Within seconds, it comes to a stop and the door slides open.

"We just traveled about twenty miles!" Seraphina exclaims.

I look at her in disbelief. "But that only took like a minute."

"It's the latest mode of transportation here in China. Fantastic, huh?"

Ander jumps out of the tube first. "That's so cool!"

Around the corner, we enter a restaurant. Seraphina smiles. "It's time for *yum cha!* Translated, that means, 'Drink tea.'"

"Is there food also?" Ander asks. "I'm starving."

"Me, too," Mare replies with a pained expression on her face.

"Oh, there'll be more than just tea. Trust me."

We sit together at a large table. "This is a bit like an American-type brunch where we'll sample many foods," Gregor explains. "There will be dim sum, many small steamed dishes served in bamboo steamer baskets. There'll be dumplings filled with vegetables and meats, flat noodles, and spongy cakes, all served with tea."

"That sounds good! How about fortune cookies?" asks Jillian. "Will we get those?"

"From what I understand, fortune cookies are not a tradition in China. They have origins in the United States, but the creator is hotly debated."

Our food arrives in the small, bamboo steamer baskets . . . tons of them! We sample a little bit of everything, until we can't stuff ourselves with another bite. The dumplings are so good—even though I have trouble picking them up with chopsticks.

"What did you think of the Buddha and the cable car?" Gregor asks as he spins the noodles around his fork.

"The cable car was fun, and that Buddha is so big," Jillian replies.

"That glass floor freaked me out a little," says Jax.

"Yeah, me, too," I say. "I felt like I was going to fall through."

When our *yum cha* meal is over, we head back up to the platform. We have a packed schedule for the next week, presenting to children at both the Hong Kong

Convention Center, where we saw the golden flower statue, and the convention center in Beijing. I lean my head back in the megacar and think about our invention—the one waiting for us up on the platform. I know we still have months before we present it to the PIPS judges, but I just wish I knew right now how we were going to make it excellent. I bet the Buddha knows. He had a look in his eyes like he knows everything about everything. I just wish he could tell me if I'm going to end up at PIPS.

THE HIDDEN COMPARTMENT

OUR INVENTION HAS been on hold, because we've spent most of January off the platform in Beijing. My head swirls thinking about all the children we presented to and all the places we visited. We're traveling to Australia tomorrow, so we jump off the aero-bus now, determined to explore this platform one last time—even though we've seen everything there is to see. First, we pass the Pooncha Tree and grab a cup of the problem-solving elixir. Then, we pass the Swiss aero-bus, Master Freeman's aero-bus, and the tree cluster right before Andora's. Suddenly, Ander turns back and jumps into the cluster. Mare peeks through the branches. "What are you doing?"

He motions for us to hide along with him and whispers, "This is where we were hiding when we saw Andora last time, remember?"

"Yeah," I say climbing into the cluster beside him. "But why are we hiding now?"

"You never know when you'll see something worth seeing."

I shrug. "True."

We're laughing from being squished when we hear her door creak open. Mare, Jax, and Jillian quickly move closer to us and we watch her. As she walks down the steps, I hold my breath, trying not to laugh. She makes her way to the back of the aero-bus, places her hand near the corner of it, and wipes something off the metal. She taps her fingers a few times, a panel opens, and she stares at it.

I'm so confused. What is she doing?

She reaches inside a small compartment and pulls out an object that I can't see very well. But by the way she holds it with two hands, I can tell that it's heavy. She brings it carefully to her chest and stares off into the distance like she's remembering something. She doesn't look closely at it. She just holds it. *So weird.*

Soon, she sets the object back inside the hidden compartment and closes the door. She touches the door after she closes it, almost as if she's missing the object already. *I wonder what it is.* She walks back up the steps and disappears inside. When we're sure she can't see us or hear us, we pour out of the tree cluster and sprint away. We run by Team France's aero-bus, and when we're near the courtyard in front of our own, we stop.

Mare tries to catch her breath. "What was all that?"

I blow my bangs away from my face. "I don't know. Could you guys see anything?"

"I saw her take something out of the back of her aero-bus," says Jax. "But that's it."

Jillian nods. "It looked really important. She was holding it so carefully."

"Whatever it is," says Ander. "She doesn't want anyone to see it. Did you see her look over her shoulder to be sure no one was watching?"

It doesn't make any sense. "I saw. But if she doesn't want anyone to see it, why doesn't she keep it *inside* the aero-bus? Why would she keep it in a hidden compartment *there*?"

We have no idea, but we agree on one thing: *that was so strange!*

Curiosity is getting to me. "Let's go back later when everyone is inside their aero-buses. I want to see what it is."

"Are you serious?" asks Jax.

"Yeah, why not?" asks Mare. "I want to see it, too. Andora won't catch us."

Ander nods. "We'll just look inside. We're not going to take it or anything."

Jax shakes his head. "I don't think we should."

"Come on, Jax," Jillian replies. "We won't even touch it. We need an adventure."

"I don't want our team to get in trouble."

"We're not going to get in trouble for going for a walk," I say. "Seraphina says to *be curious*. So, this is us being curious."

"I don't think that's what she meant, but okay . . . if we just look."

We enter the floating chamber and jump onto the floating furniture to pass the time. Seraphina talks about flying to Australia the next day, while the rest of us listen to music and float on the chairs. But I have trouble concentrating on what she's saying. What kind of object would be so important to Andora that she would hide it in the back of her aero-bus? Why would she hold it so tightly and stare into space?

The floating clock announces the time. Ten minutes until lights out. That's when we'll sneak out of the aero-bus. My butterflies stir just thinking about it. I've never snuck out of the house—or anywhere before. But Jillian's right. It's just a small adventure and then we'll come right back.

When Seraphina and Gregor leave to go to their bed-chambers, the rest of us follow them. But once they close their doors, instead of going into ours, we turn around and sneak back to the front of the aero-bus. Mare taps the button to open the outer door, and I'm kind of surprised that's all it takes to open it. No elaborate lock. No alarm. Nothing but the open door.

I expect the air outside to be cool at this hour, now that the moon is shining overhead. But then I remember that we're inside this air-controlled bubble. Changes in temperature must not happen. We stay silent and quickly walk next to the platform walls, avoiding the center courtyard. If we walked across it, we'd reach Andora's aero-bus faster, but now that it's past curfew, if one of the preceptors is hanging out there, we'd be in big trouble.

We pass the French team's aero-bus without running into anyone. Just beyond the tree cluster, we stop to be sure no one is around. Ander whispers, "Okay, so the lights in her aero-bus are off. She's probably in her bed-chamber. Let's go."

"Are you sure?" asks Mare. "Go slow, just to be sure."

We inch closer to the panel but it's hard to tell a panel is even there. Jillian walks up to it and touches it, but nothing happens. "I think she waved her hand in front of it, or wiped it or something," I whisper.

She tries both, but nothing happens. "Here, let me try," says Ander. Jillian steps aside, and Ander waves his hand out in front of it and then wipes it like it has dirt on it. "It's not working."

"Do you think it's sensitive to her handprint or some-thing?" I ask.

"Maybe," says Jillian.

I sigh. "Andora's smart. If she's trying to hide the object inside there, she probably wouldn't make it very easy to open."

"You are correct, Miss Krumpet. I wouldn't."

My stomach drops to the ground. I swing around to see Andora standing before us—still as the night. I gasp at the sight of her in her bathrobe, stone-faced. Frozen with fear, I'm sure I'm about to be in more trouble than I've ever been in, in my whole life. We all are.

Ander blurts out, "We were just—"

"Trying to open a compartment on my aero-bus."

"No, we were—"

"Were you *not* trying to open the compartment on my aero-bus?"

"Um—well."

No one on my team tries to help him, and I don't want to either. But he shouldn't have to explain. I'm the one who suggested we come here in the first place. I should be the one to tell her why we did.

"We were trying to open the panel, Andora, and we're really sorry. We know we shouldn't be out after curfew, and we know that your private property is inside that compartment. We should not be here."

Her head tilts but her eyes stay glued on mine. "Why are you here then?"

I look at my teammates, and they look as petrified as I feel inside. I take a big breath hoping the right words come out. "We were exploring the platform earlier—because that's not against the rules, and we saw you take something out of a compartment right there someplace, and we didn't mean to spy on you, but we couldn't help it and I think our curiosity got the best of us. We just wanted to see what it was."

"Yeah," says Ander. "We weren't going to touch it or take it or anything. We really weren't. We just wanted to see it."

"It seemed really important to you," says Jillian. "And so—"

We glare at Jillian. It's bad enough to say we saw her take out the object, but she didn't have to make it sound like we spied on her the whole time.

"We're very sorry," I say. "We're sorry we came here."

Andora stares at us for too long, saying nothing. Nothing at all. She looks out into the darkness, someplace in the distance beyond the Aerogel walls of the platform. My teammates and I glance at one another. I try to decide if I should say something else. I'm not sure. She's probably deciding what punishment to give us and how horrible she should make it.

She looks away from the darkness and back to us. "Would you like to see what's inside that compartment?"

Um, what?

Ander's face lights up. "I would!"

Mare smiles. "Definitely!"

Seriously? I don't get it. Why would she show us? She steps up to the aero-bus and moves her hand in an elaborate wave-like motion—nothing like the spastic wave we tried. The panel door slides open and we lean in to look inside. Without taking her eyes from the panel, she says, "Please step back."

We back up and she reaches inside. Her hand stays put for a few seconds, and I wonder if she's changing her mind about showing us. But then she places her other hand inside, too, and carefully retrieves a brownish metal object. She cradles it in her hands and holds it out to us, ever so slightly.

"Is that a statue?" Ander asks.

"No. It is not a statue."

"It kind of looks like a light bulb, a tarnished golden light bulb statue."

"It is not a *statue*."

"But it is a light bulb, right?"

"The exterior is molded and covered in bronze, but I assure you it is not a light bulb."

"What is it?"

"It is an invention."

"What does it do?" I ask.

"I'm afraid I cannot share that with you."

"What do you mean?" asks Mare.

"I would prefer to tell you a story. However, before I tell you, you must promise you will not attempt to retrieve it again for selfish reasons or for the sake of satisfying your curiosity. You were caught after curfew and that is cause for punishment. If you do as I ask, though, you will not have to suffer the consequences of your actions this evening."

She doesn't wait for us to answer.

"As you know, my late husband, Lexland Appleonia, was a creative writer who was instrumental in developing the category system used by schools today, the Piedmont Organization, and the Piedmont Challenge. He had a curious and highly intelligent mind. Before he died, we invented the—well, we made an innovative discovery. Knowing the discovery was important, something the world would be eager to see, he secured it with a complex locking system. He needed to protect our discovery from people, to keep them from using it incorrectly and suffering the consequences. He died shortly after, and the code that would serve to unlock and activate our invention died with him."

Jax gasps. "You don't know how to unlock it?"

"I do not."

"Well, what could the invention do?" Ander asks, his eyes as big as the tennis ball in his hand.

"That's all I'm willing to share. It was an innovative discovery over forty years ago and would still be innovative today. But without the blueprint to open it and administer it correctly, the invention is dangerous—more dangerous than I'm willing to take responsibility for."

Her expression is so serious, it's scary. Still, I can't resist asking. "Is that why you keep it hidden in the compartment and not inside your aero-bus?"

"This compartment is the safest place on the aero-bus. This invention is my last connection to Lexland. Just because a person is gone doesn't mean he's forgotten. This was the last project we worked on together, and this invention is fragile. My heart would shatter if anything happened to it. So, as instructed, you will focus your energy on your last task of this competition, and on your presentations to the children you meet on this tour. Besides, not all discoveries are meant to be discovered."

We stand there silent, stunned by her story, and by this strange bronze-looking object sitting in her hands. As she places it gently back in the compartment, I watch the elaborate wave she makes with her hand. I'm not sure what kind of passcode her motion contains, but I've never seen anything like it before. It's sort of rhythmic, almost magical.

At Andora's command, we race back to the aero-bus. I'm shocked and relieved that we aren't in trouble, but it stinks that we had to promise to never come back. We'll never get to look at this invention again. I mean, it doesn't look all that impressive—it's just an old bronze object, but at one time, it must have done something incredible. If only we could find a way to take back our promise, we could find out.

QUAD CAPSULES

OVERNIGHT, WE LAND on the Australian platform, our fifth tour stop. I've lost track of time, being on this tour. It's weird being so cut off from everyone else. Yeah, we see the other kids all the time, and the people in the countries we visit, but it's still strange being so separated from my family and everyone back home. All the countries blur into one when we're up on the platform. But once we step foot in a new land, that all changes. Each country has a uniqueness to it, something that makes it different from the others. Today, we'll set foot in Australia and present at a place called the International Convention Centre Sydney.

At first, I have a hard time staying focused on our presentations. All I can think about is Andora's mysterious invention. But after three sessions with the kids of Sydney, we drive to Bondi Beach, and once I see the sand, I forget all about it. We swim in the Pacific Ocean, diving in and over the waves. While we tread water, Jillian, Ander, and I do our best Australian accents. "Look, mate," she calls. "Dolphins!"

She's right! We spot a pod of fifteen bottlenose dolphins playing in the clear blue water. Later in the day, we board a ferry and glide across the harbor where the sails of the Sydney Opera House glitter in the sunshine. Ander leans up against the ferry railing. "Did you guys know that Sydney is the state capital of New South Wales?"

"Yeah," Mare replies. "If you were listening, the driver told us when we boarded."

"Well, did you know that Sydney was once a convict colony?"

Seraphina shakes her head. "I didn't know that, Ander. That's one fact I hadn't heard about."

"No worries, Seraphina. Ask me anything. I probably know the answer."

"Okay, what year was the Sydney Opera House built?"

"Easy. Nineteen seventy-three. But it went through a $200 million renovation in the year 2022."

"Wow. Remind me to ask you this afternoon about the Sydney Harbour Bridge."

"Oh, I will. It's sometimes called the *Coathanger*. I'll quiz you on that later."

"Ha ha. I know you will!"

I lean back and let the sunshine warm my face. "Do you think we'll get to see koalas or wallabies? I really want to see them."

Jax nods. "And kangaroos also."

"Probably not today, but we will at some point while we're here. I hope so anyway."

I imagine the fluffy koalas climbing up a eucalyptus tree. "Me, too."

The next day, we leave the platform early for a tour of an industrial plant that makes one of Sydney's newest inventions. I can hardly sit still thinking that we'll get to see how an invention is actually made.

When we enter the plant, we're brought into a room where we watch a five-minute movie about transportation drones—the way people in Australia travel in their biggest cities. The common name for them is Quad Capsules, and they fly four people at a time to their destination, kind of like taxis or ride-share vehicles, except it's like flying in a glass bubble.

After the movie, we're led into an enormous room filled with computers, conveyor belts, and transparent tubes. They work together to create each part, like the wheels, the outer bubble, the seats, the brakes, the navigation system, and all the other parts needed to make the drone fly to its correct destination. Very few people are involved in the process. According to the movie, the people who work there program the computers to do the construction. They assemble the tubes with the right materials, and the materials inside the tubes do the rest. When all the separate Quad Capsule parts are assembled, they pass through a final tube where they're combined into a working four-seater drone.

When our tour is over, we're led outside to the street corner so we can ride one. A metal post with a keypad stands on the curb. Gregor enters an address, and we ask him where we're going. Before he can answer, though, two Quad Capsules whiz toward us and stop at the curb. Gregor, Jillian, and I step into the first one, and Seraphina, Ander, Mare, and Jax step into the second. When our door slides closed, we secure ourselves inside the glass bubble. The seats are practically sitting on the floor and there is no driver, just a computerized voice that says, "Good afternoon, Mr. Axel. I hope you and your companions enjoy your ride to the Peppermill Café."

The capsule lifts off and we whiz through the air more like a bumblebee than a jet. We bounce and turn and dip through the air in a strange pattern. There aren't many aero-cars flying around, maybe because these Quad Capsules drive themselves, and people think that's better. Seraphina's capsule moves along next to us, and we wave to each other, but it feels more like we're on an amusement park ride than riding in a vehicle.

When we arrive at the café, the capsule pulls up to the curb. This one also has a metal pole with a keypad, and I realize that every restaurant and storefront has one. That means when we're done eating, we'll probably take another capsule back to the industrial plant where the megacar is parked.

The low hum of voices greets us as we enter the restaurant. People are scattered everywhere and when we're finally seated, we look down at the table. Menus light up in front of each of us. We order sandwiches but when they arrive, there's an extra platter that the server places at the center of our table. "This," he says, "is a local Australian favorite. Let me know what you think."

Ander reaches for a small triangle. "What is it?"

"Well, mate, it's a vegemite sandwich. Australian kids love them and eat them like American kids eat peanut butter and jelly sandwiches."

I peek between the slices of bread. It looks like a chocolate paste but smells weird. I take a small bite and quickly drink a glass of water. "It's salty!"

"Yup. It's full of vegetables and spices. Do you like it?"

I swallow hard. "A little bit."

He laughs. "You're not the first tourist to make that face. I suppose it is an acquired taste. Enjoy your time in Australia, my friends!"

AS OUR DAYS in Sydney wind down, we finally finish up the scoring program and put together more of the sensors for the Balance Blocks, knowing that soon we'll be in Germany. That means we'll finally find out Part Two of our task. Just thinking about it makes me feel like butterflies are bouncing in my stomach—just like they did when we rode around on the Quad Capsules. Our task might get even harder soon, and I'm not sure we're ready for that.

DRONE MESSAGES

MY TEAMMATES AND I sit on the window seat of chamber eight, watching the city of Berlin fly into view. The lights dot the sky like stars, but we don't fly close enough to see anything more. As we approach the German platform, the aero-bus slows down, and within seconds we're swallowed up by it. The floor closes underneath us and once again we're parked outside the courtyard. Germany is our sixth tour stop and that means one big thing. Soon we'll find out Part Two of the Piedmont Challenge final task.

"What do you guys think it'll be?" I ask at breakfast the next morning.

Jillian takes a sip of juice. "I bet they're going to make us think up another invention."

"Nah," Ander replies. "But they might make us turn the one we made inside out and backward and rebuild it or something."

"You mean like start over? I think we've done that already."

LATER THAT MORNING, we meet Seraphina in the floating chamber. She talks to us about some of the things we'll be seeing in Germany and asks us about our invention. Finally, she dismisses us so that we can work on it, reminding us that this invention is our key to getting into PIPS. That's all the motivation I need to hear, so I slide off the floating couch and grab Mare. "Okay, thanks Seraphina. We got this. Let's go, guys. Let's get inspired in chamber eight!"

The rest of our team follows as Seraphina calls after us. "Good luck! I'll stay here and read about the Neuschwanstein Castle."

A little later, while we're inside chamber eight finishing the last of the sensors, we hear a bouncing noise coming from the hallway. We race to the door and see a circular object made of metal heading toward us. We step back, and it stops midair. That's when we realize—it's a drone! It hums and whirrs and a tiny door slides open with instructions:

*Greetings, Team USA. Your presence
in the courtyard is required.*

*Be prepared to discuss your invention with
Team France and Team Switzerland.*

Jillian jumps up. "Oh, good! We finally get to hear what the other teams are working on."

I bite my pinkie nail. "But that means they get to hear what we're working on, too."

Ander leads the way as we follow the drone back down the hall. When we arrive in the courtyard, the other teams are just arriving, too. Maëlle hurries over to us. "I was hoping we'd see each other again soon."

Ander gathers everyone around. "Well, it sounds like we each have to describe our inventions."

Jonah smirks at our team. "That is what the drone said. Shall we go first?"

"If you would like," Zoe replies.

He nods. "Hannah, would you please explain our invention?"

Hannah gives Jonah a strange look. She doesn't seem to mind explaining their invention, but I think she does mind him telling her what to do. "Sure." She stands and faces all of us. "We're really very excited about our invention. We're calling it a Memory Movie. By using a screen and headphones that will link to a person's brain, helping it to recall their favorite sights and sounds, our invention will help prevent homesickness. Those sights and sounds, like a person's mom, or house or vacation place, will be projected onto a screen. The person can watch them, and by them receiving comforting thoughts from home, we hope to eliminate homesickness."

"Wow," Ander replies with his mouth hanging open. "That's really cool!"

"How do you do that?" asks Stephan.

"We'll use similar technology to that which we used in the Thought Translation Box," Jonah replies.

"Yes," says Giulia. "We found similar items on our aero-bus, so hopefully putting it together will be possible."

"What do the rest of you think?" Finn asks.

"That would be incredible," I say.

Maëlle nods in agreement. "Most definitely."

"We're planning to add scents, too," adds Lars. "For example, my grossmami's house smells like oranges. Whenever I smell them, I think of her."

"Mine does, too!" I reply, picturing the inside of Grandma Kitty's house. "That's a great idea."

Hannah looks relieved that we all like her team's invention. "We are just getting started. It took us quite some time to formulate our idea."

Gwyndol stands up. "You were able to invent the Thought Translation Box, so I bet you'll have no problem creating this Memory Movie also."

Jonah folds his arms across his chest. "Thank you. I don't think we'll have trouble at all."

"Our invention," Gwyndol begins, "is also in its beginning stages. We are mostly researching right now, trying to see if we have the materials to make a prototype."

"Yes," Zoe begins. "We are attempting to build robotic backpacks."

"What do you mean, 'robotic backpacks'?" Finn asks.

"We're inventing backpacks with mechanical pockets," Stephan replies. "They will hold every single item a child needs for school or an adventure. Weight or space would not matter because the internal system could shrink down each object."

"Yes," Danielle continues. "That way, children could carry everything they need and more. There would be a keypad on the front strap. Press a button, and the robotic brain inside the backpack resizes the item, a compartment opens, and the object is within reach."

Yikes. I'd like one of those.

"That sounds so cool!" Ander replies. "I'd use it."

"Me, too," says Mare. "But how are you going to build it?"

"Do you think you have materials for that inside your aero-bus?" asks Jax.

"Maybe, maybe not. But we're hoping to find materials that are similar enough to present our invention for this competition," Maëlle replies. "It only needs to be a prototype."

Hannah smiles. "I think that's a very cool idea. I wish we had thought of that!"

"Me, too!" I say. "I'd definitely want a backpack like that."

"What about you, America?" Jonah asks. "What's your invention?"

I glance over at Ander. Why does it bother me so much that Jonah calls our team 'America'? We do have names.

I stand up as straight as I can. "We have an invention, too, but it needs work."

"What is it?" asks Maëlle.

I bite my ring-finger nail. "Well, the girls and I have these brick-like blocks on our wall. When you touch them, they fall into your hand and light up with a motivational message."

"Really?" asks Zoe. "That's very cool."

"Yes, but only some of them wiggle and fall into your hand," Jillian explains.

"So, what's your idea?" asks Jonah.

"Well, we were searching the closets for materials we could use for our project. We wanted to see if something would inspire us."

"Did you find something?" asks Danielle.

"Yes, we found a closet full of the colorful blocks. When we picked them up, some of them connected to each other like magnets, only stronger—if they were arranged in a certain pattern."

"That's interesting," Gwyndol replies.

"We thought so, too," Jax says. "So, we examined them and wondered if there was an invention we could make with them."

"Is there?" asks Danielle.

Jillian jumps up from her chair. "Yes! We're inventing a game."

Jax nods. "It's an elaborate game of balance."

We describe the game in detail and the other kids look excited about it, especially when we tell them about the scoring system and the sensors we're adding to the blocks. They say nice things and tell us how much they'd like to play it. All except Jonah. He folds his arms across his chest like always and mumbles something about their amazing Memory Movie.

I bite my thumbnail and glare at Jonah. He doesn't see me do it, but it makes me feel better anyway.

We're barely done explaining our inventions when Master Freeman and Andora appear in the courtyard.

"Greetings, children."

I spin around at the sound of Master Freeman's booming voice. He and Andora stand before us with serious expressions on their faces. Our preceptors appear out of nowhere also and stand around us.

"I see that you received your drone messages and have shared your inventions with each other."

We nod and assure him that we have. He looks pleased and pulls a purple envelope out of his coat pocket. "As promised, the time has come for you to solve Part Two of the Piedmont Challenge final task. Andora, will you please do the honor?" He passes the envelope to her and she opens it slowly.

"Innovation is a great connector of our world. It brings people together in more ways than we can imagine. I give you now Part Two of the Piedmont Challenge final task:

You must take each of your three team inventions and work together to turn them into one new, connected invention. On the Day of Creativity, you must present your connected invention to Master Freeman, to me, to your preceptors, and to your families and international judges from your potential schools, who will be viewing remotely. As a reminder, you will have twelve minutes to present your connected invention."

* * *

ANDORA HOLDS THE task to her chest. "We wish you well and trust that you will work hard to create an inspired invention worthy of your teams."

Master Freeman clasps his hands together slowly. "Best of luck, children. I look forward to seeing what you achieve together."

They turn away and hurry out of the courtyard.

Maëlle looks at me with a smile on her face. "How wonderful. We shall be able to work together."

I'm not sure what to say, but I nod quickly. Part Two is not what I expected at all. Mare's face is twisted into a scowl, glaring at the other teams. I pull her aside and whisper. "What's wrong?"

But she doesn't whisper back. "What do you think? I am not working with them."

I stand there, stunned, afraid to look over at Maëlle. Maybe she didn't hear her, though. Maybe her English isn't as good as I think it is. Maybe just once, Mare could figure out how to be a nice person.

Mare stands her ground. "I did not sign up for this."

Jonah glances over at us and I shush her.

"Sign up for what?"

"A brand-new team."

"What do you mean? We're still teammates. We just added a few new team members."

"Yeah, like ten."

"Mare, it's no big deal. We only work with them for the second part of the task anyway."

"But we've already come up with three inventions. Now we have to do it again. What are we, superinventors now or something?"

I stare at her. "You do know that the Piedmont Challenge is an invention competition, right?"

She folds her arms. "I think of it as a task-solving competition."

I nod because she's right—but so am I.

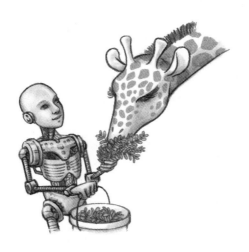

ZOO ROBOTS

THE NEXT MORNING, we drag ourselves out of bed and get ready as fast as we can, because if we're late for breakfast, Seraphina will think we overslept, which we did—but still. I guess staying up late talking to Jillian and Mare about Part Two of our task and messaging Ander and Jax was not a very good idea. My eyes are still barely open when we meet her in the dining chamber for breakfast. It looks like the food flower has already spun. Colorful bowls are waiting for us filled with bananas, strawberries, pineapple, blueberries, granola, peanut butter, and yogurt.

"Good morning, my Crimson Kids. Wow, you look like you haven't slept in a month."

None of us says a word. We just eat our breakfast.

"Don't tell me you're worried about Part Two of your task?"

I shrug.

"Okay, well, that's a conversation for another day, when you look more awake. I guess while you eat, I'll fill you in on our day. We're headed down to Germany today—Berlin, Germany, to be exact. Berlin is the capital and largest city of Germany in both area and population . . . and it's a city bursting with creativity! Through the last several decades, people have looked to this city to set trends in music, art, and theater."

"That sounds amazing," Jillian replies.

"I think so, too. We'll be spending the first part of today at the convention center called Messe Stuttgart. You have two groups to present to and two sessions of Swirl and Spark Recall tasks to administer. Then we're off to explore. There's so much to see in Germany, and we'll start with Tiergarten Park. You've been cooped up on the platform for a while. Gregor and I think an afternoon in this famous park will do you some good. Plus, we may even check out the zoo. It's Europe's biggest animal park."

Ander looks up from his fruit bowl. "Cool! I want to see the German giraffes."

Mare stares at him. "Aren't giraffes in Germany the same as anywhere else?"

"No, they're German."

She shakes her head, but I laugh. I guess she doesn't understand Ander's humor like I do. After breakfast, we fly down to Berlin. When we enter the convention center, we're greeted by a group of people all dressed in suits. They're friendly, like all the people we've met so far, and for a minute or two I forget which country we're in. It doesn't take me long to remember, though, especially when speaking with the children. Most speak German but some speak English, too. We talk to them with a similar translation invention that we've used in many of the countries, and it's a relief. Even though Grandma Kitty said to smile and do the best I can communicating with the kids, it's better when I know the words they're saying.

After meeting with the kids, we wander around Tiergarten Park. It reminds me of Central Park in New York City, because it's a huge park located inside a very big city. We pass by people, people, and more people walking, running, and riding bikes. The weather is much colder than Australia, but spring is coming, and Gregor tells us that the weather here now is kind of like how it is back home—maybe a little warmer. My teammates and I race each other down the path, and after lunch we head to the zoo. It's fun watching the animals roam and Ander imitate them—especially the giraffes. Ander's impression of them is the worst!

"It's a shame we weren't here in the fall," says Gregor as we reach the area filled with monkeys. "We could have gone to the Oktoberfest."

"What's Oktoberfest?" I ask.

"You don't know what Oktoberfest is?" Ander blurts out. "It's a huge sixteen-day celebration with a ton of food, drinks, and carnival rides. It was started as a wedding celebration for King Ludwig and Princess Therese of Saxe-Hildburghausen in the 1800s. The citizens were invited to celebrate, and it became an annual tradition after that."

"That's correct and impressive, young Ander."

Ander grins like he just won a million dollars.

Jillian and I skip ahead to see the elephants up close. We press against a plexiglass barrier and watch a mother and her baby playing in a pond. Out of the corner of my eye, I see something approach them. It looks like a person, maybe a zookeeper, but I quickly realize it's not. It's mechanical. It's a mechanical zookeeper! It moves toward them in a rigid way, carrying an enormous bucket of vegetation. The mother elephant notices it but carries on, splashing her baby with water. The robot places the bucket on the sandy edge of the pond and slides into the water; the mother splashes it, too. The robot sways back and forth, in and out of the water, not afraid, not anything. That's when I get it. The mother is playing with the robot, too!

Mare moves to get a closer look. "So, the German people invented zoo robots. Nice."

Weird! I never would have thought to invent that.

The zoo is so big, we'll never get to see all the animals that are here. But at least we've seen the zoo robots. Grandma Kitty will never believe this one!

Up ahead a group of people are gathered around a small food cart. The pretzel smell is unmistakable. "Let's stop for a snack," Seraphina suggests.

"You don't have to convince me," Ander replies. "I'll take a bratwurst and a pretzel please!"

"What's bratwurst?" asks Jillian.

"It's sausage made with pork or veal and a mix of spices," Gregor replies. "Germany is known for its bratwurst."

Seraphina places our large order while we find a spot in the grass to eat the snacks that end up being our dinner. When Gregor sees how much we like the bratwurst and pretzels, he heads back to the cart and gets a currywurst for us to try. Similar to the bratwurst, it's smothered in curry powder and ketchup and served with French fries. As we're cleaning up our grassy picnic area, Seraphina tosses each of us a small wrapped piece of candy.

"Ooh, chocolate!" Jillian exclaims.

"Not just chocolate, Jillian. This is German chocolate. Some of the finest in the world."

She's right! It's so good, I don't even want to swallow it.

THE NEXT SEVERAL weeks in Berlin whiz by as we meet more and more German children every day. We hardly have any time at all to work on our own inventions or to work with the other teams on a way to connect them. And now we're headed to Switzerland tomorrow! It's exciting that we're moving on to another new country already, but my head feels like a pin ball machine. The metal ball inside bounces from one place to the next, setting bells and alarms off every time I think of something more that we need to do. Presenting to the kids is like our job. Solving this task is our job, too. But exploring the countries is one of our jobs also. My head just wants a time out already.

When my teammates ask me if I want to stop at the Pooncha Tree before we get ready for bed, I jump out of my floating chair. A drink from the problem-solving tree is the best idea I've heard all day!

book
backpack
game

THE INVENTIONS

THE CALENDAR FLIPS to April, which means today we're on our way to our seventh tour stop: Switzerland! Sometime this month, the Swiss team will meet up with their families. I'm kind of jealous. I wish we were seeing our families this month, too. But we have a lot of work to do on our task anyway. After the five of us finish eating breakfast in the dining chamber, we head to our bed-chamber. "Maybe the creativity misters will help us think of a great way to connect our inventions with the others."

"Sounds good to me," Ander replies. "I'm up for getting my face splashed with water."

Mare throws a pillow at him. "Your face isn't going to get splashed with water."

"If you say so."

When all of us are inside our bedchamber, as if on cue, the misters turn on. "Wow," says Jillian. "The mister must really think we're hopeless—that we need all the help we can get."

Ander lies down on the floor like he's staring at the clouds. And then I realize he actually is! We lay down on the floor next to him, watch the clouds roll by, and let the mist sprinkle our faces.

Jillian points up. "I see a monkey just like Mabel floating by."

"I see a castle. There's a tower and a moat and everything."

"I see a fish," says Ander.

"What are you guys even looking at?" asks Mare. "I see a tree. It's so obviously a tree."

"What? A tree? That's a ship," says Jax. "A pirate ship, definitely."

I look at the castle more closely. It reminds me of Camp Piedmont at Piedmont University. It reminds me of PIPS. My stomach drops and I suddenly feel like we're doing something wrong. Something very wrong. I sit right up.

"What's wrong, Kia?" asks Jillian.

"You guys, can't break time be over? We need to get back to work on our invention. We're never going to get into PIPS if we don't."

"Why are you so worried, KK? We have until August."

"I don't know. I just have this feeling that we should be farther along with our own invention than we are. And I really don't like this feeling."

Mare sighs. "Don't be such a worrier, Kia."

* * *

WE LAND ON the platform in Switzerland and get a reminder message from Seraphina. We're meeting with the other teams in a half hour. "I told you guys we should be farther along than we are."

Mare grabs a notebook. "Kia, it's fine. So, we meet with them. What's the big deal?"

"Mare, it's April! We only have a few months left. Our invention is not ready and that means we're not even close to connecting it somehow to the other two inventions."

"That's not true," Jax replies. "Just because the details of our game aren't all figured out, that doesn't mean that we can't get together with them and brainstorm a way to combine them. We know what the three inventions are now, and we know that our game is going to work. That's all we need."

"He's right, KK."

I bite my pointer-finger nail and force myself to take it out of my mouth. "I hope so."

We arrive at the courtyard to find Seraphina, Elin, and Mathilde waiting for all of us. Both teams are waiting, too, sitting together at tables. All ten of them are laughing, talking about something that we can't hear. We try to join in their conversation, but I guess we're too late. Maëlle is already sitting with Hannah, Zoe, and Giulia. There's an empty seat with Danielle, Gwyndol, and Finn. I sit with them.

The chatter stops, and I feel everyone staring at us. I guess everyone *was* waiting for us.

Elin stands up, her blonde hair pulled back into a braid. "Hello, everyone. For this part of your task, you must collaborate in a large group. Doing so may be uncomfortable or even difficult, but that's part of the challenge you face. The sooner you put your individual differences aside and work together for the good of each of your goals, the sooner—and better—you will each solve this task."

Mathilde steps forward. "If you look behind me, Seraphina has accessed an air screen for your use today." She pulls a clear floating computer screen out of nowhere and turns it on. "Beginning today, you'll meet to discuss how you'll connect your inventions."

"Yes," says Seraphina. "And please do not tell a team— or team member—their idea is bad. You know that would not be in the spirit of Piedmont."

Ander's hand shoots right up. "Who's in charge?"

"What do you mean?" Mathilde asks.

"Well, like, this is a big group. *Somebody* has to be the leader of the team, right?"

Seraphina looks at her purple nail polish. "Well, you know what it's like to be on a team. You all do. So I think you already know that it's up to your group to decide whether you need a leader for your meetings."

Ander shrugs. "Well, I'll be the leader if no one else wants to."

"I certainly would like to," Hannah announces.

"I would also," Jonah replies.

Stephan raises his hand. "I would as well."

Ander looks from one person to the next, like a mouse caught in a mousetrap. "Well, then we may have to figure out who would be the *best* leader."

Mare sighs. "Do we even need a leader?"

"I suggest you remind each other about the details of each of your inventions. And then brainstorm ways to connect them. Beyond that, you're on your own." Seraphina and the other preceptors retreat from the courtyard, and the fifteen of us are left staring at one another.

Hannah stands up. "Perhaps our team should start, because we're creating a different invention than the Memory Movie we spoke about last time."

"I think America should go first," says Jonah. "Since they were late."

"Sorry," I say. "We didn't mean to keep you waiting."

"Well, you did, and we have inventions to work on also, you know. Your team is not the only one."

Ander looks at him, confused. "We know that."

"Okay, then, why don't you tell us how your invention is coming along so we can decide how to connect it with ours."

I don't like that Jonah automatically thinks we'll connect our invention to theirs. Why can't we connect their invention to ours? I take a deep breath and look at anyone but him. "Well, we reported before that we're creating a scoring system for our game of Balance Blocks. We're still working on that."

"Do you have a plan for it yet?"

"Yes. I said we're working on it."

Finn nods. "Okay. France, how is your invention coming along?"

"It is coming," Gwyndol replies.

"Yes," says Zoe. "We found materials to use for a backpack prototype. The difficult part is motorizing it."

"It sounds like a cool invention to work on," says Jax.

"It is," she replies with a smile.

Jonah stands up. "Well, our team has changed gears—switched inventions."

Jillian leans forward with her elbows on the table. "I liked your Memory Movie idea."

"Unfortunately, we could not find the materials we needed to implement our idea. So we quickly thought up something else—something that we can make with the materials found on our aero-bus."

"What is it?" Maëlle asks.

Hannah stands up next to him. "It is an invention that adds hologram images to a book. It will take thoughts from the reader's brain and cause them to hover above the pages."

"Seriously?" Ander replies.

"Yes. We hope to help people learn better by visualizing the information or better comprehending the story."

I stare at her in disbelief. "You mean like as you read, ghost-type pictures of what you're imagining will hover above the pages?"

Jonah smirks. "That's the plan."

"Wow," says Jax. "That's good. You have all of those materials on your aero-bus?"

Giulia nods. "We think so. We have the same materials we used to make the Thought Translation Box, so that was our inspiration. We're taking those thoughts and turning them into holograms."

"Wow," says Zoe. "That sounds like a great invention."

"Really great," I say, trying to sound happy for them.

"Thank you," says Hannah. "Hopefully we can get it to work."

"I have an idea about solving this next part of the task," says Zoe. "Why don't we mix up into three groups and talk about how we can connect all three of our inventions. Then when we all come back together, we can vote on the best way to do it."

"That sounds good," I say, happy to separate into smaller groups. Working in a big group like this makes me feel like our invention is terrible. Like it's the worst one. But when we're finished working in the smaller groups, we're still not ready to vote yet. Everyone has a different idea of how we should connect our inventions. Some of the ideas are okay but not great.

Maëlle stands up. "Maybe we need to look at things from a different angle. It appears we have three inventions: a mechanical backpack, a hologram book, and a game of balance. Do we need to combine them into one invention or connect them in some other way?"

"Combining them into one invention would be the most challenging, I believe," says Gwyndol.

"What other way could we connect them?" Danielle asks.

"I'm not sure," says Hannah. "Let's see what they have in common."

"That's obvious, isn't it," says Jonah. "They all relate to children."

"But they don't have to relate to children," I say. "Our game is meant for adults. And adults use backpacks and read books, too."

"Yes, of course," Jonah replies. "I just meant that the connection *could* be children."

"I think I'm confused by this whole connection part of the task," says Jillian. "Do we need to show how they connect, or actually connect them?"

None of us is sure. I think it could go either way.

"Let's use the red board to show how they're all similar," Mare suggests.

"Good idea," says Hannah. "We could make a Venn diagram showing how our inventions are different and how they are similar."

The red board records her idea.

"Well," Jillian begins. "We could create a movie showing a few of us using the invention, showing how these inventions could each be used by a family."

Jax raises his hand. "What if we actually connect them. Make a game of it with a person walking the beam attempting to win the book and the backpack?"

"That could work," Gwyndol replies.

"I think so, too," says Giulia.

I think about that for a second, but I'm not sure I like this idea. There's something about it that makes me think that we can come up with something else. "I like it, but can we keep brainstorming?"

We think of ways we could change our game so that the players would need a book or a backpack to play it. But with only one book, and one backpack, we don't get very far.

Maëlle sighs. "This part of the task is harder than I thought it would be."

I shake my head. "I thought this part would be fun—all of us getting to work together. Instead, it's frustrating."

"I'm not worried," says Zoe. "We'll find a great connection sooner or later."

"I hope it's sooner."

We organize our chairs into a giant circle, thinking a new arrangement will help us to think up some better ideas. The red board records them and soon it's completely full. With fifteen of us brainstorming together, there's a lot of ideas. We decide to think the ideas over on our own, though, to narrow the list down to our team's top five and vote the next time we meet. But still, even with so many ideas for connecting our inventions, I walk out of the courtyard discouraged. The other teams' inventions sound good—like unbelievable—and I can tell Jonah thinks our invention is lame. I hate that feeling. I want the other teams to look at our invention and wish they had thought it up themselves. I don't like Jonah. If it weren't for the other kids on his team—and that we need his invention so that we can connect it to ours—I would wish that his hologram book would fail.

THE DANCING CLOCK

THE NEXT MORNING, Mare, Jillian, and I sneak across the hall. After one knock, Ander cracks open the door, and we barge into the boys' bedchamber.

"Happy birthday, Jax!"

He sits up with a jump, his face flushed with red—almost looking mad . . . but then he slowly smiles. "Thank you. How did you guys remember? I didn't tell you."

"Just because you don't talk endlessly about your birthday, like Jillian, doesn't mean we don't know when it is."

Jillian looks at me like I just stole her craft materials. "I haven't talked endlessly about my birthday!"

"Really?"

"Well, maybe sometimes."

Seraphina and Gregor barge in. "Happy birthday, Jax! Of course, we knew it was today!"

"Hello, Jax. And I wish you a very happy twelfth year as well."

"I'm getting to like these birthday mornings," says Mare. "Cinnamon rolls are the best."

"I'll take two," says Ander.

"I think the birthday boy should get first pick," says Seraphina, "before we head down to Switzerland for the day."

Jillian picks up a cinnamon roll. "A birthday in Switzerland sounds fabulous, almost as fabulous as my August birthday in England!"

Jax takes a second one. "Will we get to see the Clock Tower? I read that it's really cool inside."

Gregor nods. "We will. And I believe it'll be cooler than you can even imagine."

I watch Jax's expression. He has a hard time hiding his smile. I think this may be one of his best ever birthdays, too.

An hour later, we fly down to Bern, Switzerland. The megacar drives us to Old Town, and we get out to walk around. "Remember," says Gregor. "There are three official languages in Switzerland: German, French, and Italian. You'll use translators, of course, when you're interacting with the children, but for now as we tour the city, it's important to know which languages you could be hearing. I believe most people will be speaking German, though."

The streets are made of cobblestones and bordered by winding sidewalks that stretch for miles. The lower levels of the buildings are filled with restaurants, shops, and bookstores. It looks like the top levels are filled with apartments. I think I'd like to live in one of those and every single day watch the people walking below.

We stop at the center of the city, where a famous landmark, the Zytglogge, a giant medieval clock also called the Clock Tower, stands seventy-five feet tall. Jax doesn't say a word. He only stares at it with a huge smile splashed across his face.

"Look at that thing!" says Ander. "It has two clock faces."

Gregor encourages us to step closer. "That's correct. It has both a traditional clock that tells the time of day and an astronomical clock that also tells the day of the week, the day of the year, and the position of the sun and stars."

"It's so colorful," Jillian exclaims. "Look at all those circles and hands."

"It looks really old," I say. "Do you know when it was built?"

"It dates back earlier than the 1500s," Gregor replies. "That's when the astronomical clock was added."

"What is that thing on the tower next to the astronomical clock?" Mare asks.

"You'll see," says Seraphina. "Let's climb up to the observation area where we'll have a better view."

We climb all 130 steps to the observation deck and when we're finally there, Seraphina lets out a breath. "It's almost time! At three minutes before every hour, the astronomical clock sets in motion something special."

"What's it going to do?" asks Ander.

"Patience, young Ander, patience."

Seraphina smiles. "Keep your eyes on the area next to the astronomical clock."

I stare at it, waiting and waiting. The clock strikes 9:57 a.m. and mechanical figurines pop out from the front of the clock. A dancing jester rings two bells, and a parade of bears, roosters, a piper, and a knight dance and put on a show.

"Hey, guys, look at the jester!" Ander exclaims. "He looks just like Freddie Dinkleweed!"

I laugh. It does look a little like him—and the show reminds me of our skits. I guess whoever built this clock so long ago wanted to present a story to people, too.

We take a tour of the inside of the tower and see an elaborate and intricate gear system. A tour guide explains how the gears work together. Jax doesn't take his eyes off the gears and now I'm positive—this is the best part of Jax's birthday.

After climbing back down the steps and walking through the historic city, we pass the parliament building and then drive to the Communication Museum. We play games and look at the exhibits that show the history of communication through the centuries, like speaking, sign language, the telephone, and the internet.

"Who's ready for a birthday dinner in Switzerland?" Jax's eyes light up, and we travel to Della Casa, a restaurant with reddish-brownish shutters. Window boxes overflow with flowers, and I can't wait to see what it looks like inside. We walk through the door to find small wooden tables covered in white linens scattered throughout the restaurant. A waiter shows us to our table and Seraphina whispers in his ear. I bet she's telling him that we're celebrating a special occasion.

Our dinner consists of a traditional Swiss meal called the Berner Platte, a dish filled with meats and sausages, cooked with sauerkraut and boiled potatoes, all served on a large platter. But the dessert is the best part. When we're finished eating, the waiter presents Jax with a chocolate Swiss roll cake filled with crème, and we sing "Happy Birthday" to him while the other people in the restaurant look on. He turns beet red, but I don't think he's mad. I think he secretly feels like a movie star.

A few days later, we head to the Congress Center Kursaal Bern, the convention center where we'll meet the children of Bern. By now, our presentations feel like a habit. We know our lines and our dances so well that, sometimes, it feels as easy as brushing my teeth. But also not like that, because every time I'm on the stage and I see the Ancestor App and Satellite Spectacles working, it's the greatest feeling in the world.

Before we leave, Gregor takes us to a special room in the convention center. "There's an invention I want to show you all. It's quite impressive."

Inside the room is a wall of giant panels, each containing a million buttons. Each button is color coded.

"A Swiss instructor was kind enough to show this to me earlier today while you were performing."

"What is it?" I ask.

"It's called the Snap Friend Maker."

Ander makes a strange face. "What's a Snap Friend Maker?"

"You can create a personalized companion."

"Like a pretend friend?" Mare asks in disbelief.

"More like a robotic friend. Watch."

He presses several buttons indicating name, age, gender, and personality type, like quiet, shy, friendly, or funny. I don't believe he's actually telling the truth about this. I think he's making the whole thing up until a metal robot that looks like a twelve-year-old kid with fake hair and everything rolls out the door.

"Hello, my name is Matthew. I am your new friend."

We stare at the robot—for a long time. "You created a robot friend, just like that?" Mare asks.

"Yes. You can bring him anyplace. He's yours to use for one day or for much longer. It's a way to be sure you always have a companion, if you want one."

"So, wait a minute," Ander replies. "Let me get this straight. You can build a friend with this invention."

"Yes, young Ander. You can."

I'm not sure what to think of this invention at all. I know it's hard to make friends, but *building* one seems weird. Whoever thought this up is smart at technology, but I'm not sure he's smart about people.

"I don't think it's a good invention," I say. "If the friend really is perfect, people won't want to be friends with real people. If it isn't, people will be unhappy."

Gregor nods. "Kia, I agree with you completely. Some inventions are better off not created. I'm afraid this may be one of those. Let this be a lesson for all of you. Be sure that the inventions you invent are ones that should be invented."

THE GONDOLIER

WE CLIMB OUT of the megacar and step into a new foreign country—our eighth. The Italian platform is located above Rome, the country's capital and home to the Colosseum, Vatican City, fountains, and palaces built during the Renaissance. Seraphina says we'll be spending most of our time in Rome, but some in Venice, too. She showed us pictures and told us it's a city built on water in the middle of a lagoon. But I'm most excited to eat the pizza here, even though Gregor says it doesn't taste anything like the pizza back home.

Today, after our presentations at the Roma Convention Center, we follow an usher into a small auditorium with a round stage in the center. We take our seats and place our translation pieces in our ears. The children seem excited to meet us, and we do our best to answer their questions—and inspire them to think up their own inventions, too.

We spend several weeks in Rome, meeting group after group. I can't help wondering how many of these kids want to become inventors and someday will be allowed to. And as much as I like talking with the kids every day, I can't stop thinking about seeing my family again. Mom and the rest of my family are so excited to see this country. I'm more excited to see all of them!

I count down the days, and when our megacar finally pulls up to a parking lot near the Colosseum, we all practically push one another out of the car!

Ryne races over to me first, with Mom right behind him. She hugs me tight—they all do—and I can't stop smiling. They ask me a million questions, and I ask them a million more. Ander's family is crowded next to ours, and I can hear him talking without even taking a breath.

"Oh, Smartie Girl, look at you!" Grandma Kitty says as we walk together toward the Colosseum. "How is your invention coming? Last time we talked, you said you had figured out the scoring sensors."

"Yeah, we did. Our invention is done. Now we just have to figure out a way to connect it with the other two teams' inventions. We're not sure how to do that yet."

"I'm sure you'll think of something."

"It's hard to get all fifteen of us to agree."

"Well, just stick to the basics. Let your mind wander in its normal way."

"But, Grandma, we have to find a way to connect them that's really good, because I don't think that by itself, our invention is spectacular."

"I'm sure it's fantastic, Buttercup."

"You're just saying that, Grandma. But this one really isn't incredible. It's cool, but it doesn't have that one special thing. It's not memorable."

"Well, then, you'll just have to make the connected invention incredibly memorable."

"I hope we can, Grandma."

"You will, Buttercup. Mark my words."

We arrive at the Colosseum, and I can't believe it. It's like something out of my Human History book.

"Now this is something memorable. Whoever built this was really talented. Can you imagine doing our presentations in here?" I ask Ander. "At one time, this held over thirty thousand spectators."

"I thought you weren't good at Human History."

I smile. "I guess I'm not that bad."

"There were also over eighty entrances."

"There were?"

"Yeah, they had to have that many for all those people."

We explore all kinds of things in Rome, like the Vatican and the Sistine Chapel. We throw coins in Trevi Fountain, walk through St. Peter's Basilica, and pass by the Arch of Constantine. It's all cool to see, but the best part is being back with my family.

When Seraphina asks us what we want for dinner, we agree in like two seconds.

"Pizza it is!" she exclaims, and we wander through the streets of Rome until we stumble upon an Italian restaurant that's dimly lit inside with beautiful arches. There's so many of us, we need several tables. Once they have them ready, the parents sit together and all of us kids sit on our own. Ryne and Malin sit on either side of me, and Ander sits across from Ryne. Ander's sister, Daphne, sits across from Malin. They talk the whole time it seems—like they've been best friends forever. That's how I feel, too.

We order margherita pizzas, the kind with fresh mozzarella, and when we're finished eating, the waiter brings us Italian-style ice cream called gelato in fancy silver cups. It's sweet and smooth, and I think I could eat in this restaurant every single day.

Later that night, when we walk down a brick-paved street, we peek in the storefront windows. The shops are closed but the window displays are lit up, filled with beautiful clothes. We walk slowly so we can look at them, but Ander groans every time we stop. "Why are we walking so slow? Who wants to look at clothes?"

Seraphina puts her hand on his shoulder and points to the next window. "I think you'll want to see this."

"What is it?" he asks.

"It's a morphing mannequin. I read about them in a fashion magazine. Watch."

I stare at the mannequin, dressed in a beautiful blue ball gown. Her hair is piled high on her head. Soon the dress shrinks, transforming into a blue shirt and jeans. Beautiful gold jewelry appears on the mannequin's arms. Brown riding boots appear on its feet.

"That's so cool!"

"Watch, it's changing again."

We continue watching as, this time, the mannequin's hair transforms into a ponytail and her shirt and jeans become a workout outfit with pink-striped sneakers.

"This is the best invention ever!" Jillian exclaims.

I step closer to the window. "Yeah, I wonder who invented it?"

"I'm not sure," Seraphina replies. "But I'm thrilled we found one. I was hoping we could watch one in person."

A few days later, on the last day with our families, we tour Venice, Italy, and take a gondola ride through the canals. As we glide along the water, guided by a man called a gondolier, I have to pinch myself. Even though we've been on this tour for so many months, I still can't believe how lucky I am, how lucky we all are to see all these places that I've only read about. If it weren't for the Piedmont Challenge, I never would have been able to.

"Isn't his costume the best?" Jillian replies. "Gondoliers always wear blue and white striped shirts with red sashes and straw hats."

I watch him paddle and think that it would be an easy costume to copy. And then it hits me. I know exactly how to connect our inventions. I can't believe I didn't think of it before. Wait until I tell my teammates!

THE PATH TO CRIMSON CATROPOLIS

THE CHAIRS IN the courtyard are arranged in a giant circle. All fifteen of us are facing one another—no, it's more like we're staring at one another. It seems like everyone's ideas for connecting our inventions have dried up—except for mine.

I have an idea, but I'm not sure if I should tell them all. It's nothing like any of the other ideas and they might shut me down. They could laugh, because it is kind of a laughable idea. I'm not even sure what my teammates will say. I wish I had asked them first. I just wasn't sure I totally liked the idea myself. But as we sit here staring at one another, with no other brilliant ideas, I need to at least try.

But Jonah starts talking again. "It appears that no one has a better idea so I think we should go with Hannah's idea and create a transparent box that will contain all the inventions. We can present them as the Trio Toys—meaning toys that belong to our three teams."

Everyone starts talking at once. Some of the kids like the idea. Some of them don't. My head beats like a drum. The toy box idea could work . . . we could build a transparent box together. But I still think my idea is better.

Jonah leans back. "Okay, do we all finally agree?"

Hannah's idea is easier than mine. It would be less work and give us more time to focus on our own team's invention. Jonah and Hannah could be in charge. If I go along with it—everything would be easier. But all three of our inventions would be better together, connected another way. I look down at my wristband, and I know I have to speak up. Seraphina says we need to be courageous. I guess this is my chance.

The butterflies in my stomach revolt, but I stand up anyway. "Wait a second, Jonah. I may have another idea to share, an idea that could go along with the toy box."

My team looks at me, surprised.

"What is it?" asks Ander.

"Our preceptor is always telling us that when you're trying to make an idea stand out in someone's mind, you need to make it memorable. By doing our skits, with all of the costumes and sets, we've presented our inventions in a memorable way. They've helped us to show the judges how important our inventions could be to other people. While we've been on this tour, I've realized there's more to Piedmont than just figuring out how to solve tasks and build inventions. It's about inspiring people with our creativity. If we want to show the judges at each of our schools how creative we are *and* how good we can be at inventing new things, then we should be as creative as we can be when we present to them."

"That makes sense," says Hannah. "What do you think we should do?"

"You've seen our skits so many times. They're set in a fictional place called Crimson Catropolis. They tell stories about a little girl. What if all of us put on a skit for the judges? Our inventions could be *connected* through a story."

"All of us?" asks Hannah.

"Do a skit together?" asks Maëlle.

"Yes! All fifteen of us. We already have the basic story created. We just need to tell a new chapter."

"That's the best idea yet, Kia!" Jillian exclaims. "We can make costumes *and* act together!"

Ander jumps up from his chair. "I totally want to reinvent Freddie Dinkleweed."

Jonah stands up. "Wait one moment. What type of story—or chapter—would connect all our inventions?"

I take a deep breath. "I've been thinking about this for a little while. What if the residents of Crimson Catropolis have never heard of school? What if the little girl tells them all about it, how wonderful it is, and tells them they should create a school there? They could disagree. She could convince them by showing them all the cool things they'll get if they enroll, like the hologram book and the backpack, and tell them they'd get to walk on the Balance

Blocks—an activity that would help them choose their futures."

They stare at me. Their eyes feel like lasers burning into my face. I knew they wouldn't like it. I knew they would think my idea was dumb. Why didn't I figure out a story with my own team first?

Maëlle stands up next to Jonah. "That's brilliant, Kia. I vote yes!"

"Me, too," says Jax. "It's a great idea."

"Really, Kia?" says Mare. "Another play? Don't you think it would be hard to coordinate all fifteen of us?"

"Yes!" I say. "It might be. But we can figure it out. I know we can. We need to impress the judges, and this will definitely do it."

Jonah sighs. "I think our hologram book will impress them anyway."

"I agree," says Zoe. "Our backpack doesn't need a play to stand out for the judges."

I bite my ring-finger nail.

"But," she continues, "I think a play would be fun, and it would be a better connector than just a toy box."

I sit on my hands. I hate to admit it, but they're right. Their inventions *are* good enough. But our invention needs something more. We need this skit.

We banter back and forth weighing the pros and cons of doing a connected skit. Finally, Jillian says, "I think we should do it. This tour is about all of us connecting, too. What better way to do that than by making costumes, building sets, and writing a script—together?"

"Yeah," says Ander. "We can split into three mixed teams. We can work on whatever we want. I want to work on the sets. Anyone else want to?"

"I would," says Mare.

That means that Mare is willing to do another skit! I try not to make a big deal about that, though, because if I do, she'll probably change her mind.

"I want to write the script," says Maëlle.

I smile at her. "Me, too."

Jonah sits quietly with his arms folded across his chest. I watch him, waiting for him to protest my idea and say how dumb it is.

"What do the rest of you think?" I ask, before he has a chance to speak up.

"Okay, America. I'm in. I can be a team player, and it seems like your team needs this great connection in order to get into your inventor school."

I stare at him. If I had my own laser daggers, they would scorch him. Why couldn't he just say yes? Why does he always have to act like he's better than me? But whatever. He agreed to it, so I guess we better get started.

We split into two groups. One will create a box, but instead of being a toy box, it will be a school box containing all the things that a person going to school receives on the first day. It will be part of the stage set and hold the backpack and the book. The second group gets to work on the script.

I hurry to the back of the courtyard with a notebook and pencils. Jillian, Maëlle, Danielle, Gwyndol, Giulia, and Finn follow. We find a cluster of trees to gather by and sit together on the cold cobblestone floor. "Our first job is to plan out the story. After that we'll write the script."

"Sounds fabulous to me," says Gwyndol. "I love writing stories."

It takes us a long time to figure out the details, but while the other group plans out the box, we decide what the story will be about. We decide that Little Girl returns to Crimson Catropolis to settle a dispute among the residents. The Jester wants to leave Crimson Catropolis to explore the world. The Gatekeeper doesn't want him to go until he's better prepared. He's heard of a place called "school" and suggests they start a school in their land. The Jester and many of the residents don't think school will be fun. So, with a little help from Madam Sparkles and Teenager Mare, Little Girl shows the residents what happens to people when they go to school. They get hologram books, they get a mechanical backpack, and they get to choose a path on the Balance Blocks that will help them to decide their own futures.

"I like this story," says Maëlle. "It's the perfect combination of all our inventions."

"I think it's fantastic," says Gwyndol. "Let's write the lines."

"But what characters should the rest of us play?" asks Danielle. "Your team already has roles. What should we be?"

"The rest of us should be the residents," Finn replies. "That would be the easiest."

"And your costumes can be whatever you want," says Jillian. "If you want to be glamorous, you can. If you want to be rugged and hardworking, that's fine, too. The possibilities are endless in Crimson Catropolis."

"This is going to be so much fun," says Giulia. "Let's write the script."

So we get to work writing our lines. It would be easier on the air screen, but we decide that we like writing the words on paper. "Some of these lines will probably change," I say. "Ander usually changes his while we're rehearsing anyway, but at least this is a start."

When we have most of the script written, the other group crowds around us, wanting to hear the story.

"Sit with us," says Jillian. "We'll read what we have so far."

We make room for them by the tree cluster and take turns reading lines from the script aloud.

"I don't know if you noticed, but everyone has at least one or two lines," says Giulia.

"That's good," says Mare. "I noticed you only gave me a couple, which is fine. I want to spend most of my time working on the sets, not memorizing the script."

I nod. "Jillian and I knew you wouldn't want too many."

"I like it," says Hannah.

"I do, too," says Ander. "It's great."

"I like it," says Lars. "And we planned out the sets, too. Hopefully we'll find all the materials we need on these aero-buses."

We finally take a short break, but only to eat. Our preceptors bring dinner to us, and we eat scattered around the courtyard. I think about our script. It's a little strange writing one with kids who aren't my teammates. But in a way they are. It's kind of good listening to all their different ideas. Maybe this last script will be even better because of them.

Later that night, after saying good night to our new teammates, Mare, Jillian, and I lie on our flower beds. Mare makes a shocking statement. "I don't really mind working with the kids on the other teams. It's not that bad. I was dreading it. But except for Jonah, it's fine."

"Is he trying to be the boss of everyone?" I ask.

"No, I thought he would, but he's not."

"What's he doing that's so bad, then?" asks Jillian.

"He acts like I don't know how to build anything, when I'm not sure he even knows how to use any tools. Sure, he's good at technology, but there's other things you need to know to be able to build something. He's so annoying."

I nod because I agree. *Wow, I finally agree with Mare.*

When we turn off the lights, the creativity misters turn on. The mist gently covers my face, and I finally feel like we may have a chance in this final stage of the competition. I can't believe we're doing another skit—all together! I finally feel like the fifteen of us have something in common—and we may even help one another reach our goals by working together.

It's strange that tomorrow we're already off to Spain. I'm excited to get there, but I wish we could stay up on the platform instead of touring the city. The script is almost done, and I want to start practicing. But I guess I'll just think about our lines while we're walking around the city. I'll think up the ones we're missing. No problem at all. And so, I drift off to sleep dreaming of the Gatekeeper, Madam Sparkles, Freddie Dinkleweed, Teenager Mare, and Little Girl all traveling around Spain together.

CUPCAKES IN THE COURTYARD

WITH JUST OVER two months to go until the Day of Creativity, we reach the platform in Spain. I never thought June would get here so fast. At least the sensors are attached to the blocks, our script is written, and one of our set pieces is complete. Now, all we need to do is complete the rest and show the other teams how to make their costumes. Oh, and memorize our lines and rehearse. Okay, maybe we still have a lot to do.

I follow Ander out of the megacar onto the ground in Barcelona, Spain. The sunshine warms my face but not for long. We follow Seraphina and Gregor into the Barcelona Convention Centre and, like so many other convention centers on this tour, it's massive. I wonder what the kids here will be like. Will they be like the kids in Brazil or more like the kids in Italy? How about Australia? But as I think that over, I decide that, except for their accents, the kids we've met on the tour have been the same— friendly and curious.

After our three morning presentations, we're led into a gigantic room where we'll give the kids Swirl and Spark Recall tasks. But this time, Team France and Team Switzerland are giving them as well, in the same room at the same time. With so many of us in here, it's like a great big party. Usually, there's only a few small groups of kids, maybe six tables of seven kids each. But there's three times as many today. Music plays in the background and balloon-like orbs float around like bubbles, filled with the words *think, brainstorm, create, build,* and *solve.*

The task I'm leading today is one where the teams need to place colorful pieces of paper in bowls of the same color. There's five in all: red, blue, green, yellow, and orange. The trick is, the person who places the paper in the bowls is blindfolded. The other kids must instruct him or her on where to place each one, but they can't use words. They need to create some other type of communication system—a way to tell them which bowl is correct, and they have to decide the way they'll communicate with the blindfolded person in one minute's time, before the task officially starts.

Some kids decide that one clap means they're about to drop the card in the wrong bowl, and two means they're about to drop it in the right one. Others tap on the table, and others snap their fingers. Seven teams of seven rotate

through my table. Some get the right colors in the bowls
before the time's up. Some don't. Some are silent, but
others forget they need to be and get a penalty point. But
during it all there are giggles and dropped papers and lots
of clapping and snapping.

When we're finished with the last group, we leave the
convention center and head to a famous open market
called Boqueria Market. We pass through the entrance,
an arched structure made of iron and stained glass, and
quickly find stall after stall of fresh fruits, vegetables,
meats, and cheeses. We wander around all afternoon and
don't even stop for lunch. We don't need to. Floating platters travel around the market like flying carpets carrying
samples of every single food item. A silver platter hovers
near Jillian and me carrying Spanish ham called *jamon*.
We try it because Gregor says it's a Barcelona classic. I'm
not sure if he's right about that, and I hesitate at first, but
it actually tastes okay.

Later, we head to La Barceloneta Beach, located at the
foot of the old fisherman's district. We swim in the Med-
iterranean Sea and listen to a guitar concert on shore.
Afterward, we visit Park Güell. But it's not a park like
anything we're used to. Instead of regular park benches
spread out over the whole place, this park has one long
wavy stone bench covered in colorful mosaic tiles with
views to the ocean. Even the buildings are different. They
look like they popped right out of a Dr. Seuss book.

When we've had our fill of Barcelona for the day, we
head back up to the platform. We camp out near the Pooncha Tree, not quite ready to go inside the aero-bus yet.

"Our next meeting with the other teams is tomorrow," says Ander. "The script is done, but we still need to finish building the sets, right?"

"Right," says Mare. "We have two signs to make: *Welcome to Crimson Catropolis* and *Path to Your Future . . . This Way!*"

"And a Crimson Clock Tower to build," says Ander.

"Why do we need a clock tower?" I ask.

"Because we thought it would look cool," Ander replies. "You know, like the one in Switzerland. Besides, we have more people so that means we can make a more elaborate set for the world of Crimson Catropolis."

Jax nods. "I wanted to build the clock tower. You can blame me."

I laugh. "It's good. A clock tower will look good."

"Don't forget the costumes," says Jillian. "We need to help the other teams make theirs."

"How will we do it?" I ask. "We better search for some materials."

"I already asked Mabel. She snuck into her secret compartment and brought back the Clothes Copier we had used in Quebec, along with a whole cart of fabric."

"Seriously?" Mare replies.

"Seriously!" says Jillian. "And if we have time, we may even add some special touches to our costumes, too."

I stand up and walk toward the aero-bus. "Okay, then. Tomorrow we work on sets and costumes."

The next morning, we meet the other teams in the courtyard and divide into two groups: the costume team and the set team. Jillian and I lead the costume team.

Mare and Jax lead the set team. Ander decides we need a team manager to oversee the whole project. I'm not sure what Jonah will think of that, though. It's bad enough he has to take direction from Mare and Jax. I'm glad I won't have to see his face when Ander tries to manage him, too.

We designate the center tables as our large group meeting spot. Jillian and I take Maëlle, Danielle, Giulia, Gwyndol, and Finn to one end of the courtyard, which will be the costume-making area. Mare and Jax lead Jonah, Hannah, Lars, Zoe, and Stephan to the other end, which will be the set-making area. As we hustle to our area, Ander calls after us, "I'll start over at the set side and be over at the costume side later."

"Okay," I call back to him. When we get to our area, we dump the fabric out on the table.

Gwyndol steps up to the table. "What's this machine?"

"This," says Jillian, "is the Clothes Copier. There's a computer attached to it. First, you research the type of clothing you want to create on the air screen. Then you feed the fabric into the tray. After that, just push the button and the outfit slides out."

"You're serious?" he asks. "That's fantastic."

"Definitely!" she replies. "But the outfit that spits out won't be your exact size. You'll need to cut it down and sew the new seams."

Danielle tugs on her sleeve. "How do we do that?"

I motion for her to sit near me. "We'll show you. It's easy."

"How did you learn to sew?"

"Jillian taught us all at our first competition at Camp Piedmont. It's kind of fun making our own clothes—well, parts of our own clothes."

We gather around the air screen and they pick outfits that they like. It's interesting seeing what each of them choose and funny seeing the giant outfits spit out of the copier. We measure, cut, and sew—and glue on glitter, sequins, and buttons. Eventually Ander appears, anxious to see our progress.

"It's going pretty well here," I say. "How about over there?"

"It's good. I got sick of painting, so I thought I would add something to my costume. I think Freddie needs more interesting shoes." He finds a clown pair on the air screen, feeds blue fabric into the tray and, with the touch of a button, out pop shiny new jester shoes! "These are perfect . . . a little big maybe, but I'll just pin the fabric." He salutes us and races back to the other group.

Jillian laughs. "He doesn't want to be a leader. He just wants to work in both groups."

"Exactly," I say. "And he has no idea that we're totally on to him."

While we're sewing, Seraphina places trays of colorful cupcakes on the center tables. Both of our groups descend on them like vultures. "I'm exhausted," says Mare. "I need a cupcake and then a nap."

"Not yet," I say. "What if we read through our lines?"

"Oh, yes," says Giulia. "Let's do that."

So Jax gathers up several air screens and we sit in a giant fifteen-person circle. I find the script file that contains our lines—the whole story of our skit—and we slowly bring the world of Crimson Catropolis back to life with ten new residents.

Ander shuts down his file. "That sounds pretty good, for a first read through, I mean."

"Well," Jonah replies. "I think it's going to require a lot more work if it's going to look professional enough. Our inventions are good, well most of them are, so this performance better match that."

We sit there with our mouths hanging open.

"Yes, Jonah. *All* the inventions are good, and our performance will match them," says Hannah. "This skit is excellent and will pull them all together."

"Thanks, Hannah," I say. "But to be sure, *Jonah,* we will practice. A lot. And we'll work on our costumes and sets *a lot*. Mare will even make us a schedule, right, Mare?"

She yawns. "Right."

I know Mare hates practicing. But I know she hates making a fool of herself in front of an audience even more. It sounds like Jonah's just like her that way. And for once, I don't mind at all. We'll get to spend every spare second over the next few weeks working on this skit.

THE PIEDMONT PROBLEM

AFTER WEEKS OF building and painting our sets, measuring and sewing our costumes, and learning our lines—all while presenting to the children below the platform, we have only one more day in Spain. Master Freeman and Andora are off the platform for the day, back at Piedmont University preparing to announce this year's winners of the first stage of the Piedmont Challenge to schools all over the United States. A new generation of sixth-grade students will follow in our footsteps. Five kids from each state will win Golden Light Bulbs today in the Day of Brightness Ceremony. They'll travel to Camp Piedmont this summer, where they'll work in teams to solve a task. The state teams will compete against each other at the end of camp in the Piedmont Challenge National Finals. Just like we did.

The announcements will take place at different times today in each of the fifty states. Master Freeman and Andora will make the announcement from the university, and students will watch the results from giant screens in their school auditoriums. Just like we did.

Most of the kids around the country will be programmed into one academic category: Art Forms, Communications, Earth and Space, Human History, Math, or New Technology. The top five scorers in the Piedmont Challenge from each state will, instead, win a Golden Light Bulb. Just like we did.

I'm not sure how I feel about it. Part of me is excited to know more kids will win today and more kids will be headed to Camp Piedmont. But part of me feels jealous, like I wish we could do all of this all over again.

We've been invited to watch the announcement of the New York Piedmont Challenge with Seraphina and Gregor today. A giant air screen has been set up in the courtyard and a bigger table as well. I sit next to Seraphina and Ander. We joke about that day last year, how excited we felt to hear our names called. They remind me that my name was called first. Like I could ever forget! I remind them that Ander danced up on stage next to me. None of them needs to be reminded of that either.

Seraphina tells us that she was watching that day with Gregor from a room inside Piedmont Chamber at Piedmont University. They had been chosen ahead of time to be our preceptors. "That day was like finding out who our new family would be," she says in a voice that sounds sadder than normal. Maybe she wishes we could do all of this all over again, too.

Gregor smiles at her, like he's thinking the same thing. But then, as if a spring erupts under her, she exclaims, "Okay, my Crimson Kids, let's watch! Let's see who wins Golden Light Bulbs, too!"

The screen flashes and Master Freeman appears looking very important in a bright white tuxedo. As soon as I see him, I remember the butterflies fluttering in my stomach while I wished with my whole heart that I would not get programmed into Math, that I would be one of the top five winners of the Piedmont Challenge, that I would win a Golden Light Bulb.

He holds the first envelope, opens it, and exclaims, "The first winner of the Piedmont Challenge in New York is Van Michael, student number 524 from Spry Elementary School." The television switches to an auditorium where a boy with blond hair and glasses races to the stage. His grin is big, and he dances. Just like Ander.

Master Freeman holds a second envelope, opens it, and reads the second name. "Raylan Clark, student number 1105 from Briarwood Elementary School!" The television switches to a second school auditorium and a dark-haired boy timidly walks up the stage steps and smiles a shy smile.

He opens the third envelope and says, "Samantha Faith, student number 812 from Martha Brown Academy!" The camera switches to a third school where a tall girl with light brown hair walks confidently up to the stage. She has a serious expression on her face, but when her principal hands her a Golden Light Bulb, she beams almost as brightly as the trophy.

The camera switches back to Master Freeman, and he exclaims, "The fourth winner of this year's Piedmont Challenge is Alba Costello, student number 84 from Seneca Falls Elementary."

A bubbly, brown-haired girl with big, brown eyes hops out of her seat and runs onto the stage in seconds. She bounces up and down as her principal places a Golden Light Bulb in her hands.

"And the final winner of this year's Piedmont Challenge is Alexandra Wilder, student number 603 from Friendship Academy." A small girl smiles, walks purposefully onto the stage where she receives her Golden Light Bulb, and clutches it to her chest.

"Congratulations to all five winners of this year's New York Piedmont Challenge!"

The camera splits into five smaller screens, and each of the five children appear on their own stages at their own schools. It's a different scene than we had at Crimson, where all five of us stood on the stage together.

Ander leans back and sighs. "Looks like we still hold the record at Crimson. We're the only Crimson kids to win Golden Light Bulbs in more than fifty years. We're still like royalty."

"And we're still the only team to be made up of five kids from the same school," I say.

"True," says Seraphina.

"Soon they'll go to Camp Piedmont," Jillian adds.

"Who will be their preceptors?" asks Mare. "Since you're here with us?"

"Yeah and what about Andora and Master Freeman?" asks Jax. "Don't they need to finish out the tour with us?"

Gregor nods. "They've already been assigned preceptors. Master Freeman and Andora will still spend their time on this tour. When they need to appear at Camp Piedmont, they certainly will."

It's weird thinking that Camp Piedmont will happen again this summer—without us, while we're in France and England.

"That was fun," says Jillian. "I liked seeing who the kids on this year's team are."

Seraphina purses her lips. "Yes, I liked seeing that, too."

Something about Seraphina is off. She says she liked seeing all this, but she isn't acting like it. I wonder why.

Gregor stands up. "Seraphina and I have a meeting with the other preceptors in just a few minutes. Therefore, you are dismissed. Perhaps you can work on your final task."

"Yeah, sure," says Ander. "Come on guys, let's go."

We enter the floating chamber and hop up on the couches and chairs. We hover above the room, trying to figure out what's going on with Seraphina.

"She seems sad," I say.

"Even Gregor was acting a little weird," says Mare.

"Maybe they wish they were going back to Camp Piedmont," says Jillian. "*I* wish we were. I miss the floating playground."

"Me, too," says Ander. "And Nacho Cheese Ball."

"I don't think that's why she's sad," I say. "I saw her look at Gregor in a weird way."

"What do you mean?" asks Jax.

"I'm not sure."

"Do you think it has something to do with their preceptor meeting?" asks Jillian.

Ander jumps down from his chair. "Only one way to find out the answer to that! Let's see if we can hear what they're talking about."

Mare stops to tie her sneakers. "They're probably talking about our schedules for France or something. But whatever, let's casually walk near that end of the courtyard. I want to grab a drink from the Pooncha Tree anyway."

We race off the aero-bus and walk as close as possible to the platform windows. On the way, we stop at the Pooncha Tree and find it full of colorful slushy drinks. I pull a sunshine-yellow Pooncha cloth from a branch, wrap it around the small cup, and take a sip. "Mmm, it tastes like cherries, blueberries, and coconut."

Mare takes one, too, places a blue starlit Pooncha cloth around it, and the rest of our teammates follow. We creep our way closer to the table we sat at earlier for the Day of Brightness Ceremony on the big screen. It sounds like the six preceptors are sitting there speaking in hushed voices. We stop at the largest tree cluster on the whole platform, one that's about ten feet away from it. The leaves on the trees are thick; we can barely see through them. We can't see the preceptors or the courtyard, but we know they're there. Their voices are unmistakable, so we freeze like statues and listen close.

"It sounds as though Andora's efforts to change the committee's minds were not successful," says Mathilde.

"No, they were not," Gregor replies. "This situation is more serious than we had thought."

"So, this is it?" says Elin. "This could be the end of the Piedmont Challenge?"

"I'm afraid so," says Levin.

"How long have you all known?" asks Gabriel.

"Seraphina and I found out a short while ago."

I peek through the branches. Elin shakes her head.

"Why are you all acting like it's hopeless?" says Seraphina.

"Because it is!" says Mathilde.

"No, it's not! The children still have a chance. Their inventions are good!"

"Yes, but are they good enough to convince the World Government Bureau that creativity and inventing are important? They still believe that *all* children should be separated into categories—that they are more useful to society that way."

"But what about the creative children of the world?" Seraphina exclaims.

"That's right," says Gabriel. "What about them? They are not just daydreamers. They are our future."

"Of course, they are," says Levin. "Except that the WGB believes that innovation is dead. They believe there are no more inventions to be created, especially by children. They believe the world has advanced as much as it needs to."

Elin sighs. "That's horrible."

Levin continues: "Apparently this tour is Piedmont's last hope to convince the WGB and the people around the world that our future becomes our own through innovation. This final task that the children have been given is the Piedmont Organization's last chance to show the government the amazing things kids can create if they work together."

Seraphina taps her purple nails on the table. I could recognize the pattern anywhere. "And the kids can still do it."

Gregor nods. "Yes, I believe they can. But now we know that it won't just be the judges at PIPS and the other elite schools who will be watching them—and judging remotely. On the Day of Creativity, the WGB will be watching and judging, too. The fate of Piedmont is in their hands."

I move a branch just a bit and see Seraphina cover her face with her hands. "It's so unfair. The whole future of Piedmont lies in the hands of fifteen children. If they can convince the WGB that inventions still make a positive impact on our world, *that they can*, Piedmont will go on as it always has. If not, there'll be no more Piedmont Challenge, no more Camp Piedmont, no more PIPS, no more of any of it. How is this even happening?"

"I don't know," Gregor replies. "But it's up to us to give the children the tools they need to work together and be their most creative. That's what Piedmont has always been about and that's what it will continue to be. That is not going to change. I believe in the children. They will come through."

"Gregor, we do, too," says Mathilde. "But we must be realistic. By the time we return from the tour, the Piedmont Organization may be no more."

The preceptors stand up and walk together out of the courtyard. We wait until they're out of sight and climb out of the tree cluster. Liquid drips down my hand, and I realize I've let my slushy drip out of the cup. We stand together stunned into silence right there on the cold, silver platform floor.

THE MISSION

THE RIDE TO France feels like a funeral. Seraphina and Gregor have been spending most of their time locked away in the dining chamber, with no idea at all that we know about the WGB, that we know about the problem at Piedmont. We squish together in the boys' bedchamber, inside their hot air balloon, where the floor between their beds is hard, like the pounding in my head.

"How can they shut down Piedmont?" I ask. "It's the best thing in the whole world!"

"I don't get it either," says Jillian. "Master Freeman and Andora are like the leaders of the universe. How can the world government tell them what to do?"

"They're the leaders of Piedmont, that's all," Jax reminds us. "They're an organization, like a company. They still have to follow the rules of a country and the rules of the world."

"But they're a good organization," I say. "It's not like they're hurting anybody!"

"The WGB thinks that what we're all doing is useless, that our ideas and inventions are like cotton candy at a carnival. Sure, kids like it but it doesn't help them—or anyone."

"That's a horrible comparison," says Mare. "I think the Ancestor App, the Satellite Spectacles, and all the inventions that have come from the Piedmont Challenge are more important than cotton candy."

"They are," says Jax. "But did you hear what the preceptors said? They don't think there are any more inventions to create. They think kids can be more useful being taught to do specific jobs."

"Yeah," I say. "By getting programmed."

Ander pulls his pillow onto his lap. "That's why Master Freeman and Andora gave us this new task. That's why we have to earn our places at PIPS again."

"Yeah," says Jillian. "That's probably the only way they could think of to get us to create another incredible invention."

Ander shakes his head. "Why didn't Master Freeman just ask us? Why didn't he just say, 'The future of Piedmont is in your hands. We need you to create an amazing invention or else you can't go to PIPS because PIPS will be closed and so will all the competitions and camps at Piedmont.'"

"Yeah, that would have been great," says Mare. "No pressure on us at all."

"Well, we have pressure on us now anyway."

My brain tangles like seaweed. "So, what do we do now? PIPS cannot close. Piedmont cannot be shut down!"

"Well," says Jillian. "We go down to France. We present to the kids. We show everyone there that there are so many more inventions to be created—by kids like them."

"You're right. And when we come back up here, we find a way to make our team invention even better. We have to. The future of Piedmont depends on it."

A SHORT WHILE later, after arriving on the French platform, our entire group touches down in France. Maëlle and her teammates bounce out of the megacar, thrilled to be back in their home country. Even though most of them don't live close to Paris, where we'll be presenting, their families will make the trip here sometime this month.

The Paris Convention Center and all the children inside are ready for us when we arrive. The crowds are larger here than we're used to, and I bet that's because the French team is here. The children's cheers sound like they're coming from a rock concert when Maëlle, Danielle, Gwyndol, Stephan, and Zoe take the stage! It's crazy but it makes me so happy. They're the nicest kids I've ever met, and they should be treated like rock stars.

The cheers for us are not as loud, until we finish our first skit. Then the children jump to their feet and scream. I guess they think we're like rock stars, too. When we administer the Swirl and Spark Recall tasks, I realize how much the kids here want to be inventors someday, just like the kids on the French team. It makes me want to save Piedmont even more than I already do.

"Before you leave the convention center, there is something we would like to show you." I spin around to see an usher motioning for us to follow her. "It is our latest invention created right here in Paris." She leads us to a colorful wall with laser beams flashing in front of it. "This, my friends, is called Voice Choice. It will alter the sound of your voice. If you find your voice too squeaky or high pitched, you may lower it. If you find it too low, you may raise the pitch, or frequency, of the sound."

Ander looks at her in disbelief. "Really?"

"Yes, most certainly. Simply place your hand on the surface and raise or lower the dials to your desired specification. Your voice will then be altered. Would anyone like to try?"

"Is it permanent?" Seraphina asks.

"It is semipermanent. It will wear off eventually."

Mare scratches her nose. "So, what if you don't like the way your new voice sounds?"

"Then you will have to get used to it for a time."

"That's a really cool invention," I say, but I don't actually mean it.

"So . . . who would like to try first?"

Gregor gathers us together. "Unfortunately, we are on a tight schedule. Perhaps next time. But many thanks for showing this to us. It's quite remarkable."

We hurry away, and it feels more like we're escaping. I think that's an invention that needs more work.

Later that morning, we begin our tour of the city of Paris. We visit the Louvre museum, Notre Dame Cathedral, and the Arc de Triomphe. The buildings are some of the oldest I've ever seen and some of the most incredible. We look at the Eiffel Tower from the ground, climb to the top, and even eat lunch inside. The server brings us a platter of fruit crepes, bacon quiche, baguettes, and croissants. While we snack on an assortment of colorful macarons for dessert, I think about Mom, Malin, and Grandma Kitty. I wish they were here with me now, looking out over the city. They would love it. People and cars whiz by, and I feel like I'm on top of the entire world. Seraphina takes our pictures and promises to send them to our families. I hope it makes them happy and doesn't make them miss us more.

When we get to ground level, Jillian asks Seraphina when we can go shopping, but I don't care one bit about shopping in Paris. Tomorrow we have our next meeting with the other teams. They still have no clue about what's happening at Piedmont, and we can't tell them. We just need to make sure they make their inventions and our connected invention as great as they can be.

We meet in the courtyard the next day and rehearse our skit for the first time. We say our lines, but, even without including each of our inventions, our skit is too long.

"It's okay," I say. "When we all know our lines better, it'll go faster. We're hesitating, so that takes up time." Ander and Jillian give the kids performance tips, too, and it feels like we've become theater directors. On our next run through, we're still two minutes over. And the next time we're over by one and a half. But we know from doing two skits already, we need to cut some lines. Going over time will give us a penalty, and we need all the points we can get. Only a score of excellence will get us into PIPS—and save Piedmont.

When we're done rehearsing, we test out our inventions and it doesn't go well. It seems we all have problems to work out. We can't find a way to move the Balance Blocks into the courtyard without dismantling the whole structure, so we pretend we're actually walking on them. The French team's backpack malfunctions twice, and the Swiss team's hologram book fizzles. The images appear and then disappear quickly in a puff of smoke. I watch Jonah as he tries to adjust the settings, and he catches me staring. "What are you looking at, America? At least when it's working it's life changing. I don't think you can say the same for your Balance Blocks."

I walk away from him before I say something mean, even though I want to. But he's right. Our invention is not life changing, and if Piedmont closes forever and we can't go to PIPS, it's our own fault.

When everyone else leaves, our team stays in the courtyard. "I can't believe this. The Ancestor App and the Satellite Spectacles are life changing. The Balance Blocks are only pretty good, not excellent. Now that it really matters, for more than just a competition, we're blowing it. Our invention is not good enough to save Piedmont."

Jillian slouches in a chair. "What will Andora do without Piedmont? It's her whole life."

"My head hurts," I say. "I'm going for a walk."

Ander jumps out of his chair. "I'll go with you."

We walk toward the platform window, and I stare at the sky, basically looking at nothing.

"KK, what's up. You haven't said much for a while."

"I don't know. I'm worried about our invention."

"Don't you think it's good enough?"

"Not really. Do you?"

"I think it's awesome. But I think it needs something more special."

"That's what I think. I just don't know what's wrong with me. At home, while I'm flying on my aero-scooter, tons of invention ideas swirl in my head. But here they're just gone."

"They aren't gone. Maybe they're just taking a break."

"Maybe. But break time is over. We need to work on something big—something incredible."

We near Andora's aero-bus and see her walking outside again. What does she *do* all day anyway? We stop and wait. We can't see her face, but even with her back to us, we can see that she's looking out into the sky. I wonder if she's thinking about Lexland. I wonder if she's thinking about their mysterious invention. I bet she is. She said it was an incredible invention. If I was her, I would be thinking about it, too.

We wait until she's back inside and keep walking, right by the compartment where the invention is hidden.

"Do you think she's mad that she can't figure out the code that Lexland locked their invention with?" Ander asks.

"If there was an invention that I helped invent and it was locked up somehow, and I didn't know the code, I would be mad. I would be curious, too. I'd want to figure it out."

"Yeah, me, too."

Suddenly my brain starts swirling. Just a little at first, and then more. "Wait, that's it, Ander."

"What's it?"

"Ander, why are we not trying to crack that code? Andora told us not to try to retrieve it for selfish reasons—just because we're curious. But what if our reasons aren't selfish? What if we did it for her? Isn't that what this competition is about? Taking things that are already here and finding ways to make them better? Well, all Andora has right now is a statue. Sure, it's filled with memories of Lexland, but it's also filled with something that could be important. She said the invention was life changing. What if we unlocked it for her—as like a surprise? Seraphina's always telling us to be courageous. Why isn't Andora trying to unlock it? It could be the one thing that saves Piedmont! Why isn't she being courageous? I think she's forgotten how. Maybe it's up to us to remind her."

Ander nods. "Let's do it, KK."

"Really?"

"Sure, but what about *our* invention . . . and our skit?"

I bite my ring-finger nail. "Maybe you were right before. Maybe our brains need a break from it. We'll still work on it, but we're kind of stuck anyway. Maybe it would help to have another project to work on. We have time."

"What if we can't open it."

"We won't know until we try, will we?"

"So, you really think we should?"

I smile without any hesitation. "Yeah."

We quickly walk away and call an emergency meeting with the rest of our team. They meet us in chamber eight, and we tell them what we want to do.

"Are you guys serious?" asks Jax. "We could get into so much trouble."

Mare laughs. "Andora said we should never touch it for selfish reasons. Kia's right. We'd be doing it for her—and for Piedmont."

"Exactly. If we can open it and give it to Andora, she can show it to the WGB. If it's as good as she says it is, it has to convince them to keep Piedmont open."

"But what about our final task?" Jillian asks.

I tighten my ponytail. "We need a short break. Then we'll start working on it again. But first, we'll try to crack the code. "Come on, you guys. We need to do it for her."

"And for the rest of the world," Ander replies.

"Hold on," says Jax. "What if we get caught with it? What if Andora goes back to that compartment and it's gone?"

"Then we'll work on it when she wouldn't be looking at it."

"When?" he asks. "In the middle of the night?"

I smile. "Exactly."

"You guys can do that part," says Mare. "I need my sleep."

"Ugh, Mare. You can take a nap tomorrow during our breaks."

"Wait, can you repeat that, Kia?"

"Mare, if you help us in the middle of the night and still need more sleep, you can nap during our breaks."

She grins. "All right. I'm in."

"Me, too," says Jillian. "Andora looked so sad when she told us the story. I can picture her face already when we tell her we figured out how to unlock the lock."

"It would be the best present ever!" I say.

Ander grins. "What do you say, big guy? Are you with us? We really need you to be with us."

Jax shakes his head. "I don't want to get caught. And what if it is dangerous—like Andora said?"

I sigh. "If it looks like it'll be dangerous for some reason, then we'll stop. Agreed?"

Ander, Mare, and Jillian agree. Jax considers that for a minute. "Okay, agreed."

"Yes! When do we start?" I ask. "How about tonight? We aren't leaving the platform until tomorrow afternoon, so if we're up late, at least we don't have to wake up super early."

Jax lets out a breath. "We better do some research first. We need to figure out what kind of lock is on the compartment. That might help us get started."

"Good idea," says Mare. "I'll grab the air screen."

Later that night, after Gregor and Seraphina go to their bedchambers, we sneak down the hall and off the aero-bus. The platform is dark, and we rely on the glow from the courtyard lampposts to guide us. We don't say a word. We stay silent the entire time. We'll attempt to open the compartment, and if we succeed, we'll shine a flashlight inside and take pictures of it. Once we're back at the aero-bus, we'll examine them.

When we get to Andora's aero-bus, it's completely dark. There's hardly any light shining from the courtyard, so Mare shines a light from her watch at the door. Jax holds his hand in front of it, waves it in a pattern like Andora did and taps four knocks then two. The door slides open without a sound. My eyes get big. How did it open so easily? I guess our research was right. These aero-buses are all equipped with a standard compartment lock.

Mare moves her watch light over the opening. Ander aims his and presses a button. He takes nine or ten pictures, pulls his watch away, and Jax waves his hand in front of it again. The door slides shut, and we hurry out of there as quietly and quickly as we can. My heart is beating like the footsteps of a giant; the walk back to our aero-bus takes forever. When we finally reach it, we open the door and slip inside. We've just entered the floating room when Gregor appears in the doorway to the dining chamber. We freeze like the statue we just took pictures of.

"Out taking a nighttime stroll?"

"Um, yeah," says Ander. "We were just exploring."

"You're out past curfew."

"We are? Oh, yeah, it's later than we thought."

"If I recall, we said good night to all of you and you were headed to your bedchambers—because at that time it was already past curfew. So, unless time ticks backward here on the platform, you knew you were breaking the rules."

"We're sorry. We just wanted an adventure . . . to see the platform at night." Jillian explains.

"I understand. However, that's not allowed. Get to bed. Explore tomorrow if you must."

"Okay, we will!" says Jillian. "Good night!"

We walk quickly away from him, go into our own bed-chambers, and shut our doors.

"That was close," I say.

"Close?" says Jillian. "We totally got caught!"

"But at least it wasn't Andora."

"I'll message Ander and ask him to send us the pictures so we can examine them, too."

"Yes," Mare replies. "From the comfort of our beds."

A few minutes later, after we've changed into our paja-mas, the pictures appear on our watches. We climb into our flower beds and stare at the screens.

"It looks like a bronze light bulb–shaped statue to me," says Jillian.

"Zoom in," says Mare. "It looks like the bulb has lines on it, like vertical lines."

"Oh, I see them," says Jillian. "The bulb is separated into sections or something."

"Look closer—at the bottom," I say. "There's writing. I can't read it, though. Can you?"

Jillian squints at the picture. "I think we need to take a close-up."

"Let's talk to Ander and Jax about it later in chamber eight," I suggest. "If we wait a while, Gregor and Seraphina will be sound asleep."

"Okay," Mare replies. "Then I'm sleeping now while I still can."

Before we go to bed, we set our alarms. At exactly midnight, Mare, Jillian, and I crack open our bedchamber door. Ander and Jax open theirs and together we hurry into chamber eight.

We huddle together in a circle, staring at our watches. But not because we're wondering about the time. We're wondering if there's a clue to the pictures Ander took of the statue. By examining them closely, maybe we'll find one.

"What kind of lock could be placed on a solid statue?" Ander asks.

"Yeah, it's really weird," Jillian replies.

"If the lock is on the bottom of the statue, we're going to have to go back, you know," says Mare. "These pictures are only of the statue from the front."

"Sorry. It was the best I could do without moving it."

"I'm not questioning your picture-taking skills. I'm just saying."

I zoom in on the first picture. I still think it looks like a light bulb.

Ander rubs his eyes. "Do you guys notice the vertical lines on the top of the statue, the part that looks like the light bulb?"

"I did," Mare replies. "There's three of them."

"Yeah," says Jillian. "They look like they're dividing the bulb into sections."

"Maybe they are," Jax replies.

"Why?" Ander asks.

I think about that. "I have no idea."

I look at the other pictures. They all look the same. I zoom in on each of them, just to make sure. When I get to the last one, I see parts of letters written on the bottom. "Did you guys zoom in?"

"Yeah," says Jillian. "I did."

"Look at the last picture. Ander, I think you held your watch closer on that one, because when you zoom all the way, you can see the tops of letters showing."

"I don't see those. Oh, wait, yeah, now I do."

"So do I," Jax replies. "But they must be really small."

Jillian sits up on her knees. "I wonder what it says."

"Maybe it's the clue we need," says Ander. "Instructions of some type."

"I doubt it's going to give us directions to open it," says Mare.

"Probably not," I say, "But it might say something that will help."

"Okay," Ander replies. "Then we need to go back and take a closer look."

CALCULATING THE CLUES

A FEW WEEKS later, with just days to go until the Day of Creativity, we sneak out to take more pictures. This time we're going to have to move the statue, which is kind of scary. It's Andora's most treasured possession. If something ever happened to it, she would be crushed.

We stand in front of the compartment in darkness and in silence. Since we've rehearsed exactly what we're doing once the compartment is open, we don't have to say a word. We can't say a word. Andora could hear us. Jax waves his hand in the pattern, just like the last time, and taps four knocks then two. The door slides open without a sound, and this time, I hold my watch light over the compartment. Mare reaches in, carefully grabs hold of the statue and tips it back a few inches. Ander takes pictures of the bottom and pictures of where we saw the letters.

She quickly turns the statue in a circle, so that he can take pictures of the sides and the back. When he's done, he pulls his watch away, and she turns the statue back so that it's facing forward. Jax waves his hand in front of the opening and the door closes quickly.

Without saying a word, we continue walking around the platform.

"Hurry up and get changed for bed," Ander whispers. "We'll meet you in chamber eight."

Mare, Jillian, and I take turns in the bathroom, throw our pajamas on, and sneak out of our bedchamber. Ander and Jax are waiting inside and we quietly close the door. Our watches blink at the same time, telling us that the pictures he took have arrived. We huddle close again, so our voices won't carry out of the chamber, and click to examine them. I zoom in on the picture of the bottom first but don't see anything at all, just solid bronze. And that reminds me of a question.

"Mare, when you turned the statue, did it feel heavy?"

"Yeah, kind of. Like the weight of a bowling ball, I guess."

"A heavy bowling ball or a light bowling ball?" Ander asks. "Because the light ones are about six pounds, but the heavy ones are sixteen."

"I don't know. I didn't exactly have time to weigh it. But I think maybe five pounds."

"Wait," I say. "Look at the bottom of the front. Do you guys see numbers?"

Jax clicks something on his watch and holds it up to the picture.

"What is that?" asks Ander.

"It's a higher magnification zoom. It lets me see closer."

"Do you see anything?"

"It's a keypad."

"Wait, seriously?"

"Yeah, the naked eye would never notice it."

"That must be how we unlock it!" Ander replies. "We just have to figure out the numbers."

Mare groans. "That'll be a nightmare to figure out."

"Guys, I'm looking at the letters right now," says Jillian. "It definitely says something."

We lean in and look at the letters magnified by Jax's light.

Throughout history, secrets paved the way.
A warning to us once saved the day.

"Whoa," says Ander. "It *is* a clue."

"It sounds like it," says Jillian.

"But what does it mean?" asks Mare.

I read it again.

Throughout history, secrets paved the way.
A warning to us once saved the day.

"Secrets?" I ask. "What secrets? And who does it mean when it says, "A warning to us?"

"I'm not sure," says Jax. "But whatever the answer is, I bet we type it on the keypad."

Ander straightens up. "Well, you guys better get ready to go back to the compartment because that clue is easy."

"What do you mean?" I ask.

He looks at me in disbelief. "Don't you know any Human History at all?"

I shrug. "Human History? Nope."

Ander springs up to a stand. "During the Revolutionary War, Paul Revere was part of the secret system set up by the patriots to warn that the British were coming. One of the best-known lines of the poem 'Paul Revere's Ride' is 'One if by land, and two if by sea.' It's the way he would signal his comrades—by hanging one or two lanterns in the belfry of the Old North Church. One lantern meant the British were attacking by land and two meant they were attacking by sea. That's got to be the code to unlock the statue: a one and a two!"

I tighten my ponytail. "Whoa. That could be it."

"That seems too easy, though," Jax replies.

"Not really," says Mare. "Andora said that Lexland was a creative writer. That means he may have been interested in poetry. And he made the keypad and clue so small that someone—even Andora, looking at it with the naked eye couldn't read it. So, yeah, it may seem easy, but it makes sense."

Ander looks hurt. "But none of you knew the answer."

I pat him on the back. "You're right, Ander. Your knowledge of history is saving the day now, too."

He grins. "Why, thank you, KK."

"What do you guys think? Should we go back now? Try the code?"

"Hold on," says Jax. "That keypad is tiny. How do we even press the right buttons?"

"We have to use a really small tool, like a pen or a pin or something."

"Okay, let's bring both—just in case."

Jillian tightens her watch. "So, we're going back tonight?"

"Midnight," Jax replies. "We wait here for a little bit, just to be sure everyone is asleep."

"It could be loud, you know. We could wake up Andora."

Ander jumps up on the bench. "Yeah, like what if it lets off steam in the compartment or something?"

"You watch too many movies," I reply. "Once we enter the code, it'll probably just start doing whatever it's going to do."

"Yeah, maybe," says Jax.

Ander jumps off the bench. "I want to go right now, but okay, we'll go at midnight."

So, at exactly midnight, we sneak down the hallway. But this time it's riskier. We have to pass both Seraphina's and Gregor's bedchambers, and we don't even know if they're in them. They could be out in the floating chamber. They could be in the dining chamber. We think up an excuse, a reason we're out of our bedchambers, just in case. We'll tell them we were all hungry. They definitely would believe that. But we don't need the excuses. We make it out of the aero-bus without them noticing and hurry across the courtyard to the compartment at the back of Andora's aero-bus.

We gather around the compartment, Jax waves his hand in the weird pattern, then knocks four times, then two. I shine the light and Mare reaches in to grab the statue. My butterflies explode into a full-on rebellion. She lifts it up, and tips it back so that the bottom is facing us. Even with me shining the light from my watch, I don't see a keypad. Jax steps closer. His watch has been set to the maximum magnification mode, and he shines it on the spot where he thinks it's located. Mare leans in with the end of a straight pin. I think she sees what she's looking for, because she moves the pin closer. She stabs at it once and then moves the pin just a little. She stabs it again, quickly pulls her hand away, and sets the statue back down. We stare at it for like a millisecond before the top part of the statue clicks and turns about two inches. The base hasn't moved, but the top round part has!

We look at one another, frozen, not sure what to do.

Ander holds up his watch and points to the statue. We realize he wants to take more pictures, and the rest of us stand back. He makes a move with his watch but hesitates. I open my eyes wide at him, urging him to hurry. Instead he motions to us that we should bring the statue with us. Jax and Jillian shake their heads. Mare nods and I motion for him to take it. He grabs it but then pulls his hand away. Jax lets out a breath, grabs hold of the statue, and waves his hand in front of the compartment door. It closes and we fly out of there like a flock of birds trying to outrace a hawk.

My heart beats as I realize we have Andora's invention. We took it! I convince myself that we're doing this for her so that I don't feel guilty, but I still do. We're steps from our aero-bus when we see Gregor standing at the door like a bald eagle, and skid to a halt.

Uh oh.

"I assume your watches are broken and you think it's 9:00 p.m."

We say nothing. Nothing at all.

"That's the only reason I can think of that the five of you would be out roaming the platform at 12:30 at night."

Ander replies, "We know it's late, Gregor, and we're sorry. But we were working on our invention and we just wanted to get some fresh air before we went to bed. None of us could sleep."

"And this air is so much fresher than inside the aero-bus?"

Ander shrugs. "We really wanted to see France at night."

"I suggest you all get inside. We're meeting for breakfast at 8:00 a.m. You better not be even one second late."

We know we shouldn't, but after Gregor disappears inside his bedchamber, we hurry into chamber eight. My heart is beating so fast—everyone's heart seems to be, so we take a few seconds to catch our breath.

"It worked!" Ander exclaims.

"Shhhh!" says Jillian.

His eyes get big and he whispers, "Sorry! But did you guys see that?"

"Yeah, it totally turned," I say.

"I don't think we completely unlocked it, but we did something," whispers Mare.

Jillian twists her hair into a bun. "Maybe there's more than one lock on it."

"Yeah," says Jax. "If Lexland really wanted to protect whatever the invention is, that would make sense."

"That's why I wanted to take it with us," says Ander. "Now we can see if there's another clue."

Mare lies down on the floor. "I'm so tired. Can't we just go to sleep?"

I shrug. "You can but I'm seeing if there's another clue."

"Me, too," Ander replies.

"Fine. I want to see if there's one, too."

Ander unwraps the statue from Jax's sweatshirt and places it in front of us. I zoom in with my watch as far as the lens will let me. "There's definitely a second message."

Mare leans over my shoulder. "I can hardly read what it says, though."

"I'll access the magnification mode on mine again," says Jax. He leans in and holds his watch light up to it.

"What does it say?" I ask.

"It looks like another riddle:

A cake can be made of carrots,
but it's a treat some will not try.

Some prefer sweets of fruit,
particularly one turned into Pi.

"What does that even mean?" asks Mare.

Jillian shakes her head. "It's a clue about desserts, but the answer needs to be a number so we can enter it on the keypad."

Ander laughs. "I guess we know he liked carrot cake."

"And that he left out the letter *e* in *pie*," says Jax.

"Oh, no, he didn't," I say. "He spelled it exactly the way it's supposed to be spelled."

"What do you mean?"

"If the answer to this clue needs to be a number, I know what the number is. It's 314."

"Why would it be that?" asks Jillian.

"Pi—spelled P-I—is a math term. It's used to measure the perimeter of a circle. It's a never-ending number that's commonly rounded to 3.14. I bet the answer to this clue is 314."

"So, it's a Math clue?" Mare asks.

"It could be," Ander replies. "The first clue was a Human History clue."

"If that's true, then there could be more clues after this one—one in each category," I say.

"It would make sense," says Mare. "Lexland and Andora did create the category system in our schools."

"And there are six," says Ander.

Jax nods. "That means there could be six locks—six clues."

"But," Mare replies. "We don't know yet if Kia's right about 314."

"Okay," I say. "Let's find out."

Mare gets her straight pin ready. Jillian carefully tips back the statue so that Jax can magnify the keypad. Mare holds the pin carefully, reaches in, . . . and drops it next to the statue.

I gasp.

I shine the light so she can find the pin on the floor, and she picks it up. I take a breath as she leans closer. She presses the pin into the three, then the one, and then the four. Jillian rights the statue and pulls her hand away. We wait, hoping the statue will react again. Nothing happens at first, but then the statue clicks, and the top turns a few inches to the right.

Yes!

"It worked!" Ander exclaims.

"Shhh!"

"We have to try the next one, too," I whisper.

Jax leans in again with his magnifier and reads:

> *When asked how old she was, a girl replied, "Well, in two years I'll be twice as old as I was five years ago." What age is she attempting to communicate?*

"Even though it sounds like a Math problem, I think it's a clue in the Communications category," says Ander, "because we already solved a Math one."

Jax nods. "All these answers need to be numbers, so obviously this one is, too."

"This seems hard," says Jillian.

"I need paper to figure it out," I say.

"Do you know how to calculate it?" asks Mare. "Just use your watch."

"I like using paper." I grab a notebook and pencil from the window seat and get to work. It takes me a few seconds but just as I set down my pencil, Mare looks up.

"I got it," she says. "It's twelve."

"That's what I got, too."

"Me, too," says Jax.

Ander and Jillian agree. "That was easy," says Jillian.

"Okay," says Ander. "When do we try it."

I tighten my ponytail. "What time is it?"

Jillian bites her lip. "One o'clock in the morning."

"If our theory is right," says Jax. "There'll be more clues to unlock the remaining locks. We can't stop now. I say we keep going."

"Yes!" I reply, and just like before, Mare enters the code and the top of the statue turns. Only a few inches like the other times but it totally turns.

"Well," Jax replies. "It looks like we were right. There must be six locks, and we just unlocked three."

Three more? Three more to go. Then we'll have unlocked the bronze statue and uncovered the secret invention!

We stare at the statue for way too long, trying to magnify the fourth clue. But we don't see anything at all—except for the letter D. "There has to be more to the clue than that."

"Maybe we need different light, like daylight," Jillian suggests. "We've been using the flashlight, but maybe shadows are in the way."

"But we don't have any daylight. What about moonlight? Do you think that might work?"

I hold it up to the east side window of chamber eight while Jax aims the magnification light on his watch. "Cool," says Jax. "I can see it now."

Ander jumps on the window seat. "What does it say?"

Mare sits up. "Read it aloud, Jax."

Diamonds are mined, we know
it's true, from caves as dark as night,
but these men have pure hearts of gold,
for them it was love at first sight.

"This sounds like it's from the Earth and Space category," says Ander. "You know, mining diamonds from caves and all that."

"I don't know," I say. "What about love at first sight? It sounds like it's from a movie or a book."

Mare laughs. "Hah! This one's easy. It's not Earth and Space at all, it's a clue about *Snow White and the Seven Dwarfs.*"

"I knew that one!" Jillian says with a proud look on her face.

I high five Mare. "And the answer must be seven!" We quickly press the button and watch the statue turn a few inches yet again.

"I was beginning to think we'd never get this one," says Jillian. "Figures that the clue would be easy—just reading this one was the hard part."

We huddle together and find that the fifth clue is much easier to read, and easier to solve.

The fifth one from the sun,
and the largest of its kind.

With rings not one but four,
so many moons there are to find.

"Well, at least we know that it's from the Earth and Space category," I say.

"Let's look up the planets," says Ander. "Maybe it's one of those."

I pull down the air screen and we learn that Jupiter is the largest planet, and the fifth one from the sun.

"Wait, look!" says Mare. "It has seventy-nine moons."

"That's it," says Ander! The answer is seventy-nine."

"We got it," I say. "Five down. One more to go!"

"This is awesome," says Ander. "I feel like the jester on the Clock Tower in Switzerland!"

"Or maybe the rooster," says Mare.

"If not the jester, I prefer to think of myself as the knight."

Mare grabs her straight pin and we get to work. Jax shines his magnification light, Jillian tips the statue back, and as soon as Mare enters a seven and then a nine, the top clicks and turns an inch to the right.

When I look at the statue, my stomach flips over. There's some kind of incredible invention locked inside it, like a treasure. But this invention could be better than all the gold and silver coins hidden on a pirate ship. And right now, the sixth clue—the last clue is the key to seeing what it is.

Ander jumps on the window seat again. "One more and then we unlock this thing!"

Jax shakes his head. "It's really late, guys. I think we should wait until tomorrow."

"But we have to try!" I say.

"Even if it means keeping the statue here overnight?" says Jillian.

"Once we unlock the last lock, the statue will probably open. We may need time to figure out what's inside. I heard Andora and Master Freeman talking this morning anyway. They're leaving the platform tomorrow. They have a late dinner with the tour organizers in France."

My eyelids can barely stay open. "Okay, let's put the statue inside the closet. It should be safe there overnight."

"You mean for a few hours," says Jillian. "It's already 2:00 in the morning."

It's so late! And even though I can't wait to know what Andora's mysterious invention is, I can't wait to sleep more.

POPPING THE BRONZE BALLOON

A FEW DAYS later, after rehearsing nonstop for the Day of Creativity with the other teams, we're back in chamber eight, staring at the bronze statue. It's sitting on a white cloth, just in case. In case it explodes, in case it gets the floor dirty—in case something.

"Jax, can you shine your light? I'll read the last clue."

Ideas are the source of all new technology.

How many great ideas does it take to create the world's greatest invention?

"I don't know," says Jax. "A million."
"The answer could be any number," says Jillian.
"Yeah," says Ander. "Every invention is different."

Mare sighs, "It figures that the last clue would be impossible. It could be anything. Who even knows what the world's greatest invention will be?"

"It's one," I say. "It only takes one idea to create any invention!"

"One?" says Ander. "Wait, yeah, it is one!"

Mare laughs. "I guess that's it. Time to unlock the last lock."

I hold my breath as they get to work. Jillian tips the statue back, Jax shines his magnification watch on the bottom keypad, and Mare taps the number one with the pin. We wait in silence and watch the top of the statue click and then turn—again. Just like before. And then we wait.

But nothing happens.

Until something does. A message in small letters slowly appears across the center of the statue.

My fellow inventor,

You have solved my clues and unlocked the many locks of this object. But only a person with a connected lineage to my beloved Andora or myself will one day open the final lock. Family is and always will be of the utmost importance to us.

Best of luck in your future endeavors,
Lexland Appleonia

"What?" Ander exclaims. "It didn't work?"

I bite my bottom lip. "I can't believe it. That's why Andora couldn't unlock it. She has no direct connection to Lexland. They were married but they don't share the same bloodlines."

"I don't get it," says Mare.

"He must have thought that it would be passed down to their children," says Jillian.

"Except they never had any," says Jax.

"Oh, my gosh," says Jillian. "That's so sad."

"So that's it?" Mare replies. "Lexland never had any children, so no one will share his bloodline. No one can open it? All of this was for nothing?"

Ander grabs hold of the statue and lets out a yell in frustration. "This is the worst!"

"Ander, shhh. Put it down," I say. "It'll break."

"Who cares? Maybe then it will open."

He grabs onto it with his other hand like he's going to shake it. "I just want to see what it can do!"

I look at the statue held hostage in Ander's grip. "Ander, be careful with it. I want to see what it can do, too, but we can't break it."

He quickly sets it down on the floor and pulls his hands away. "Ouch!"

"What? What's wrong?" asks Jillian.

"It's hot!"

"No, it's not." I reach out to touch it, but before I can, smoke seeps from the statue and I pull my hand away. "Ouch! The smoke is burning hot!"

"What do we do with it?" screams Jillian. But just as I begin to panic that chamber eight will catch on fire, the smoke disappears. The bronze cracks, and pieces of it chip away from the top of the statue, one section at a time. One by one, they break off—crackling, popping, and exposing six colorful sections of a hot air balloon. The bronze pieces lie shattered on the floor. The bronze coating is gone; the Bronze Balloon has popped out of its shell!

"It's a balloon!" I say. "It wasn't a light bulb at all. It was a balloon the whole time."

Mare moves closer. "It looks like the miniature hot air balloon from the Piedmont Global Championships in Québec—the one that led us to that room with the task we had to solve, and finally to the tree suites."

We stare at the balloon for a long while. "But I don't get it," says Jillian. "Andora said it was an incredible invention."

Ander reaches into the small bronze basket and pulls open a door to a tiny hidden compartment. Inside is a folded piece of paper.

"Open it," I say. "But be careful."

Ander unfolds it and reads the message.

January 9, 2023

My Dear Descendant,

If you've found this note, then you've also discovered a most important invention—one that can help you decide your future. But with every great invention comes great responsibility. When left unprotected, it will cause more harm than good. If you have Appleonia blood running through your veins, then you know right from wrong, the importance of loyalty and teamwork, and the necessity for hard work. And you must also know the importance of dreaming big.

Use this Bronze Balloon to wonder, question, and imagine your future. Only then will the balloon truly soar. The source of every invention is imagination. This invention was created with the intention of bottling up and storing imagination. But what my beloved Andora and I discovered instead is that imagination does not need to be bottled up, because even if it could be, it cannot be accessed without first having a dream—a wish for what could be in the future.

This invention, when used properly, will help anyone who uses it to imagine the possibilities for the future. But be very careful, because it cannot and should not be used to predict the future but only to help you imagine what could be. By placing your hands around the basket, your personal energy will pass through the balloon. You need only to do four things:

Wonder. Question. Imagine. And watch the balloon soar.

Best of luck to you, and to all you deem worthy to use this invention. May your future be bright—and yours alone to decide.

Sincerely,
Lexland Appleonia

We look wide-eyed at one another and then stare at Ander.

"What? Why are you all staring at me? Don't you want to try it? It's open. It's here. We have to see it work!"

"Didn't you read the note?" asks Mare.

"Yeah, you heard me read it."

"Didn't you notice who it was addressed to?"

"Yeah, one of Andora or Lexland's ancestors."

Jax shakes his head. "Aren't you wondering how it opened? How the balloon popped?"

"I guess we were lucky."

"Lucky?" I say. "It said it could only be opened by someone with connected lineage. Someone related to them."

"So."

Mare lets out a huff.

"Well, none of us are related to them."

"You're right. None of us are related to them. But you are."

Ander jumps back. "Me? But how?"

"I don't know," I say, "But you were holding it when the pieces chipped away—when the balloon popped."

Ander's forehead crinkles up. "How can I be related to them?"

"It doesn't matter," says Mare. "You can figure that out later. Don't you think we need to try the invention?"

"Wait," I say. "Look! There's another note in that tiny compartment." I pull it out and Jillian reads it over my shoulder.

My Dearest Andora,

If you're reading this note, it must be twelve years or more in the future. As agreed, I've sealed our invention in bronze. I've locked it away with a six-step lock of clues for our future children to solve—so that they will

be the first children to use it. It seems the time has come
for at least one of them to plan his or her own future—
to see possibilities with the help of the Soaring Balloon.
  I hope that today, with the help of this invention, our
children will be the first to soar and that millions of
others will follow.

With love,
Lexland

We stand in chamber eight stunned.

"Are you serious?" says Mare. "This invention was meant for their children—to help them figure out their futures?"

Ander looks like he's in shock. "I wonder how it works."

I'm wondering the same thing, but we don't have to wonder for long. The balloon lights up and flashes the words *wonder, question, imagine,* and *soar* . . . and I realize those are the same four words on our team shirts! A message slowly appears:

The balloon is here to show you, all that you can be
when far too many options make it difficult to see.
The right paths can be confusing . . . or even covered up.
Let this invention show you, what you might be when
    you grow up.

The future is yours to see.
Wonder what it will be?
To watch the balloon take flight,
hold the basket tight.

Wonder first and ask a question,
imagine what you wish to be.
Then watch the balloon show you,
a future that could be.

"Wait, what?" says Ander. "This will really show me my future?"

"I think it'll show you *many* of your futures," I say. "It'll give you options!"

"That's impossible," says Mare. "Seriously."

"Try it," says Jax. "See what it does."

"Me first?" asks Ander.

"You first," I reply.

Ander grabs ahold of the basket. "What do I do?"

"It said to wonder what your future will be, ask a question, and then imagine what you want to be, like when you grow up."

"So, do I do it in my head or what?"

"Say it out loud so we know what you're doing."

He looks nervous, for like the first time ever.

"Okay. I wonder what I'll be when I grow up. Will I be a professional hockey player? I imagine that I am a professional hockey player."

No sooner does he say the words when the balloon lights up. An image of Ander riding in a hot air balloon appears—on the balloon itself. But then the image swirls into a different image. Ander looks older. It's still his face but he's bigger. He's wearing hockey gear. There's a huge hockey rink, and a crowd cheers as he skates around the ice.

"No way!" says Ander. 'That's me! That's me as a professional hockey player. Look at my jersey. It's a Buffalo Sabres jersey, and I'm number fifteen!"

Jax scratches his face. "It's like the balloon listened to what you wanted to be and showed a simulation of you being it—when you grow up."

"Try something else," says Mare. "Just to see what it does."

"Okay." He lets go of the basket and wipes his hands on his shorts. The image disappears. He grabs hold of it again and says: "I wonder what I'll be when I grow up. Will I be president of the United States? I imagine myself as the president of the United States."

Mare laughs and the balloon lights up. It shows an image of Ander riding in the balloon again. The image swirls into older Ander again but this time he's wearing a suit and sitting behind a desk with his hands folded—in the Oval Office of the White House!"

"Oh, yeah, that's me!"

Jillian laughs. "Wow, Ander, when you're dressed up like that, I can totally see you as the president."

"This is incredible," I say. "Can I try it?" Ander moves to the side and I kneel in front of the balloon. I grip the basket and say, "I wonder what I'll be when I grow up. Will I be the inventor of the first underwater bubble bike? I imagine myself as the inventor of the first underwater bubble bike."

I stare at the balloon and it lights up again. This time it's me soaring inside it! I watch myself floating through the sky until the image swirls and I'm standing in a convention center. My face looks different, but I can still tell it's me. I'm standing in front of a small crowd, next to a large object that's covered with a cloth. I pull the cloth away and it's there. My underwater bubble bike is there! "It's exactly like I imagine it when I think about it! You guys, that's me! I'm an inventor and I invented the underwater bubble bike!"

"What an unbelievable invention," says Jax. "I've always wondered what it would be like to be a lawyer. I don't actually want to be a lawyer, but I have wondered."

"Try it!" I say. "See what it would be like."

He grabs hold of the basket and we see Jax, standing tall in a courtroom, speaking to a jury, and then speaking to a judge. Then he looks through his papers and speaks to the person sitting next to him, his client. It's so weird seeing Jax all grown up, doing a grown-up job.

Mare tries next and I'm surprised by what she wants to see—herself as a builder. She measures and cuts a large piece of wood and carries it over to a building under construction. Most of the building is made of glass, but some of it is wood. It seems to be the final piece, because when she's done attaching it, the sign on the front of it comes into focus. It says, *Mare's Medical Supply Company*!

After Jillian grabs the basket, we watch her ride the balloon—and then walk up to a stage to direct a play. She's dressed in wild, colorful clothes, and her face is covered in strange makeup. She lets go of the metal basket, but her smile stays splashed across her face.

"Andora was right. This invention could change the world," I say. "If a person isn't sure what a certain job is, they can watch themselves doing it, and then they'll learn more."

"And not just kids," says Mare. "Grown-ups could use it, too."

"We have to tell Andora," says Jillian. "She'll be so happy we unlocked it for her!"

'But what if she isn't?" Mare asks.

"What do you mean?" asks Ander. "Why wouldn't she be happy?"

"Oh, I don't know. We snuck into her aero-bus and stole her most prized possession."

"But it was for her," I say.

"I know and I think she'll be happy to see it and use the invention. But . . . it was invented for her kids—hers and Lexland's. It might make her even sadder."

"Yeah," says Jax. "What if she disqualifies us from the competition. She told us to never go near it."

"She said not to do it for selfish reasons or out of curiosity. Our reasons weren't selfish," I say. "We did it for her! And now we have to tell her. It's the only way to save Piedmont!"

"Wait a second," says Ander. "If we tell her, we could get disqualified. But it might save Piedmont because the WGB would see this incredible invention."

"Right," I say. "And if we don't tell her, we won't get disqualified. We might get into PIPS, but they might close Piedmont down anyway."

"This is terrible," says Jillian. "What do we do?"

"I say we go to Andora," says Mare.

"Me, too," says Jax.

"But I don't want to get disqualified," says Ander.

"Me, either," I say.

Mare shakes her head. "I don't know."

"This stinks. Why didn't we just invent something amazing? Then we wouldn't have this problem."

"I like our invention," says Jillian.

"I like it too, but we didn't actually invent anything," says Mare. "We found the blocks. We found the stuff to build the sensors, and we put them all together."

I feel the tears coming and purse my lips. I feel like sprinting out of the room and screaming, like I did at Camp Piedmont after we found the ghost gallery smashed, and in Québec after Grandma Kitty got hurt. I didn't know what to do so I ran. But it didn't help. I'm not going to do that again.

"I know what we need to do," I say.

"What?" asks Ander.

"We need to talk to Seraphina and Gregor."

"She's right," says Jax. "They need to know what we did—and they need to know why. Besides, they'll know what we should do."

"But we can't go now," says Mare. "It's late. The Day of Creativity is tomorrow."

"Then we better get some sleep because we need to tell them before we perform."

THE DAY OF CREATIVITY

THE CLOCK STRIKES 7:00 a.m. We march into the courtyard behind Gregor and Seraphina. Andora and Master Freeman await us, sitting on their thrones where cameras flank them. We take our places in rows of seats set up on the side. The French and Swiss teams march in next and take their seats behind us.

"Welcome, children, to the morning of compulsory judging. The judges from the Piedmont Inventor's Prep School are viewing from Piedmont University. The judges from L'Académie des inVenteurs de Quimper and the Institut für Innovation are viewing as well. This is your chance to explain your inventions to all of us, so that this afternoon, on the Day of Creativity, we will know precisely what details to look for. Each of your teams will have two minutes to introduce your inventions. Team USA, you will introduce yours first."

I bite my pointer-finger nail and then my thumb. This is it. It's our time to show the Piedmont Organization what we have invented. Seraphina and Gregor give us a thumbs up. We stand in a row lined up by height and walk to the taped off area. I know that's not how we planned it, but that's how it looks right now.

Master Freeman smiles. "I now introduce the team from the United States of America and Part One of their solution to the Piedmont Challenge final task." He starts the timer, and I step forward.

"Hello, Master Freeman, Andora, preceptors, and judges at Piedmont University. Later today, on the Day of Creativity, we will present to you an activity called Balance Blocks. It is an activity that can be used by people all around the world, but it does more than test balance. It can be played as a game, which will encourage friendly competition and teamwork, and teach decision-making skills."

I step back and Ander steps forward. "As you will see later today, our invention uses a set of blocks that we've connected to form an elaborate beam-like structure with three different paths. Teams race to step onto as many blocks as possible before the time is up. The team that covers the most blocks wins."

Ander finishes and Mare steps forward. "There is an element of strategy involved in the activity as well. Participants can play alone, choose an end point they wish to reach, and navigate the hills and valleys of the structure in order to reach the end point as quickly as possible."

Mare returns to her place, looking happy to be done, and Jillian steps forward. "You will notice that the blocks are colorful. But they are also filled with motivational messages. These messages appear at random, encouraging the participant to keep going and stay strong, even when they fall off or take the incorrect path."

Jillian steps back, and it's up to Jax to finish. His face, though, has turned redder than an apple. "In order to account for the points accumulated by each participant, we have attached touch sensors to each block. We have also created a program that adds up the points. However, the game is designed to be played either with or without keeping score, which makes this activity useful in two ways: for entertainment and for skill and confidence building. Thank you for the opportunity to invent for this competition this year. We hope you enjoy our presentation today."

Jax steps back and I let out a breath.

"Thank you very much," Master Freeman says. "You may return to your seats." His face doesn't reveal anything. I can't tell if he's impressed or disappointed. The faces staring back at us from the screens are stone-faced, too. But this time, I don't think they're stone-faced because they have to be. I think they're stone-faced because they were not impressed.

We sit back in our seats and Team France explains the mechanical backpack. Next, Team Switzerland explains the hologram book. And I sit there noticing that everyone—Master Freeman, Andora, and the preceptors, all look more impressed than they did watching us. I've never

felt this way before. With every invention we've presented, the crowds of people watched wide-eyed. Some
even gasped. Today, none of them did that. They nodded
their heads and smiled. But smiling won't get us into
PIPS. It won't save Piedmont.

MY TEAMMATES AND I sit at the table in the dining
chamber where we eat a late breakfast with Seraphina
and Gregor. But I'm not hungry. My stomach is tied up
like a pretzel. I feel like I could throw up all over this
table. But I can't do that. Today is the Day of Creativity,
and puking instead of presenting our invention is not the
way to save PIPS—or get into it. Besides, Seraphina's face
tells me that what we just told her and Gregor is worse
than we thought.

Gregor sits up. "So, this invention you're speaking of,
Andora showed it to you?"

"Yeah," says Ander. "When we were exploring the platform in China. Back in January."

"And she specifically told you not to unlock it?"

"Well," I say. "She said not to touch it for selfish reasons. This wasn't for selfish reasons. We wanted to open it
as a surprise to her. We wanted her to be happy."

"Do you think we should tell her now?" asks Mare. "Or
after we present?"

"Do you think she will disqualify us?" asks Jillian.

Seraphina folds her hands and sets them on the table.
She looks at Gregor and he looks at her. "I would like to
know what the five of you think you should do."

We all talk at once. I can't understand what anyone is saying. My brain jumbles and my head pounds. Finally, I say, "Can I please be excused? I know you want us to talk this over, but the Day of Creativity is here now and none of us knows what to do. I need quiet to think."

I sprint off the aero-bus. But where am I going to go? The courtyard? It's being set up for the presentation. I can't walk by Andora's aero-bus or any of them. I stop in front of the Pooncha Tree and let out a breath. One cup after another grows from its branches. Another incredible invention. How can the WGB think inventions aren't important?

I take a drink from the Pooncha Tree, hoping the problem-solving elixir will help me solve this one. I play with the small door on my watch, opening it up and closing it again.

A few minutes later, Seraphina comes walking toward me. "Come on," she says and leads me to the closest bench. She pats the spot next to her and smiles.

"I'm sorry. I always do this."

"Always do what?"

"Run away when things get bad."

"I don't think you're running away. I think you're trying to find a place to think."

"I am trying to think. I look at this tree, this amazing invention, and I just want to know how they thought it up. You always tell us to be curious and I am. But I guess we were too curious about the Bronze Balloon."

"I don't think you can be too curious, Kia. Any more than you can be too creative, or too collaborative, or too colorful, or too courageous."

"So, you don't think it was bad that we unlocked Andora's invention?"

"That's not for me to say. The invention does not belong to me."

"Yeah, I know."

"But I do think a dream is born to become a dream come true."

"What do you mean?"

"Lexland and Andora had a dream, and it became an invention. But circumstances prevented the invention from becoming their dream come true. He died far too young, and of course he didn't foresee that. He and Andora created an invention for their future children, but life had other plans, ones that didn't include biological children. Instead, they created a place of joy, where countless numbers of children have grown up to make incredible things—their own dreams come true. Their legacy is Piedmont. But their invention—their dream has been waiting to become a dream come true. Andora has been like a fairy godmother to so many children and so many dreams. Maybe it's time she was reminded how wonderful it is to see an invention, like a child, reach its full potential."

"Seraphina, I really want to go to PIPS, but Andora needs to be happy. I think seeing her invention again will make her happy, and it may save Piedmont, too."

"So, you know what to do?"

I glance at my balloon message shining at me from inside my watch compartment.

The future is yours to decide.

"I think I do. Thanks, Seraphina! We need to surprise Andora during our presentation. It's the only way we can show the WGB what inventions can mean to the world."

We work quickly to revise our script and tell the other teams. Of course, Jonah protests. "Why are you adding something to the ending—thirty minutes before we present?"

"We have a good reason and it's life changing," I say. "Trust me. It's worth it." But he doesn't believe me. It doesn't matter. Piedmont is bigger than all of us combined.

WE MARCH INTO the courtyard, wearing our costumes, and take our places surrounded by our sets. My heart is beating so fast, I'm not sure it will slow down enough for me to say my lines.

Master Freeman stands up from his throne with Andora by his side. "Welcome, children, preceptors, distinguished judges, and representatives from the World Government Bureau. This Day of Creativity will surely be remembered as an important one in the history of Piedmont. It will long be remembered as a day when our children, our world's future, shared with us some of their most exciting discoveries. Andora and I look forward to today's presentation. Best of luck, children!"

I swallow hard and try with all my might to stand still, to not bite my ring-finger nail.

"I now present to you the teams from France, Switzerland, and the United States of America and their connected invention."

We stand up, take our places by our sets, including our colorful Balance Blocks structure, and freeze in position.

Seraphina stands up, too. Her purple platform heels make her look way taller than she is. She smiles her purple lipstick smile and says, "Global Team, are you ready to show us all how imagination is the world's most important resource?"

In unison, we exclaim, "More than ready!"

"You may begin."

At the sound of her words, our skit begins, and we transport our audience to the land of Crimson Catropolis. Little Girl spins out from behind the transparent toy box and over to the Gatekeeper.

"Hello, Gatekeeper, here I am! I'm back in Crimson Catropolis. Why did you summon me again?"

The Gatekeeper flairs his black cape, but the Jester jumps out and tips his jester hat before he can respond. "Hello! Hello! Hello, Little Girl! We're happy you came back!"

"Why am I back?" Little Girl asks.

"Your assistance is needed, I'm afraid," says the Gatekeeper.

"Ah, dahling!" Madam Sparkles exclaims. "There's drama in Crimson Catropolis. You know how these things go." She throws her pink feather boa over her shoulder as Teenager Mare walks out from behind the town sign. The townspeople, gathered on either side, move closer to the center of our courtyard stage.

"When isn't there drama?" asks Teenager Mare. "Jester wants to take a worldwide trip. Gatekeeper thinks he should attend school first. The townspeople have chimed in. Some say school is fun. Some say school is boring. But since none of us knows what school is really like, we need you to show us." She snaps her gum and folds her arms in front of her.

"Can you do it? Can you? Can you?" asks the Jester. "Can you tell us about school?"

"Me?" asks Little Girl. "Well, I can do more than tell you. I can show you." I open the toy box, pull out the backpack, and hand it to Maëlle. "If you go to school, you get to carry one of these."

The townspeople gasp. Maëlle steps out from the crowd. "Look at all these compartments. They work like magic. Look everyone! Look at what this magical backpack can do!"

The townspeople hand her several large items. The mechanical pockets open and close with the touch of a button. She places the objects inside. The backpack shrinks them down and they fit easily—ready to fit even more. The preceptors gasp, too, but I try not to let their reactions mess up my lines.

"But the backpack needs a book, too, and you'll have many books like this one to bring to school."

"What kind of book? What kind of book?" the Jester asks.

I pull the hologram book out of the toybox and bring it to Jonah. He takes it from me and reads the first two pages. Ghost-like images with pictures of the story he's telling appear above each one. The preceptors gasp again and shuffle in their seats.

"I think going to school would be fabulous!" Madam Sparkles exclaims.

"There's more," says Little Girl. "You can even walk the path to the future!"

"Show me how," says Teenager Mare.

Little Girl goes up onto the blocks to show her. "Choose a path. The blocks will encourage you, keep you on track, and lead you toward your destination." She activates the first block, jumps off, and steps aside.

Teenager Mare hops on and picks a path. The motivational messages light up as she walks, and they warn her when she steps on a block taking her down the wrong path.

She walks with her arms extended, trying to keep her balance, over hills and down the valleys all while the blocks help her decide which way to go. When she reaches the end, she jumps off and the Jester jumps in front of her.

"What happens after you walk the path?" he asks.

Little Girl takes a breath and says: "Now that you've walked the path, you'll have some of the tools necessary to decide your own future. But not all of them. Sometimes you need to see for yourself before you can make the right decision, and this balloon will help you do that. First grab hold of the basket. Then wonder, question, imagine, and soar."

And when he does, the balloon pieces pop off, and an image of grown-up Ander flashes on the Bronze Balloon. But this time he's not a hockey player or the president. He's inventing the first platform house in the sky.

The preceptors are wide-eyed as the last moments of the skit play out. All three of our inventions light up one right after the other. And then on cue, the Jester grabs hold of the balloon and it pops again, but this time, it shows him wearing the backpack, reading the book, and crossing the Balance Blocks while the words *decide your own future* flash on every single block and on the colorful balloon.

Master Freeman and Andora nod. The preceptors clap. And I can tell by the expressions on the faces of the other two teams that they are amazed at our secret invention. Master Freeman thanks us for our hard work and creativity, but I'm afraid to look at Andora. I can't read her mind, and I wish I could.

The room goes quiet. A judge from Piedmont speaks through the monitor. "There seems to be some confusion. There are four inventions but only three have been entered into the competition. Each team may only present one. We must know which inventions to score."

Gregor stands and asks the judges if he and Seraphina may speak with our team. They agree and we huddle off to the side. "It appears as if you have a decision to make."

"You mean we can use the Bronze Balloon for our invention?" asks Ander.

"It appears so."

"The Bronze Balloon is a better invention," says Mare.

I shake my head. "But that's not our invention."

"Yeah," says Jillian. "Ours is the Balance Blocks.

"Then we use the Balance Blocks," says Mare.

"Yup," says Ander. "Definitely."

"What do you think, Jax?" I ask.

"The Balance Blocks, for sure."

We deliver the news to the judges, and even though we might have gotten into PIPS with the Bronze Balloon, it would not have been right. Master Freeman dismisses us, and the screen goes blank. The preceptors gather around. "That was wonderful!" says Mathilde.

"Excellent," says Elin. "What a wonderful way to showcase all of the inventions."

"What was that fourth incredible invention—the balloon?" asks Levin.

My teammates and I look at one another.

"Oh, that?" says Ander. "It's the invention that's going to determine the future."

"Well done, well done," says Gregor. "Whatever happens, you've all done a superb job."

MAËLLE, DANIELLE, AND I talk about the performance, and I can tell from their faces they liked performing for the audience as much as I did. "I thought I would be so nervous," says Danielle. "But I wasn't. It was fun!"

"I wish we could do it again," says Maëlle. "But that was the one and only time we will be in a play together, I suppose."

I nod. "I guess so. But it was fun, wasn't it?"

"Now, we hope, the judges will agree that our inventions should receive a score of excellence."

In the chaos, I watch Andora retreat to her aero-bus. I motion for my team to follow her. She sees us but holds up her hand as if to tell us to go away. I bite my thumbnail because just when I thought we may have saved Piedmont, we may have also betrayed Andora's trust in our team.

"What do we do now?" I ask.

"I suggest you return to the aero-bus for now to be sure you have all of your belongings from the platform," Seraphina says. "We leave for England tonight. Besides, Master Freeman will not announce the judges' decision until tomorrow at the Night of Shining Ceremony."

We're in the floating chamber, wondering if we made a big mistake, when Seraphina pops her head in the door. "Hey, my Crimson Kids, Andora would like to speak with you."

"Oh, no," I say.

Seraphina leads us to a hidden patio area behind Andora's aero-bus and leaves us alone with her. She's standing with her back to us, staring out into the sky.

"We're really sorry, Andora," I say.

She slowly turns around.

"We didn't mean to disobey your orders. We just wanted to make you happy and unlock your incredible invention. We know we should have told you right away when we unlocked it, but we heard about the WGB and wanted them to know how important inventions are. We wanted to help save Piedmont."

She says nothing at first, and I realize I'm holding my breath.

She folds her hands in front of her and looks at each of us, one right after the other. "From the moment your team was selected to represent the state of New York, I suspected that you were special. Perhaps I had thought it was because you all came from the same school. *Special* means you are distinctive or unique. However, in reality you are five children who earned your places in a creativity competition—like all the other children in this competition."

I feel the tears well up in my eyes.

"I realize now that to call you *special* would be inadequate. You were meant to be more than unique participants in a competition. You were meant to be the team to save Piedmont.

"You have given Piedmont—and me—a gift. I don't know what the WGB will decide. But you can rest easy knowing that your futures will be bright. Each one of you sparkles like the twinkle star in our vast sky. Those exact words are the way Seraphina described you during the first week at Camp Piedmont, and she was right. You have brought back to life an invention and a dream I thought was long dead. Lexland's invention may very well be the invention that saves Piedmont today. But children, how? How did you do it?"

It takes a very long time, but we tell Andora everything, the whole story of how we popped the Bronze Balloon. When we're finished, she thanks us and looks at Ander. "So it seems, young Ander, that you're related in some way to Lexland or to me."

"I guess so," he says, like he's afraid she's mad about that.

"You have the same bright blue eyes that Lexland had. I will research the lineage, but I have my suspicions already."

Ander smiles his huge Ander smile, and inside I'm smiling, too. Andora's not mad at us, and soon we'll know if we've made it into PIPS . . . and if Piedmont will be saved. I don't know about my teammates, but I don't think I'll sleep at all tonight.

THE NIGHT OF SHINING

WE LAND ON the platform above England, and Andora is waiting for us when we step off the aero-bus. She hands a slip of paper to Ander with no expression on her face at all.

"What's this?" he asks.

"This is the connection we were looking for. You, my dear, are the great-nephew of Lexland Appleonia."

"I am?"

"Indeed, you are. Lexland had a sister and they were very close. She had a son and he had a son as well. And that son is you. That is why you were able to unlock our invention."

"So, I'm related to the founder of Piedmont?" Ander exclaims.

She smiles. "Yes, Mr. Yates. You are related to *one* of the founders of Piedmont. And now perhaps I know why I always expected great things from you."

Ander smiles and for the first time ever, turns redder than Jax ever did.

"Perhaps that is why I always expected great things from all of you. Family does that, you know, and in a way, you have all been mine. Families help each other, especially when they cannot help themselves. From the bottom of my heart, I thank you for your innovation and perseverance. Because of you, my dream with Lexland will live on, and the children of the future will be able to dream bigger dreams than ever before. No matter what the future of Piedmont may be, the Bronze Balloon will soar, like Lexland and I believed it one day would."

LATER THAT NIGHT, we follow Seraphina and Gregor into the courtyard. We stand in line with the other teams, listening to the Piedmont Challenge theme song playing in the background. We shuffle in our places, waiting for the Night of Shining Ceremony to begin. The chairs are arranged in a semicircle facing the small stage. I'll be sitting with my teammates, Seraphina, and Gregor. The French team will sit next to us on one side and the Swiss team will sit on the other. We'll march in together with our families watching. I know the whole town of Crimson will be watching, too, because Principal Bermuda will make sure of it. I'm sure he's puffed up with pride, but he has no way of knowing that we failed this time. We aren't as incredible as the whole town thinks.

We've traded our matching team shirts for matching red blazers with white shirts. The boys are wearing stiffly pressed blue pants. Mare, Jillian, and I look just like them wearing stiffly pressed blue skirts with tall socks. Our shoes are shiny—almost sparkly. I just wish I felt sparkly, too. If things were different, I would love this outfit, this ceremony, this moment. But things aren't different and it's all my fault.

Master Freeman and Andora take the stage and sit on their thrones. He's dressed in a purple tux. She's wearing a lilac-colored gown. Her bun is wrapped in flowers, and her hands are folded gracefully in her lap. We wait in silence watching them, and as we march in, they watch us. Their expressions are serious, and it makes me want to throw up all over the courtyard bricks. Maëlle smiles at me as I pass her, and I try my hardest to smile back. We take our places, and I can feel the lenses of the cameras, the ones recording the ceremony, watching me. They feel like a million lasers burning into my skin.

Once the music fades, Master Freeman stands up. "Greetings, children and preceptors, and those watching all around the world. It is our great pleasure to welcome you to the Night of Shining—the final awards ceremony of the Piedmont Challenge."

He continues. "As you know, over the last year, these three teams from France, Switzerland, and the United States have been traveling together, sharing their innovative creations with children all over the world. They've educated them, befriended them, and inspired them. And for that we are truly grateful. But these three teams have been educated, befriended, and inspired, too, by this experience they have shared with one another. Over the last year, each team has been challenged to devise an invention and then combine their inventions into one. This was the final task of the Piedmont Challenge. Judges from their countries have evaluated their work and determined if they shall be accepted into their elite inventors' schools for the next academic semester. Tonight, we will learn what those decisions are."

He makes a dramatic pause before continuing. "Children, it is only fitting on this night, one of the most important in each of your lives, that the stars would be shining down on you, illuminating the stars you are—and the creative spirit that lies within each of you. For every single one of you, as both individuals and as teammates, has shown us your creative and imaginative spirit firsthand."

He continues with a smile. "The annual Piedmont Challenge began for each of you just over a year ago in June 2071. Back then, you were sixth graders, competing in your countries' creative, task-solving competitions. Now fourteen months later, you've competed in the national finals in your home countries, and the Piedmont Global Championships in Québec. You've done this in order to be awarded enrollment in your countries' elite inventors' schools for children. You have worked tremendously hard, and we wish to commend you on your efforts and achievements thus far. You have much to be proud of—no matter what the outcome."

The air becomes electric. "It is now my great honor to announce the results. We ask that the team from France please stand up."

The butterflies in my stomach jump. Master Freeman may not be announcing the results for our team yet, but this is the French team. I know how badly they want to be selected. Maëlle, Danielle, Zoe, Gwyndol, and Stephan rise. Maëlle glances over at me and smiles a small smile. She, Danielle, and Zoe hold hands, and I hold my breath for them.

"I have here the completed evaluation of your teamwork skills, your problem-solving skills, and your invention-building capabilities. I will provide your preceptors with a copy of the entire evaluation at the completion of this ceremony. However, allow me to read a short comment from the team of judges. 'We at L'Académie des inVenteurs de Quimper are honored to grant enrollment for the 2072 academic year to Danielle, Gwyndol, Maëlle, Stephan, and Zoe.' Congratulations. You have very bright futures ahead of you."

Yes! The French kids squeal, and we cheer with them. They did it and I'm relieved. They deserve a chance to be great inventors one day.

With grins on their faces, Maëlle and her teammates sit back down. Master Freeman instructs the team from Switzerland to stand next. I knew we would hear our results last, but waiting is the worst! I bite my thumbnail hard. As much as I hated Jonah at first, he does have good ideas, and he really wants to be an inventor. So does Hannah and the rest of their team. I cross my fingers that they get in, too.

"This paper indicates the results of your evaluation as well. It is with great pleasure that I read yours next. 'On

behalf of the entire judging committee at Institut für Innovation, we welcome you to our newest class of inventors!'
Congratulations, Finn, Giulia, Hannah, Jonah, and Lars!
We are extremely proud of your achievement and look
forward to seeing you at the beginning of the next term."

The team from Switzerland explodes into celebration.
They did it, too, and I'm happy for them. Their hologram
book is spectacular.

At Master Freeman's signal, I stand with my team. I'm
standing in the middle with Jillian and Mare on either
side of me and Ander and Jax on the ends. We hold hands
and I look around at all my new friends, waiting, wishing
good things for us. Beyond the courtyard, as far out
through the platform walls as I can see, the stars twinkle.
I wish that was a good sign, but I know it isn't. We won't
be getting into PIPS. Our invention wasn't good enough.
Our game was not amazing. We got distracted by our
curiosity—by our wish to unlock the Bronze Balloon. But
I would do it again to make Andora happy. She's done so
much for us and the children before us. She deserves the
gift of the Bronze Balloon. I just wish I didn't have to give
up PIPS to give it to her.

Master Freeman holds a large purple envelope and
pulls out a piece of paper. "In my hand, I have the evaluation results from the team of judges at the Piedmont
Inventor's Prep School. I would like to read their initial
comments. "Ander, Kia, Jax, Jillian, and Mare have proven
their excellent ability to work as a team. Over the last
several months, we have seen that they are already very
able inventors as well. The Ancestor App and the Satellite

Spectacles will be valuable inventions one day. By their achievements at the Piedmont Global Championships, they have earned the right for that to happen. However, when we consider the game of Balance Blocks, their latest invention, on its own merits, and weigh it against other inventions of its kind, we have not been able to assign them a score of excellence. Although children and adults would no doubt enjoy the activity, we must remember that the blocks already existed. The game created is not original enough. Even though it was changed from motivational bricks to an activity for children and adults, that alone is not enough to guarantee their spots at PIPS.'"

The girls let my hands drop. My eyes fill with tears and I can't catch my breath. I knew we weren't going to get in. I knew it. But I just thought that, somehow, someway, we still had a chance. I blink back the tears as Grandma Kitty's words whisper in my ear—*Winners have good posture and hold their heads up high.* I know we're not winners today, but I stand up straight anyway because she'd still want me to act like one.

Andora stands up. She takes the paper from him and continues. "I would like to say something before I read the last portion of Team USA's evaluation."

I swallow hard. I want to hear what she has to say, but I wish we could get this over with. All the other kids are staring at us, so is everyone at home, and it's the worst feeling in the world. Jillian and Mare grab my hands again, and I look over at Jax and Ander. We've formed a team chain, like we always do, and I'm not sure why. I guess we all need one another to get through this last part.

"I developed the Piedmont Challenge, it's corresponding competitions, and the Piedmont Inventor's Prep School more than fifty years ago. It was my dream, a dream I shared with my late husband, Lexland. Our goal was to encourage children to wonder, to question, to imagine, and to soar. To soar wherever their wondering and questioning and imagining could take them. Our goal was to create an environment that would do that. It is my greatest joy to see that we have achieved that, and with the help of Master Freeman, we have continued to do so."

She continues. "But the Piedmont Challenge has always been more than simply following rules of a competition. Team, keeping that in mind, please listen closely to this last part of your evaluation from the judges at PIPS. 'Based on your individual invention score alone, you would not be admitted to PIPS. However, when it is considered together with your teamwork and problem-solving skills—which were made evident in your ability to lead all three teams in the formation of a connected invention and your ability to unlock an invention that was long considered impossible—all for the good of the Piedmont founder and children all around the world, we have made the only decision possible. It is our final decision to reserve a place at PIPS for each of you this fall!' Congratulations, Miss Barillian, Miss Krumpet, Mr. Lapidary, Miss Vervain, and Mr. Yates. As always, I expect great things from you in the future."

She smiles at us and I don't know what just happened. I don't know who to look at first. It's like a flip just switched and everything is bright again. First, we weren't being accepted into PIPS, but now we are! My teammates erupt into cheers and I shake out of my fog.

"We're in, KK! We're in!" Ander beams and we slap each other's hands.

THE OTHER TEAMS crowd around us. We did it. We all did it—with a little help from each other. Seraphina and Gregor stand together beaming like they're our proud parents—and then I think of mine and Grandma Kitty . . . and I remember they're watching!

Master Freeman steps up to the microphone. "Congratulations to all of you! We now look forward to the last days of the tour and then to hearing and seeing the discoveries and inventions you are sure to create."

Balloons fall from the top of the platform. Before we can catch them, they pop like fireworks. I look down at my fancy USA uniform and I never want to take it off. Ander turns around and nudges me. "We really did it, KK."

I fight back my tears. "We really did."

I turn around, and Jonah walks toward me with a strange look on his face.

"Hey, America, I heard what you all did to unlock that Bronze Balloon."

"Um, yeah."

"You managed to create an invention, lead our three teams' performance, and unlock a life-changing invention that's been locked for decades."

I smile. "Yeah, we did."

"I'm impressed. One day, I'm sure I'll hear even more about your team's inventions."

I guess Jonah's not so bad after all. "Thanks, Jonah. I bet I'll hear about yours, too."

"Congratulations, America, I mean Kia. Sorry. I like using nicknames."

"Thanks, but I don't really mind. It's better than my student number. Oh, and congratulations to you, too."

THE BALLOON PIECES have disappeared into the table tops and Master Freeman gathers us around. "Before we leave you to your celebration, Andora and I have one additional announcement to make. Please take your seats."

We sit back down in our colorful chairs, and my teammates and I suddenly realize what his announcement is probably about—the WGB's decision.

"I want to say, one last time, to all of you, children and preceptors included, how very grateful I am that you decided to be a part of this creativity tour. You have made your countries proud, you have made your families proud, and you have made Andora and I proud. And I am certain that Lexland himself is watching tonight and is proud of what you have accomplished in this year's Piedmont Challenge as well. I am certain that he is proud of the work Andora has done to keep the spirit of imagination and creativity alive as well. It has been an honor for me to play a small role in helping her to do that, and it's an honor tonight to bring her and all of you this news sent to me from the World Government Bureau."

Master Freeman takes a breath and continues. "After months of careful examination, the World Government Bureau has decided to continue its support of the Piedmont Organization. We feel strongly that imagination and innovation bring the people of the world together, and it is the children with those skills who will lead us all into the future."

I look at my teammates. *Seriously? Piedmont is saved? PIPS is not being shut down!*

Andora is beaming brighter than the stars above her as she makes her way to the podium.

"Thank you, Master Freeman. I am more than grateful to hear that our work at Piedmont will continue. With that in mind, I have an announcement to make. There will come a time when Master Freeman and I are no longer able to lead this organization. I've wondered who our successors will be when we leave our positions at Piedmont. I've questioned what qualities I will look for. I've imagined different individuals in the role. Change is inevitable, and I now know that it is time for that change. It is time for us to pass the torch to someone new, someone who will guide the way for creative children of the future and lead the Piedmont Organization in the right direction. I assure you that, until I take my last breath, I will remain at Piedmont. But change is a part of life. Lexland believed that, too. I was recently reminded of that in a note I found in a long-hidden invention. I'd like to read a part of that letter to you."

Andora, I think often of the Piedmont Organization now that our dreams for a better system of learning have come true. But I wonder if one day we will still think the category system is best. I hope that in the far-off future, we will be open-minded to new ideas for Piedmont and do what it takes to make those changes when necessary.

Andora looks up from the letter and continues. "In order to take Piedmont into the future, we must put it in capable hands. Master Freeman and I must now mentor those who will be the future of Piedmont, those whose ideas will help it to soar and will lead us to places we can't even imagine today—but one day will."

Wait, so there'll be new leaders of Piedmont?

"It is with great excitement that I announce the future leaders of Piedmont. I hope that each of these individuals will accept their new roles, with us here to guide them. My wholehearted congratulations to Miss Seraphina Swing and Mr. Gregor Axel."

FAREWELL FOR NOW

OUR WEEKS IN England have passed like a rocket soaring to Saturn. Maybe because we have no more worries, no more pressure. Maybe it's because there's royalty here, and every time I walk around, I imagine myself living in a castle—one big enough to hold all the inventions I could ever dream up. Maybe it's because this is the last country we'll tour. We had thought we would be touring the USA also, but with all the excitement that's happened, Andora has decided that our three teams will return to our homes after England. Instead, we'll reunite in the United States next summer to explore our country together more extensively than planned. It's her gift to all of us for saving Piedmont.

At times while I was on this trip, I wished it would go by faster so I could be with my family again. But now that it's almost over, I wish it would never end.

On our next-to-the-last day in England, we wake to the sound of someone singing. I pull the covers away from my face. Jillian has already hopped out of bed. "It's my birthday! It's my birthday!"

I lean up on my elbow and blink until my eyes are awake. "Happy birthday, Jillian!"

She skips around the room, tapping the motivational blocks like a piano, seeing which one will fall into her hand. Mare is oblivious to the whole thing because, just like she does every day, she's sleeping like a corpse. I nudge her awake and she grunts. "Happy birthday, Jillian."

"Thanks, girls. Look! I found a Happy birthday block!" She smiles, holding the glowing pink block like a baby bird.

"Knock, knock!" Ander calls from the other side of the door. "Happy birthday, Jillian. Can we come in?"

"Hold on," calls Mare. We grab shorts and sweatshirts and change into them quickly.

"Come in!" Jillian sings.

As we expect by now, Seraphina, Gregor, Ander, and Jax are waiting in the doorway, carrying birthday gifts from Jillian's family and a tray of cinnamon rolls.

"Happy birthday, Birthday Girl!" Seraphina sings as she swoops into the room. "We have birthday treats. Your family is calling in about a half hour, but we can eat them now."

"Thank you! This is the best birthday ever already. I get to wake up in a flower bed and go to England. What could be more fabulous than that?"

"Absolutely nothing," she exclaims. "We'll explore the English countryside. We'll see cottages with thatched roofs and elaborate maze-like gardens manicured to perfection. If you think your bedchamber garden is amazing, wait until you see these. And . . . you may even have a bit of custard tart while we're out and about. Apparently, it's a popular birthday dessert."

"Well, then, that's what I'll have!"

THE NEXT DAY, our last full day together on this tour, we take the megacar to London with Teams France and Switzerland. Of all the places in England, London is the one I've wanted to see most. And now today, even in the rain, it's better than I had imagined. Not just because we get to see Big Ben and Buckingham Palace and ride on double-decker buses. It's because I get to explore it with my team—and my new friends from France and Switzerland.

Later tonight, we'll have to say goodbye. But Seraphina tells us not to use that word. So instead, Gwyndol suggests we say "farewell for now." I know we'll see each other next summer, but that's so far off. And after that, I don't know when I'll ever see Maëlle, Danielle, or Zoe—or even Gwyndol, Hannah, or Jonah again. But I hope one day I'll be lucky enough to. And maybe, now that I really get to go to PIPS, I'll invent a teleporter, and we'll meet each other with the spin of a light bulb, the flip of a switch, or even the pop of a balloon!

We cross London's Tower Bridge under the cover of our umbrellas and stop to look over the side. The River Thames below us rushes by, and I think of a game that Malin and I always played when we were younger. As much as I'm going to miss my new friends, soon I'll be back with my family again, and I'm counting down to those days, too.

When our walk is over, it's time for afternoon tea—which according to Seraphina is an age-old English tradition. But first, Gregor leads us to an old-fashioned red phone booth. I've seen them in movies and read about them in books but I've never seen them in person. As the rain drips over the sides of my umbrella, I think he's bringing us there just so we can see it. But that's not the only reason.

"I'd like you to see something created by inventors in England. These are newly remodeled phone booths called Rain Booths located on most street corners in London."

"What do they do?" I ask, peeking inside.

"For a small fee, you can step inside and dry off. The heaters will instantly dry out your clothes and even your hair by eliminating any excess moisture. About one-third of London's days each year are rainy, so it's a wise renovation."

Wait until I tell Grandma Kitty about this!

Gregor steps inside and sets the booth up so that each of us can dry. By the time we step out, we're dry enough for tea!

We enter a café called Mayfair's Sketch, and the rooms are right out of a storybook. With each room decorated in its own theme, it feels like we've been transported into another world every time we move from one room to the next.

The room we eat in is completely pink. "This is so fancy!" Jillian exclaims in her best English accent.

"It will definitely do," I reply with a laugh.

We each order a small pot of tea. I choose vanilla raspberry. Soon the waiter brings us an assortment of small sandwiches and tiny desserts. "Dahlings," I say, "this my favorite restaurant of this whole tour!"

Seraphina picks up a lavender-colored tart. "I had a feeling you'd like it."

"I like it, too," Ander exclaims. "These sandwiches are outstanding."

Later, we head to the South Bank of the River Thames and board the London Eye. From a distance, it looks like a carnival Ferris wheel, but it's really a huge wheel that overlooks all of London. It's Europe's tallest cantilevered observation wheel and holds eight hundred people! When we get closer to it, we count the thirty-two enclosed oval capsules, which represent the thirty-two boroughs of London. Each capsule holds twenty-five people so that means we can all ride in one together. I tell all this to Ander, because I guess I'm not so bad at Human History after all.

We step inside the clear bubble capsule and find a place to look from. I peer out as far as I can and watch the people and places of London below.

"KK, look!" Ander exclaims. "The people look like ants." The wheel turns and he grins. "Now we're like gerbils, running around a wheel."

I imagine all of us that way, running on this wheel, and laugh at him. Only Ander would think of us as gerbils.

When we're back on the ground, we stop for dinner at an English pub and eat traditional fish and chips and sticky toffee pudding. The pub is a happy place full of people laughing and talking and having fun. We have fun, too, but when we leave the pub, the purple megacar is waiting outside for us and I suddenly feel a little sick. This dreary rainy night reminds me that, right now, this is the last foreign country we'll stand in together as a team. We're about to take our last trip back up to the platform. It's our last ride in this big flying car.

We climb inside, but this time, we don't sit in rows by team. Instead, we mix up all together because tonight, teams don't matter. We're just friends from all over the world, who met because of something we have in common. We have big ideas and we like to turn them into something real. It's funny, though. After meeting so many little kids during this tour, I realize that all kids like to imagine things—and most of them wish they could turn them into something real, too. Who knows, maybe some-day *all* kids who want to be inventors can be. It won't be a job for just a few. Maybe someday, I'll be the next leader of Piedmont, like Seraphina, and I'll change the rules.

When we get to the courtyard, all fifteen of us plus our six preceptors stand forlorn—like we're about to lose a piece of ourselves. We say, "Farewell for now," not once but over and over as we hug and high five one another—all the kids and all the preceptors. As the lamplights cast shadows over us, I try to hold in my tears, but it's hard to say goodbye. I'm going to miss all of them, especially Maëlle, Danielle, and Zoe, and even Jonah for some reason. The air around us feels heavy and I can't put it off any longer. I hug Zoe. Her curls bounce as she pulls away. I hug Danielle, but her usual shy smile is nowhere to be found. And then I hug Maëlle. I never knew that someone who lives so far away could feel like a very best friend. But I know now that someone can.

"We shall message each other all the time, yes?" she asks, blinking very fast.

I nod quickly. "Definitely. Like tomorrow."

She laughs, and that helps this whole goodbye feel less awful. When they disappear together, we're left alone in the courtyard—just the five of us, with Seraphina and Gregor. We trudge over to our aero-bus, and Master Freeman and Andora are waiting for us by the door.

Master Freeman smiles. "Farewell to each of you, Team USA. Congratulations once again on a job done extremely well. It has been a privilege to know you. You are remarkable children, and I look forward to seeing you in the fall—if you decide to take your places at the Piedmont Inventor's Prep School." He shakes our hands, wishes us a safe trip back to the United States, and walks back toward the courtyard.

"Before you leave," Andora says. "I'd like to have a word with all of you as well." She stands quietly for a moment and we inch closer to her, waiting. Her voice crackles until she clears her throat. She stands tall besides us, even though Gregor, Seraphina, and Jax are taller than her.

"I never had children of my own, as you know. With Lexland gone, the children of Piedmont became my family. All of those who competed before you were special to me. During their time at Piedmont, I felt that I could nurture them and teach them, and I must say that I grew fond of all of them through the years. Some of them became quite memorable, for different reasons. Some because of their innovative inventions, some because of their creative attempts to do what seemed impossible, some because of their determined spirits. But none of the children or their preceptors have ever felt like my own children—until now.

"The lengths you have gone to, to ensure my happiness, to rekindle my courage, have left me overwhelmed. No one has ever done for me what the five of you have done. By unlocking the Bronze Balloon, you have given me hope for my own future and hope for the future of Piedmont. You have shown me compassion, and that is what life is truly about.

"You are all my children, and I will forever be grateful for your gift. Thank you for reminding me that innovation is not the only hallmark of a bright future. Compassion is as well." She smiles a smile that tells me that her heart is happy. And that makes my heart swell to twice its normal size.

Andora nods at Seraphina and Gregor. "I meant it when I said that I believe the two of you are the future of Piedmont. I will need your decisions once you arrive in Crimson Heights. The paperwork will be waiting after your team's performance at the amphitheater. I trust you will have made your decision by then. Paperwork for all of you, with your decisions about PIPS as well, will be waiting."

Gregor glances at Seraphina and nods. "Thank you, Andora. You will have all our decisions at that time."

"It is imperative that I do."

"Of course," Seraphina replies. Andora nods and slowly walks away, leaving us to step onto the aero-bus for the last time. Her words weigh heavy on me, but Seraphina's words do, too. Before I get on the aero-bus, though, I hurry around to the front of it to take another peek at the courtyard. Seraphina says we shouldn't be sad, but she was right before. This has been a trip of a lifetime, and I don't ever want to forget any of it. We spent a year up on this platform—and the others exactly like it. It's been like our backyard, our neighborhood, and it's hard to leave it behind. But I do have to leave it behind. Besides, we have a big decision to make.

We head back to the United States tomorrow morning, and we'll fly all day. But we must decide if we're really going to PIPS. When we step off the aero-bus, we'll be welcomed by the educators at PIPS. We'll perform for a group of children there, at the amphitheater at Crimson. But then we need to give them our decision. What if one of us decides not to go? I know that's a real possibility. It always has been. And so, I guess I have some convincing to do—and one last aero-bus ride to do it.

THE PIPS DECISION

I STEP ONTO the aero-bus and decide that maybe all the convincing I need to do can wait until the morning. We must make our last night in our bedchambers the best one yet. But it looks like Seraphina and Gregor decided the same thing, too, because when I enter the floating chamber, it's been transformed into the floating playground from Camp Piedmont!

"Come on, KK, go change! I'll race you on the blobs!" Ander calls to me while bouncing on a blue blob and hitting his head on the marshmallow clouds.

I race into my bedchamber and change into shorts and a T-shirt. When I get back to the floating playground, I grab the orange-yellow blob and hop on. It bounces me up to the clouds and I chase Ander onto the flying carpets. I shimmy myself forward and Jillian jumps on the back of mine. It picks up speed as Ander's dumps him onto a rope wall that's hanging midair. He struggles to get down while Mare swings on swings that hang over a blue carpet that's quickly turning into a pool.

"Wait, are those the idea swings? Is that the creativity pool?"

"Just like the one at Globals," Gregor replies. "It's your last chance to figure out the problem-solving bars."

"No way!" Ander exclaims. "I've been wanting another crack at those since that summer!"

Once the pool is filled up, the bars pop out of the floor on one side, take a sharp turn over the pool, and make another sharp turn down the other side. The rungs of the ladders fill in by the time the bars are in place, and we stand on the ladder waiting in line.

We spend the next hour trying them over and over, with no luck. We jump for each rung and drop into the water—no different than last summer in Québec.

"What is up with you, my Crimson Kids? Have you learned nothing in this competition?"

"What do you mean?" asks Ander.

"I mean, *Be curious. Be creative. Be collaborative. Be colorful. Be courageous.* What else would I mean?"

We stand there dripping and thinking. I look at the tall bars and the poles they're made out of. And suddenly I get it.

I tug at the pole. It pulls out of the floor with ease, like it was just held there with tape, even though there's no way it was. "Come on, guys help me reach this section of the pole. It's got a seam. It must come apart."

"What for?" Jillian asks.

"I think I know!" says Mare. She motions to Jax, stands on his back, and grabs onto the pole. She unscrews it easily and hands the piece to Ander.

"What do I do with this?"

"We can unscrew the bottom section of all the poles and then make the problem-solving bars shorter."

"Okay, but how does that help us get across?" asks Jax. "Each of the rungs across the top are still at least six feet apart."

Ander jumps onto the ladder. "We can use these extra sections. Look up there. There's spaces already there to screw them in!"

I count the legs of the problem-solving bars. There are at least sixteen, some buried under water. "We'll have enough sections to add bars in between the bars that are already there. That way they'll be less than three feet apart. We can definitely cross the creativity pool then."

Jillian races out of the floating chamber, calling behind her. "Save the poles in the water for me. I want to get those."

I shrug. "Okay, whatever you say."

The rest of us get to work unscrewing the other bottom sections. Jillian returns, wearing a pink polka dot bathing suit. "I never got to wear this last time we were in this pool, so I am now." She dives in, grabs hold of the first submerged bottom section, and unscrews it. By the time she reaches the surface with it in her hand, we've set the pole back into the water. It re-attaches itself to the pool floor and we move onto the next one. Before long, Jillian has unscrewed all of them, and we have a pile of pole sections lying next to the pool."

"Okay, now what?" asks Ander."

"It looks like we need two sections to make each bar long enough to cross the pool, so why don't we connect the pairs, and Mare and Jax can climb up."

Mare climbs the ladder at one end, and Jax follows her. She hoists herself up to the top on one side, Jax does the same on the other side. We hand the bars to Jax, and he does his best to balance the bar and pass it over to Mare. She reaches over as far as she can, but when she's almost touching with her fingers, she falls off the rung and into the pool!

"Ugh!" she screams when she reaches the surface soaking wet. "I couldn't reach it!"

I don't dare laugh, but when I glance over at Seraphina and Gregor talking in the corner, I can see that they can barely stop laughing either.

"What if I climb up with Jax," suggests Ander. "I'll help him balance the bar so he can reach out farther across the pool."

"And I'll climb up with you, Mare," says Jillian. "I'll hold onto you so you can balance better as you reach for the pole—and screw it into the sides."

"Good idea," I say. "Let's try it!"

It takes a while, but soon all the bars are attached. That means there are twice as many bars and half the distance to reach between each one. This should be easy now.

"Let's do it," Ander calls, already heading for the ladder. He reaches out to the first bar with one hand and grabs onto the next with the other. It takes a few bars for him to get into a smooth rhythm, but once he gets going, he crosses quickly and steps onto the ladder at the other side of the pool. Mare, Jillian, and I try it next, and we make it across easily without even making a splash. Jax crosses last, and as soon as he steps onto the other ladder, Seraphina and Gregor clap.

"Yay! My, Crimson Kids, you did it!"

"Well done. Well done. I knew you'd figure it out eventually."

Gregor's right. We crossed the creativity pool—we solved the problem-solving bars!

Seraphina smiles. "This is your last night, so we're giving you a later curfew. But remember, after our flight home tomorrow, you have a performance upon your arrival at the amphitheater . . . and a decision to reveal after that. So, don't stay up too late."

After swinging on the idea swings and playing one more game of yellow pole tag, we head back to our bed-chambers. We change into our pajamas and decide to hang out in the boys' bedchamber—inside their balloon fort. They finally let us take the beds for a spin, so Mare, Jillian, and I jump onto one and Ander and Jax hop onto the other. Ander tugs on the rope, *you are the future* lights up, and we spin around and around faster than the Ancestor App.

When the beds finally stop spinning, I clutch my side. I've never laughed until it hurt that much before. We slide onto the floor between the beds and sit together in a circle, with just the light from the balloon sign shining over us.

Jax tucks the balloon rope behind his bed. "I can't believe we're leaving tomorrow."

"A year seemed like such a long time. And now tomorrow it's already September." I start to bite my ring-finger nail but twist my wristband instead.

"We only present to one school tomorrow, our own—at the amphitheater," Ander replies. "That's it. Then we're done."

"Yeah," says Jillian. "Done with our trip of a lifetime."

Mare leans back against Ander's bed. "But we get to see our families—and not just for a few weeks. We get to be with them for a whole month—unless we decide not to go to PIPS. Then it would be forever."

I sit up straight. "I've already decided. I'm going."

"How can you be so sure, Kia? Don't you worry that you may not like it?"

"Grandma Kitty always says that worrying is just imagining the worst possible outcome, and I never want to imagine the worst possible outcome. I want to imagine the best. I want to imagine that PIPS will be everything I've ever dreamed of, and more. Besides, I decided when I was seven years old that I was going to PIPS. I promised myself I would get there—and I can't break a promise to myself."

Mare looks at me like I just spoke to her in Norwegian. "It's okay, Mare. I know you're not sure. I know the rest of you aren't sure either. But I have the whole aero-bus ride tomorrow to convince you!"

* * *

THE NEXT MORNING, we sit on the floor of chamber eight, taking turns giving reasons why we should go to PIPS. I start, because it's easy for me to explain.

"So, if I go to PIPS, I'll get to be with all of you and build my sixty-seven inventions. If I don't go to PIPS, I'll be programmed into Math."

"Okay, I'll go next," says Jillian. "If I go to PIPS, I'll get to be with all of you and keep thinking up inventions. But, if I go to Crimson Academy, I'll get programmed into Art Forms. I'll get to be surrounded by paint and clay and fabric. I'll be able to sew my own clothes—create my own fashion line."

I swallow hard. Jillian *would* be a good fashion designer.

"Well," says Ander. "I want to go to PIPS for the same reason. You're all my best friends, and I want to build the first homes in space. Now that I've seen the Piedmont Platforms, I'm sure it can be done—and I want to be the one to do it. But, if I don't go to PIPS, I can stay with my mom and dad and my sister. I don't know if I can leave them forever."

"If I go to PIPS," says Jax. "I'll get to experiment with anything, not just New Technology. I guess I'd like to see what I can do without being restricted by one category."

"Exactly!" I say.

"But," he continues. "PIPS is in Maryland at Piedmont University. It's six hours away from home."

"Yeah," says Ander. "That's the bad part."

I bite my pinkie nail. "What about you, Mare?"

"I want to go to PIPS because I now think I want to be a builder. I want to build the first homes in space, too. My dad taught me a lot about that kind of stuff, and I know I'd be good at it. But I just don't think I can leave my mom again for so long. I'd really miss her."

"I'd miss my family too," I admit. "A lot."

We sit quietly for a few minutes and I know I have a lot of convincing to do. I start with Jillian because she's the only one with a really good reason for wanting to be programmed into one category. "Jillian, so you know the Costume Copier?"

"Yeah, the one we used to create our costumes for the opening ceremony in Québec and for our skit with the other teams. It's the most amazing invention I've ever seen. A team from Canada created it. How did they think to take an old-fashioned paper copier and turn it into an invention that lets you look up an outfit, feed fabric into the tray, push a button, and watch the outfit slide out?"

"If the Canadian team could invent something like that, imagine what you could invent. No one loves art and clothes more than you."

She considers that for a second. "Yeah, maybe."

"I think you would like to get programmed into Art Forms, but I think you'd like studying at PIPS, too. You could work on art projects and every other kind of project too."

"Kia, we know you've made up your mind, but aren't you worried at all about being so far away from home— again?" Mare asks.

"No, because we've been far away from home—really far away from home, for a whole year. Going away to school at PIPS will be so easy compared to that. It's only six hours, so our families can visit way more than when we were on this tour. And we get breaks. Longer breaks."

My teammates stare at me. Not like I just landed here from Saturn, but like they're thinking—thinking about what I just said. But I can't tell if they're wondering if what I said is true—that they won't feel homesick because they can see their families more often. And as I sit there waiting for them to say something, I realize I'm wondering the same thing, too. I say that I'm positive that I want to go to PIPS, and I am, but Maryland is not New York. Living at Piedmont University will not be the same as living at home with my family.

I'm just beginning to feel worried that one of my teammates won't choose PIPS when Mare screams out, "I don't know! I want someone to make the decision for me."

Ander throws his head back. "Yup, me too!"

"That's what I want!" Jillian exclaims.

"That would be easier," says Jax.

"But that's what programming is!" I exclaim. "Don't you guys get that?"

Just as I say that, my head spins and it feels like the room is turning. Not spinning—but turning. I place my hands on the floor to grip it, or to at least steady myself, but my hands lift away from the carpet and my body follows. My teammates turn also and as the room turns more, we turn with it.

Ander's eyes get huge. "What's happening?"

"I don't know!" Gravity pushes me up, I think—or down, I'm not sure. Suddenly, the skylight is underneath us and the floor is a few inches above us. It's like the aero-bus has turned upside down, but I'm not sure it has. Maybe we have.

We float through chamber eight, like magic, or something else—turning, rolling, twisting. I reach out to move myself like I'm swimming. I kick my legs, but they don't go in the direction I'm aiming for. It's like my body has a mind of its own, telling me where to go. My teammates float by me, one by one, some upside down and some sideways.

Before long, the aero-bus flips—or we do. Then our bodies readjust, and we all turn upright. We float toward the center of the room, high above the carpeted floor, and end up in a circle just a few inches below the skylight. We hover, like it's no big deal, with no idea what to do.

"What is happening?" Jillian squeals.

"I feel like an astronaut," Ander replies. "We're floating in midair!"

I turn a somersault. "It's like there's suddenly no gravity in the room."

Jax shakes his head. "I don't understand it. We have no control over ourselves at all."

"I don't like it!" Mare says. "Make it stop!"

A flash of light catches my eye and I turn toward it. Another light flashes, escaping from the closet door. The light floats toward us and turns into colorful letters. The letters float out of the closet, one right after the other and dance around the room. They link together forming words and then phrases.

Be true to yourself

Create your future   *The choice is yours*

Believe you can   *Live your dream*

The words encircle us and drift in between us. They bounce, flash, and shimmer, reminding us of the things we've known all along. Soon tiny sparkles join the dance, but they're not sparkles at all . . . they're tiny golden light-bulbs, silver switches, and bronze balloons.

The show ends and the images drift away, back into the chamber eight closet. We slowly drop back down to the carpet. First me, then Ander, then Mare, then Jax, and then Jillian.

Mare brushes herself off—from what I'm not sure—and whispers, "Okay, I get it. I'll decide my future myself."

"Me, too," says Jillian.

A smile spreads across my face. "That was fun."

"But what was it?" Ander asks.

"I don't know," Jax replies. "But I have some thinking to do."

"Me, too," I say. "Tomorrow is Decision Day. That's not a big deal. Not a big deal at all."

"You know," says Mare. "We could use the Bronze Balloon to help us decide."

"We could," I say.

"Nah," says Mare. "I'm going to decide this one on my own."

My teammates agree with her and I do, too. With great inventions come great responsibility. Just because we have the Bronze Balloon doesn't mean we have to use it for everything.

THE CRIMSON FIVE FINALE

OUR MASSIVE AERO-BUS lands near the schoolyard parking lot, in a grassy area close to the amphitheater. We peek out the window of the floating chamber to see a cheering crowd—the entire town of Crimson Heights is awaiting our arrival. None of us is surprised, though. Principal Bermuda wouldn't have it any other way.

Before we exit the aero-bus, I glance around one last time, and I know it *is* the last time. I can't help but wonder. Is this it? Is there no other way for us to ride on one of the Piedmont aero-buses again? I know in my head that there isn't. The aero-buses are used for the Piedmont Challenge, and we've already aced the challenge. But my heart still hopes that someday, somehow, it will be possible.

We follow Gregor and Seraphina down the staircase and step onto a carpet that's been laid across the grass.

The carpet is red probably in honor of Crimson Heights. But it's sprinkled with gold, silver, and bronze stars, too. And that's when it hits me. Today, we get to present our inventions—all of them—to the entire town of Crimson Heights for the first time. We get to spin the Golden Light Bulb, flip the Silver Switch, and pop the Bronze Balloon. We get to show them our skits and transport them to the imaginary world of Crimson Catropolis, the world we created together.

Principal Bermuda is standing on the stage waving his arms as he speaks, running his fingers through his greasy hair. I can hardly hear what he's saying through the applause, but it's nice to feel how proud he is of us—how proud they all are. I hope we do a good job. I hope they love our inventions as much as we do.

When we reach the stage of the amphitheater, Seraphina and Gregor stop and we gather around them. Principal Bermuda turns to us and says, "It is now with great pleasure that I present to you The Crimson Five—Kia, Ander, Mare, Jax, and Jillian—and welcome them back home!"

The crowd cheers and Seraphina whispers to us: "Well, my Crimson Kids, are you ready to show them what you've got?"

My butterflies wake up, and I almost bite my pointer-finger nail—almost. We race onto the stage. "Yup de dup dup dup. We're ready to show you the wonderful world of Crimson Catropolis!"

I look out from the amphitheater stage, dressed as Little Girl, and see Mom, Dad, Malin, Ryne, and Grandma

Kitty sitting in the front row. Their smiles match mine, and I know that as much as I love being on this stage and being a part of Piedmont, there's no place like Crimson—no place like my home.

Our performance for Crimson Heights is one of a kind because it's the one and only time we'll perform with all three of our inventions together. As I stand on the stage feeling like a star, performing with my team, saying my lines, walking along the Balance Blocks, spinning the Golden Light Bulb, watching the Ancestor App activate, flipping the Silver Switch, putting on the Satellite Spectacles, imagining my future, watching the Bronze Balloon pop, and singing our finale song, I realize this is not the finale for us. It's only the beginning.

The audience cheers, and we take a bow, holding hands. I'm happy we made our skit about the imaginary version of the town of Crimson. I hope it makes the kids who have so much imagining to do feel special—like stars, too.

We race down the steps of the amphitheater and to the other side of the schoolyard lawn. I remember crossing this schoolyard on the first day of the Piedmont Challenge—marching single file with the rest of my class to solve my first task. We followed the Piedmont ushers, and entered Crimson Elementary while teachers in red robes held open the doors.

But today, it's just the five of us. No one is leading the way to our signing table but us. I jog alongside Ander. He's smiling even bigger than he usually does. "Are we really doing this, KK? Are we really committing to PIPS? Are we making it official?"

I smile back at him and can't believe that this day is finally here. Wait until Grandma Kitty and my whole family hears!

We take our places at a round table while Seraphina and Gregor stand watch, looking at us with pride splashed all over their faces. They give us a thumbs up, and we know what that means. They've decided yes—they're going to be the new leaders of Piedmont! I imagine Gregor welcoming a new class of Piedmont Campers. And Seraphina? She'll be the new Queen of Piedmont, and I bet she'll be wearing a sparkly purple crown!

A document sits in front of each of us, waiting for us to sign our names. We each have a red pen, too, the color of Crimson. I used to hate Crimson Elementary, but not anymore. Now we're The Crimson Five, the kids from Crimson Elementary, the first kids to do something no one from the whole town of Crimson Heights had ever done before. We placed in the top five of the Piedmont Challenge. We placed second at the Piedmont Challenge National Finals, and we placed second in the Piedmont Global Championships, too. And, we just took the trip of a lifetime touring the world and unlocking a long-lost invention together.

When I think of it that way, it feels like a dream. All I ever wanted was to win the Piedmont Challenge, so I could go to PIPS, so I could meet kids who appreciate my ideas, who wouldn't think they were strange. So I could finally build my sixty-seven inventions.

But that wasn't my only dream. My true dream was to have a true friend again, and I wasn't sure I'd ever find one. Sure, by being placed on the New York team, I found teammates. But my teammates turned into friends. I finally found my true friend—and another and another and another.

So, in a way, my biggest dream has already come true. And now the five of us are all sitting here together, ready for what's to come. By signing this document, I'll be going to PIPS . . . finally! But I couldn't have done it without Ander, Mare, Jax, and Jillian. There's just no way, because sometimes it takes a friend—or four—to help make your dream come true, and that's what they did for me. I guess Seraphina was right. Dreams *are* born to become dreams come true. You just need the courage to try—and a few friends to help bring them to life.

I pick up the Crimson pen and as carefully as I can, I sign my name, Kia Krumpet—*and* my number, 718—on the dotted line. I mark the *i* in Kia with a five-pronged star because the number five means we've been part of something amazing together, and I don't ever want to forget any of it.

We set down our pens and as we do, an opening in the table releases hundreds of balloons. They float gracefully above the schoolyard, like wishes for the future, turning the sky yellow, orange, pink, blue, green, and purple. But soon five of them pop. It's a faint, colorful symphony of pop, pop, popping! Confetti-like paper flutters, falls from the sky, and a balloon message falls onto my lap. I'm afraid to read it, though, because this is the last balloon message I'm ever going to get. I take a breath, wondering if I should look at it, but when my teammates hold theirs up to the sun, I can't resist.

I pick up the slip of paper and feel it change in my hand. It wrinkles, hardens, and transforms into glass. I hold it up and the letters, shimmering in the sunlight, appear like a message from the sun itself—a message I've been wishing for since even before the Piedmont Challenge began:

Welcome to the Piedmont Inventor's Prep School!
Where New Dreams Are Born.

I smile and clutch the glass in my hand.

The PIPS theme song erupts from speakers in the grass. Ander hops off his chair and breaks into an Ander-ish dance. "It's official!" he shouts. "KK, we're going to PIPS!"

"I know! I know!"

Mare and Jillian grab my arm, and the five of us hug in the schoolyard, jumping like we did on the Day of Brightness stage more than a year ago. The balloons sail higher and higher and my stomach fills with its own popping balloons. This is really happening. It is! I can already imagine the inventions we'll build together.

I used to wonder why I was picked to be on this team, what my role was. But I don't wonder that anymore. Each of us is good at something. Sometimes it just takes a while to know what it is. Even though it may take a whole team to bring an invention to life, it can't be born if it isn't imagined by someone first. And I'm good at imagining things that aren't things yet and believing that someday they will be.

At PIPS, someone has to dream the big dreams. I pick me.

ACKNOWLEDGMENTS

Writing the ending of a trilogy feels so final, like saying goodbye to a piece of myself. This world of the Crimson Five has been a part of me since I first imagined the premise more than nine years ago. Never in my wildest dreams did I think that it would become the story that it has. Creating the Piedmont Challenge, in all its splendor, with these characters who are so dear to me, and watching it all come to life on the pages of *Spin the Golden Light Bulb*, *Flip the Silver Switch*, and now *Pop the Bronze Balloon*, has truly been a dream come true. A privilege.

Seraphina always says: A dream is born to become a dream come true. Well, now mine truly has. But just like Kia, I couldn't have accomplished any of it without the support of the people who mean the most to me. Although there isn't a big enough way to say *thank you*, I'm going to try my very best.

To my husband, Jim, my one and only: You've been by my side the whole time—even before this adventure began. Because of you, I know what it means to love wholeheartedly and to support each other's dreams, no matter what. Thank you for supporting my dream, being the rock of our family, and believing in me—always. You are everything to me and more.

To my daughter, Danielle, dreamer of big dreams and my best girl: I see myself in you in so many ways, like when you look at the world and see all that's possible—all that's bright. Keep dreaming like only you can! Thank you for constantly encouraging me to be the best version of myself and for reminding me, when I forget, that life *is* sparkles and sunshine if you decide it is. To my son, Adam, the boy of my heart: Ander is *all* you on the pages of this book, but you are so much more than just him. Keep shining like the star you are. Thank you for always having my back and reminding me that spreading your wings is a good thing and that just because you're separated in miles from the people you love, you're not truly separated in any other way. No matter where you both are, always know how much I love you and that you'll always have your place here at home.

To my parents, my Mom and Dad: I've gotten to the point where I know that life has ups and downs. I realize the sacrifices you've made for our family to create our happy home. *Thank you* seems too small, when my heart is overflowing with gratitude. I dedicate this book to you because you are everything to our family and have truly always welcomed me (and all of us) back home—no matter where our adventures have taken us. Thank you for being the most incredible parents in the world. I treasure you both more than all the stars in the sky.

To my mother-in-law and father-in-law: I knew when I met your son that I was a lucky girl. But when I met you, I knew I would be lucky to be a part of your family too—and I was right. I'm so grateful to you for being amazing and supportive, for cheering me along on this journey. Thank you both for everything!

To my family and friends: It's not every profession where you get to tell those closest to you what they mean to you. But because I can, I will! Being a writer is a solitary lifestyle, which suits a homebody like me just fine—well, sometimes! Thank you for being there for coffee dates, phone calls, wine nights, and dinner catch-ups when I've needed them. And thanks for supporting me on this journey. You all mean the world to me!

To Melyssa Mercado and Joe Burns, my incredible critique partners and friends: I don't deserve all that you've put into making my books stronger, but I'm beyond grateful. Joe, thank you not only for calling me out when I try to make life too easy for my characters, but for your detailed notes on the culture of Hong Kong. This book is better because you shared your experiences there with me. Mel, thank you for being the best CP turned friend a girl could ask for. Your positive feedback in purple always encourages me to keep going and is the very reason the theme color of Piedmont is purple. I bet you never knew that! One day I *will* see both your books on bookshelves, too, and I'll be clutching my signed copies. So, please do not give up. Ever. Your words are too good, your stories too amazing, and children are waiting to read them!

To Rebecca Angus, my first literary agent: Thank you for being my ally, advocate, sounding board, cheerleader, and constant through this roller coaster adventure. This series wouldn't exist if it weren't for your belief in me and in this story. I'm so grateful that you found my pitch on

Twitter all those years ago! And to Jessica Schmeidler, the founder of Golden Wheat Literary and my new literary agent: Thank you for being in my corner all these years and for swooping in and showing me all that's possible going forward!

To Dayna Anderson, my first publisher: This book would not have been created if it weren't for you. From the start you saw potential in both *Spin the Golden Light Bulb* and *Flip the Silver Switch*, and you knew there was more of the Crimson Five story to be told. You championed for *Pop the Bronze Balloon* to be written, and I will always be grateful. I'm a published author (three times!) because of you. Thank you. Thank you. Thank you!

To Cassandra Farrin, the most insightful editor there is: You helped me through more than one publishing crisis and made everything okay again! You pushed me to find the heart of *Pop the Bronze Balloon* and to create a better title too. I'm so grateful that our paths crossed when they did.

To Cherrita Lee, my amazing editor at Amberjack Publishing: Thank you for your expertise, patience, and work on my behalf. *Pop the Bronze Balloon* is a more thoughtful and complete book (with better inventions!) because of you. Thank you for pushing me so hard to make it better! And to the entire team at Amberjack Publishing: I've said it before, but it's worth noting again. Thank you for turning my stories into such a beautiful series of books. I'm so proud to call you my publisher.

To Cynthia Sherry, Michelle Williams, Chelsea Balesh, Alex Granato, and each member of the talented and hardworking team at Chicago Review Press: I appreciate you all so much. Thank you for everything you've done to bring this book to life and for creating such an incredible home for the Crimson Five series. I'm honored to have a place among your amazing authors!

To Gabrielle Esposito, illustrator extraordinaire: You are the real hero of this book. Your gorgeous illustrations and cover design make the pages of *Pop the Bronze Balloon*, and all the books in this series, sparkle in ways my words alone never could. Thank you for your vision, talent, and hard work. I'm so grateful that we were paired up together!

To Erin Varley at Byron Bergen Elementary School and her fifth-grade students—my very first mentor class: Thank you for being my biggest fans and for your unique title suggestions. They inspired me to keep brainstorming too. *Pop the Bronze Balloon* was created out of your imaginative suggestions!

To the writing and book community: Social media has made my world bigger in ways I didn't fully expect. Thank you to every writer, reader, bookseller, blogger, teacher, and librarian who has connected with me and championed my books. Interacting with you has made the solitary parts of being a writer a lot less solitary! And to my blog readers at swirlandspark.com: Thanks for reading my rambling posts through the years and traveling with me on the road to publication again and again.

For the third time, to Kara Davis, Adam Yeager, Meg Bilodeau, Jake Leach, and Julia Vanill: Thank you for your endless support and for being the catalyst for this series.

Somewhere along the way, Kia, Ander, Mare, Jax, and Jillian took on lives of their own, and it has been such a fun journey leading them through this creative, task-solving, invention-building competition. Almost as fun as coaching your Odyssey of the Mind team through regionals, states, and the World Finals! We may not have traveled together on a worldwide tour like the Swirl and Spark Creativity Tour, but I'll never forget when our Odyssey of the Mind team had a year to remember and took a trip of a lifetime to the University of Maryland—when you were just eleven. I hope you'll always remember our adventure together—and never forget to wonder, question, imagine, and soar. If you're not sure what I mean by that, you'll just have to read the book!

And finally, to the kids and grownups who've read this series: Thank you from the bottom of my heart for choosing my books. I hope the story of the Crimson Five inspires you to *Think More* and *Work Hard* and *Dream Big* because I know you can! And as Seraphina would say:

Be curious. Be creative. Be collaborative.
Be colorful. Be courageous.

**Because dreams are born
to become dreams come true!**